WELL CONSIDERED

WELL CONSIDERED

A NOVEL

RICHARD MORRIS

iUniverse, Inc.
New York   Bloomington

Well Considered

Cover Design By Audrey Engdahl

iUniverse books may be ordered through booksellers or by contacting:

iUniverse
1663 Liberty Drive
Bloomington, IN 47403
www.iuniverse.com
1-800-Authors (1-800-288-4677)

ISBN: 978-1-4502-0388-3 (sc)
ISBN: 978-1-4502-0390-6 (dj)
ISBN: 978-1-4502-0389-0 (ebk)

Library of Congress Control Number: 2010900023

Printed in the United States of America

iUniverse rev. date: 02/01/2010

For Barbara

ONE

Red taillights flashed in the pre-dawn glow. Ron jammed on the brakes of his white, four-door Ford Taurus, glanced at the rearview mirror to see if the car behind would hit him, and then looked ahead again. *Shit. I almost rammed him. But why did he stop? What is it? A wreck? A pedestrian?*

Cars were stopping at the traffic light even on green, drivers staring across the four-lane highway toward the new subdivision of town homes, straining for a better look, pulling onto the shoulder, jumping out, grabbing cell phones. He stopped too and climbed out. On the shoulder a young black woman was talking on her phone. He saw her scanning him as he approached and imagined what she saw—a tall, slender man, medium brown skin, handsome, very short hair, forty-ish, dressed for the office.

"Excuse me. Can you tell me why everyone is stopping? Is it a fire or something?"

"Hold on," she said, pressing the phone against her chest. "Can't you see it?"

"What?"

She pointed across the road. "That wall over there. By those houses."

He turned, focused, and saw it—racist graffiti in huge white letters spray-painted on the sound barrier by the Big Oak subdivision, facing the highway.

"Damn. Thanks."

"No problem," she said, returning to her call.

A man in his mid-thirties with dark brown skin wearing business attire jumped out of a black Mercedes sedan. Frozen, he gazed with his mouth wide open for half a minute before returning to his car with his lips curled into a snarl. Next to him on the shoulder, a white man with graying hair, in similar professional dress, stared from a cream-colored Buick LeSabre, reading the wall and slowly shaking his head.

Ron pulled out his cell phone and speed-dialed Wilma. "Listen, don't bring the kids on the highway today. Take the back way."

"Why?"

"Oh, they don't need to see this. It's really obscene." He told her about the graffiti, not before looking around to see if anyone could hear him. "The wall says, I HATE and then they use the n-word, and then it says WHITE POWER, KKK, I HATE KOONS, and HITLER IS BACK. Whoever did this must be neo-Nazis. I'm not kidding. And then it says DIE the n-word, and then FUCK the n-word. And there are two swastikas. I've never seen anything like it. I'd like to grab the sons of bitches who did it and ram their heads down a toilet."

"Now, Ron."

"They must have been up on ladders to do this. And it was right out there for everyone to see. I don't know how they did it without being seen from the road."

Wilma was quiet for a moment and then agreed to keep the children away. Ron hung around for a few minutes gaping with the others in an angry demonstration of solidarity before climbing back in his car. He turned on the light jazz station and resumed his commute.

Shit, he thought, shaking his head and recalling the advice his mother Mildred had given him two months earlier, before he and his family had moved from California into the Washington DC area. *Maybe she was right.*

~

He remembered her sitting at the head of the table in her dining room in Oakland, white curly hair framing her tan face, her blouse a brown-and-white African print. Ron was beside her, his hands folded on the lace tablecloth, Wilma in the kitchen, and the children nearby in the family room.

"Things are different back east—you'll have to be more careful there," she said. "Those were slave states, you know—Maryland, Delaware, Virginia, and—"

"Yes, yes, I know, Mother—Frederick Douglass and Harriet Tubman were slaves in Maryland—"

"—and they keep building those suburbs out in the farmland, Ronnie, where the rednecks and racists live."

"Racists are everywhere, Mother. You haven't forgotten about the cops beating up Rodney King."

"I remember. And him saying, 'Can't we all just get along?'"

"Yeah."

The sounds of cartoon villains from the family-room TV intruded, mixing with the clinking of dishes from the kitchen. Aromas of leftover ham and sweet potatoes lingered in the air. A basket of cold white rolls, a tray with butter, salt, and pepper, a few plates, and two stray glasses littered the table.

Mildred put her hands on the edge of the table and looked straight at her son. "But listen, Ronnie, I never told you this before, but I think I should now. The reason our family moved to the West Coast was something really ugly that happened back east."

Ron sat up straight and looked at her quizzically. "What?"

"I hate to even think about it. That's probably why I've never told you."

His brows furrowed. "Told me about what, Mother?"

She spoke hesitantly. "Well, the thing is that my grandfather—your great-grandfather—was lynched back there."

Ron sat back. "Lynched? My God! That doesn't happen to people you know."

"It did to us."

"Where did it happen?"

"East of Washington somewhere—we don't know exactly where—in a farming area. He was a farmer."

"Great. That's near where we're moving."

"I know it is."

"When did they do it?"

"In 1907. That's when the family moved."

"But why did they lynch him?" he asked, raising his hands in supplication. "What did he do that led to it?"

"We don't know why they did it. It was a long time ago. I never even heard about it till I was sixteen. I guess my mother and father didn't want to lay that load on me until I was old enough to carry it."

Ron's eyes narrowed. "Load?"

"Oh, you know—people assuming he was lynched for some supposed good reason—like he raped or murdered someone—and us having to explain it if anyone found out."

"But that was generations ago. Who would care now?"

"You never know who. And you never know what people whisper to each other."

Ron nodded. "So when did you find out?"

Her eyes gazed away into the past. "My father told me in 1956, not long after California integrated the schools and public places and repealed those laws against mixed marriages and interracial sex."

"Hmmph. 1956."

She said her father had spoken to her as she got ready to go out on a date. He wanted her to know how dangerous some white racists could be, and where she shouldn't go in the city. Then he told her about the lynching. It had happened when he wasn't much more than a baby, so he didn't remember anything except going to live with his grandparents afterward and not having a daddy. Not much later, his mother had moved the family to Chicago, where they lived with relatives for a few years, and then to California, where she cleaned houses. She remarried when Ron's grandfather was ten or eleven.

Ron slowly shook his head, his eyes never leaving Mildred's. "Sounds like she wanted to get as far away as she could."

Mildred spoke in a bitter tone, her eyes squinting, shoulders tense. "Uh-huh. And what my father remembered most was his mother's rage. How she never stopped hating white people and never ever trusted any of them. She told him how the white people back there treated his family like they were animals and strung up his father even though he never did anything wrong."

"Damn."

He took a pen out of his pocket and picked up a paper napkin from the table. "What was his name?"

"My grandfather was named Thomas Phillips."

"Thomas Phillips. He was the one who was lynched?"

"Uh-huh."

"In 1907."

"Most likely." She waited for him to finish writing. "And your grandfather's name was Benjamin Phillips."

"Right."

"Anyway, Ronnie, I know things have changed a lot since then. But my father had enough hate in him for a thousand men because of what happened. I want you to promise me that you'll be careful back there. There are still bad, bad people out there."

"I will, Mother. You convinced me." He grinned and relaxed his body. "I'm going out to buy some guns today."

"Ronnie. My handsome boy. It's nothing to joke about ..."

He left his mother sitting in the dining room and carried the remaining dishes to Wilma in the kitchen.

Marty appeared from the family room. "Hey, Dad. Who got lynched?" Marty was four-and-a-half feet tall and slim, with his dad's color, good looks, and short hairstyle.

Ron threw Wilma a helpless glance as she looked up from loading the dishwasher. Her medium build was clothed in black slacks and a short-sleeved white blouse, her hair a shoulder-length curly shag, her skin a shade darker than Ron's. Ron looked down, shook his head, and said, "No one you know, Mr. Big Ears." He took Marty by the shoulders and pulled him into a hug.

Not satisfied, Marty pushed away and looked up at him. "Come on, Dad, who?"

His first diversion failed, Ron said, "Nine years old—do you even know what that word means?"

"Sure," said Marty with authority. "Means they hang someone in a tree."

Ron laughed humorlessly, and then told his son that sometimes lynch mobs didn't hang their victims—sometimes they murdered them in different ways.

Marty asked, "Like shooting him or drowning him?"

Ron explained that there were two other requirements for a lynching: a mob of people did it, and they did it before a court could prove the victim's guilt or innocence.

"Yeah, but *who* got lynched?" Marty asked, not giving up.

Ron tried again. "Lots of people, a long time ago. But not anymore."

"Why not?"

He put his hands back on Marty's shoulders. "Because, my man, if people tried to lynch someone today, they'd get arrested and sent to jail."

"But then the police might let them go like they did those guys that killed Emmett Till," Marty said.

"Emmett Till?" Ron frowned as Till's name welled up from his childhood memories.

Wilma stood up straight and stared at Marty. "Where'd you hear about Emmett Till?"

"On TV. Some white men shot him and threw him in the river."

"Yeah," Ron said. "But that was a long time ago too. I read about him when I was growing up."

"His face was all bashed in."

"I'm sorry you had to see that, Marty," Wilma said, shaking her head.

"It's okay, Mom. I've seen lots worse on TV. But there's one thing I don't understand."

"What's that?" Ron asked.

"I don't get what he did."

"Who?"

"That boy—Emmett. What did he do that was so bad they killed him?"

Ron hesitated. "He didn't *do* anything," he said, shaking his head and glancing at Wilma.

Marty's eyes widened. "You mean they killed him for nothing?"

"Well … they said he whistled at a white woman," Ron explained.

"That's all?"

"That's right."

Marty frowned. "And they didn't even put the murderers in jail?"

"Nope. They were evil murderers, but the courts let them go."

Ron looked at Wilma, still shaking his head. She responded with the same gesture.

What did he do that was so bad they killed him? Ron thought. *Some day Marty's going to ask the same question about his great-great-grandfather Thomas. Then Rosy will ask it. Shit! I asked just about the same thing myself when Mother first told me about the lynching. People are always assuming that the victim is guilty of some crime. But I can't let my children grow up thinking that their great-great-grandfather was some kind of criminal. And I don't want to have to rely on what Mother said about Thomas's innocence—I want hard evidence to show the children when they find out about it …*

∼

Neo-Nazi racist graffiti, Ron thought as he ended his commute. *That's all we need.*

He turned down the ramp into the garage below the Internal Revenue Service building, grabbed his suit coat, took the elevator, put on a smile, and greeted his administrative assistant. "Good morning, Jennifer."

"Good morning, Mr. Watkins. I scheduled the conference room for ten for your meeting and put a packet with the new tax forms on your desk."

"Well, great! Glad you're so efficient, and so early in the morning." He went into his office, sat down, and began to prepare for the meeting. The graffiti coiled around his mind like a snake as the lynching and Emmett Till stood by watching, but he concentrated and shook them away, and his meeting went well.

~

On the way home, he thought about how he had applied for the job, and after long talks with Wilma, had accepted the promotion. Now, after seeing the graffiti, he wondered if they had made a mistake. They could always return to California, but he had to take the DC job if he wanted to keep moving up.

He remembered the house-hunting trip he and Wilma had taken several months ago. The residential area that had attracted them most was outside the Beltway, east of Washington. From what they'd learned, the county was rapidly changing from white to black, increasingly affluent, and growing fast. As they drove through the neighborhoods, it had seemed that developments of large homes were sprouting up everywhere, on every abandoned tobacco farm. He'd heard from people at work that the buyers here were mostly upper-middle-class black professional couples long trapped in older housing in the city and inner suburbs. Houses had seemed to be rising like new grass—fertilized by double incomes, low interest rates, low land costs, and immigrant labor—two-story Colonials dubbed McMansions by critics, homes that made normal lots look small and the historic mansions they passed shrink in comparison. Friends and acquaintances had told Ron that Patuxent County was *the* place to live for rising black families—an area of intense pride, ambition, and power. Enormous new African-American churches they passed further attested to the wealth of thousands of families. When Ron and Wilma had stopped at a new mall, they had found it filled with mostly black shoppers. In the neighborhood where they eventually bought, however, they did notice some white children.

"Some of our neighbors will be white," he remarked to Wilma in the car.

"That's fine," she said. "You know I don't want our family to be part of the problem. We don't need to contribute to racial separation."

"Yeah. Like DuBois said a hundred years ago: 'shut out from their world by a vast veil.'" He steered around a traffic circle and drove to the end of the street.

"Residential segregation—it's like he said," and she modulated her voice to a deep, authoritative tone, "'The problem of the twentieth century is the problem of the color-line.'"

"The twentieth century? How 'bout the twenty-first? Segregation's still one of the last great divides. Most whites still don't want to live with us. They want their purity."

He stopped at a light and looked at the other cars. In this neighborhood, most cars were late models, with lots of SUVs and pricey foreign makes. Most of the drivers were black.

"I think white people are even afraid to talk to us and afraid of us physically—like we'll bite them or something," Wilma said.

Ron chuckled. "They run like hell when they see us coming. What did that guy at work tell me? The county has eight hundred thousand residents overall, and since the schools here were integrated in about 1970 and that housing act in the late sixties eliminated the deed restrictions that kept blacks out, it's lost almost a third of a million white people."

"That's some serious white flight." She pulled the Washington newspaper out of her bag and opened it to an article she'd skimmed earlier on the populations of cities. "Let's see. That's like having all the people in Pittsburgh sell out and leave town. Or Bakersfield, New Orleans, Corpus Christi, Anchorage, St. Paul, Toledo, or Buffalo. And only a few people would remain in St. Louis, Anaheim, or Tampa. A whole lot of white people sold their homes and moved out of this county."

"I believe it. They're afraid black people will rob them or do them in. Or reduce their property values. Or beat up their kids at school. Or beat them out of the first teams in sports. But frankly, I don't care if they stay on their side of the line and we stay on ours. Then they can't fuck with us."

"Ron," she scolded.

He laughed. "We black folk can do fine on our own."

"We can if we will. Hey, listen to this! This county has more people in it than the cities of San Francisco, Atlanta, Seattle, and—what do you know—Baltimore and Washington DC."

"Put that thing down before you became a mad statistician, with two fingers on the light bulb over your head and two fingers in the wall socket … and your hair sticking straight out in all directions."

~

Three months later, in the summer of 2005, and a couple of months after Mildred's warning, the family was moved in but far from settled. Closed doors hid piles of boxes and stacks of unhung pictures. Marty and Rosalie's rooms were finished, and the computers, stereo, and big-screen high-definition TV were up and running. Wilma's African-American figurines were displayed in the glass cabinet in the entry, and she'd had an interview for a teaching position at a high school. It was July, and she hoped to hear soon.

~

As Ron drove past the graffiti on the way home, he saw that someone had draped a large blue tarp over the unsettling message. He parked in the garage and walked into the kitchen, where Wilma was preparing a shrimp salad for dinner.

"Oh, hi," she said. "Any news on the wall? I heard that the fire department hosed it down, but couldn't get it off."

"It doesn't matter. They killed it with a tarp."

"What?"

"They threw a tarp over it to hide the indecent exposure. It won't gross out anyone else."

"Good."

"But I don't know—maybe people *should* see it, so they don't forget that racists still exist."

At the breakfast table the next morning Ron found an article about the graffiti in the newspaper. English muffins had popped out of the toaster, butter and jam were on the counter, and the aroma of coffee was strong in the air. Wilma was pouring herself a cup, and Marty and Rosalie were upstairs.

"It says that some people went home when they saw the wall because they felt a need to protect their families."

"I believe it," Wilma said. She blew across her coffee to cool it, and slurped a sip.

"And the Southern Poverty Law Center called it the worst racist graffiti they had seen in the Washington area in fifteen years. They said it was clearly a well-organized effort by a white power group."

"Did it say whether they caught the guys?"

"No. They haven't. They're still out there."

"That's reassuring."

"I'd like to see the chickenshits try something like that in broad daylight with brothers around."

"Well, I hope you can get your mind off it soon, honey. There's unpacking to do."

"Of course I will. My mind's a blank slate."

"That's nothing new."

Not totally blank, he thought. The vision of the wall faded, replaced by memories of his mother telling him how they "strung up" Thomas "even though he never did anything wrong," and Marty asking about Emmett Till. "What did he do that was so bad they killed him?" *I want evidence that proves Thomas was innocent. That's what's on my slate.*

TWO

Jimmy pulled open the door and stepped out of the late afternoon swelter into the cool, smoky haze of Jake's. Nothing felt better after working outside all day. Perspiration glued his brown shirt to his back and chest and soaked the brim of the motor-oil-logo cap that covered his close-cropped blond hair. His sleeves were rolled neatly just past his elbows, and his loose, faded jeans fell over grimy black steel-toe boots. His face and hands were rough and tanned, his build wiry.

Soon he felt a chill from the air conditioning and evaporation from his skin. The bar reeked of cigarettes, stale beer, and sweat, and the tile floor was sticky. The moth-eaten head of an eight-point buck looked down vacantly over the long, dark wood bar, which was illuminated by hanging lights with multicolored glass. Liquor bottles lined the back wall under a long mirror, and neon signs advertised brands of beer. Three young men lounged on stools talking with the bartender at the middle of the bar, and an old man sat alone near the door. A man and woman occupied a booth in the back. Everyone in the bar was white.

"Hey, Jimmy," greeted the bartender, a short man with protruding belly, graying hair combed over a balding pate, and ruddy complexion.

"Whaddya say, Jake?"

He walked past the three men, sat down at a stool at the far end of the bar, turned toward the door, and put one boot on the rail.

"You look tired tonight," Jake said. "Long day?"

"Yeah, I'm beat."

"What'll you have? The usual?"

"Yeah, and gimme some cigarettes."

"Sure thing." Jake took a fresh pack out of the wall rack, tossed it onto the bar with a pack of matches, and then went to the tap. He drew a glass of beer and set it in front of Jimmy.

"Thanks." Jimmy pulled the cellophane strip around the pack, peeled the foil off one end, tapped out a cigarette, and lit up. *Where are those guys?* he thought, looking at his watch. He took a long gulp of beer, set the glass down, and glanced down the bar. The three men were in their early twenties, all dressed in jeans and T-shirts. One was smiling and telling a story Jimmy could not quite make out; the others were laughing and gesturing.

"You stupid fuck!" said one, pushing the storyteller on the shoulder.

He replied, grinning, "Yeah, well, you would have done the same thing!"

Assholes, Jimmy thought. Bored, he took another drag and exhaled slowly. He turned and looked at the couple in the rear booth. They got up to leave and walked to the door, and Jimmy watched the man's hand slip from around her thick waist down to her rear and give it a squeeze. The door opened, filling the place with light, and they were gone. *Whore*, he thought.

He drained his glass and ordered another.

The door opened again, and a man walked in—younger, taller, and more muscular than Jimmy, with a head covered with brown stubble. His boots struck the wood floor with a crunch as he marched back to Jimmy's stool. "What's up?" he asked.

"Not much, Bill. You seen Dan?"

"Nah. Prob'ly got tied up in traffic."

"Long as he ain't tied up with some girl."

"Might be. There are a shitload where he works."

"Fooling around with women is a good way to get clap or AIDS," Jimmy said.

"Well, it ain't like he's queer. You wanna die, do what they do."

"Fucking queers. They get what they deserve."

Jake brought Bill a beer. Jimmy drained his glass and asked for a third round.

"Get any sleep today?" Jimmy asked.

"A few hours."

"Hot today."

"Hotter 'n hell," Bill said.

"Makes it hard to sleep. I turned the fan on in the office. That helped."

They talked until they ran out of words. Then they waited.

The door swung open, and a shorter man in his early twenties wearing an Orioles cap came in. A tight T-shirt covered his barrel chest, and his biceps and forearms bulged with muscles.

"Hey, Dan," Jimmy said. "Where you been?"

"At the club. One of the weight machines broke and I had to fix it before I left."

"You sure you weren't pressing three or four hundred pounds, showing off for some girl?" Bill teased.

"Nope."

Jimmy ordered a pitcher and led them back to a booth.

"That's why you like working there, ain't it?" Bill asked. "Seeing all them sluts all day long running around in tight shorts and halters."

"I don't mind," Dan said, grinning.

"And you weren't late 'cause you were sticking it to some girl in a closet?" Bill asked.

"No way. Not today."

"Hmmph," Jimmy snorted. "You shouldn't do that, Dan. One of these days you're gonna catch something bad."

"Don't you worry about me, Jimmy. I ain't dumb."

They sat down. One of the trio at the bar got up and dropped quarters into the jukebox. An old country music star filled the bar with sad crooning, and the trio began a lighthearted argument over the choice of music. Jimmy restrained himself from shouting at them to shut up, and soon their voices receded.

"Did you ever do a black chick?" Bill asked, continuing his teasing of Dan.

"Maybe."

"Black?" Jimmy said. "What about brown or tan?"

"You mean African-American?" Bill asked.

"I ain't callin' 'em that," Jimmy said. "That's bullshit. My ma was right. She said to call them colored, at least out in public where you can't call them what they are. That's good enough for me."

Jimmy and Bill nodded.

"Colored ... people of color," Dan said.

"Like that association of colored people," Bill said.

"Uh-huh," Jimmy said. "They got their associations, and we got ours. And you know what, Dan? In my daddy's time, mixing with colored women was against the law. You could get two to five if you had a kid by one, and two to ten if you married one. They didn't change that law till Daddy was mostly grown up—in the 1950s. That was a good law, Dan, and you know why."

"Yeah, I know," Dan said. "We gotta keep the race pure."

"That's right. It's against God's law to be mixing up the races. And we don't want that black blood poisoning everything till there ain't nobody left but coloreds. That's why we gotta keep the races apart as much as we can, to keep the colored girls from tempting white boys like you, Dan. I know some of them are pretty—I've been tempted plenty of times myself—but thank God, I've been able to resist."

"Yeah," Bill spoke up. "But it's harder and harder to keep the races apart, with them moving in on us like they are, and the government outlawing segregation and making laws that any tree-swinger can buy a house in any white neighborhood."

"I know," Jimmy said. "The worst thing the federal government ever did was to throw us all together in the same schools and stores and restaurants and everything. Lot of people who think they're headed for that heavenly kingdom are gonna find themselves in hell for doing that, you better believe it."

Bill leaned in on Dan and lowered his voice. "You know, one day they'll get you for doing their women. Some night they'll get you in an alley, and there won't be no mercy. They'll kill you dead. Carve you up. They're animals."

"I can take care of myself," Dan said, his eyes on fire. "They tried that before. Three of them jumped me, and they wished they hadn't."

"One pop and you're gone," Jimmy said. "They all carry guns."

"I ain't afraid of them. They're the ones that better watch out." He took off his cap, ran a hand over his short brush-cut, and replaced the cap. "I got guns, too."

Jimmy poured the last of the pitcher into their glasses, looked up to catch Jake's eye, and pointed to the pitcher. The bartender nodded. Bill and Jimmy lit up again.

"We done good last night," Jimmy said. "That'll tell them boys they better watch out."

"Man, you were beautiful, Jimmy," Dan said. "How do you keep your hand so steady? Unbelievable. No mistakes, everything neat. It was a work of art."

"Yeah, up on that ladder in the fog and at night, with just the light from that little street lamp. That was awesome," Bill said.

"Guess you forgot I used to detail cars."

"Yeah," Dan said.

"You just gotta be careful and patient."

"I almost shit when that cop pulled up down by the intersection," Dan said.

"Let's keep it real low, boys," Jimmy whispered, looking around the bar. No one had noticed their conversation. Bill and Dan nodded at Jimmy. Then Jimmy whispered, "Yeah. So next thing I knew I heard

Bill say, 'Jimmy. Car,' and saw him fall on the ground. And I said, 'Car, Dan,' and I dropped behind that bush."

"And then I slipped behind the wall," Dan whispered.

"And we all waited seemed like forever for that light to change and that cop car to move on," Jimmy said.

"But it finally did," Bill said. "And after that, I kept watching the highway, and a few cars went by, but most were traveling fast, and the sky was still dark, and nobody seemed to notice us, so I didn't even bother warning you guys."

"And nobody ever did come at us from the subdivision," Dan said.

"You guys done good," Jimmy said.

Dan frowned. "Too bad they covered up the wall so quick."

"It don't matter," Jimmy said. "They all saw it. Everybody. They know what's under there. People took pictures, e-mailed them to friends and relatives all over the country. And it'll be in the papers. The big thing is they know we're here. And they know that means they got trouble."

Two bikers came in. One was middle-aged, fat, and balding with black hair to his shoulders and tattooed arms. He wore a black leather vest with an American flag on the back and a black T-shirt with the sleeves cut off. The other had a droopy brown mustache, shaved head, and mirrored sunglasses. Jimmy watched them impassively as they walked to a booth, their boots thudding on the floor.

"Okay, let's forget about last night," Jimmy said. "The bar's got ears now."

Jake brought a new pitcher of beer to the booth.

"Thanks, buddy," Jimmy said.

They let Jake get back to the bar before resuming their conversation. Jimmy refilled their glasses. He took a long swig, and felt the cool, bitter liquid going down his throat. His blood rose in his cheeks, and a flood rushed into his brain, licking at the dam of his inhibitions.

"What gets me is how they think they own the world—with all their big-ass cars and houses," Bill muttered.

"They're moving in on us, trying to take over," Dan agreed.

"But it don't matter how much money they got or how much education," Jimmy said. "They're still niggers. And they'll always be niggers, too."

"They think that just 'cause they got education that they're better than you," Dan said. "That's what makes me mad. Them people actually look down their noses at you and treat you like shit. And they act like they hate you!"

"They forget whose country this is," Jimmy growled. "They forget who built this country. This ain't their country, this is *our* country. This country's white. This country's fucking Anglo-Saxon! We cleared the land. We fought the Indians and the British. We built the roads and factories and ships and airplanes. It wasn't them. This country's ours, not theirs." He drained his glass, and crashed it down on the table. He looked at Bill and a thought occurred to him: "You put in any applications today?"

"After I caught some zees. No one was hiring. They only want Africans and 'latrinos' and gooks 'cause they work for nothing. Shit, I ain't about to work for nothing. Fuck that shit. I'd rather stay in bed. Till my unemployment runs out, anyway."

"First they get you laid off at the tool rental. Then they take all the jobs by working for nothing."

"That's what my boss said. He said I wasn't nice enough to them. Didn't talk nice enough. Didn't smile at them enough. Made them load their own lawnmowers and tampers into those stinking SUVs and big-ass pickups. Well, they can all kiss my ass. Why should I strain my back? Why shouldn't they strain theirs? Yes, Mr. Negro. Yes, Mr. Spic. Nice to see you, Mr. Cabbie. Be sure to have it back on Monday, Mr. Chink. I'll shoot the fuckers before I kiss their butts."

"Fuck yeah," Jimmy said. "They work for nothing, but then you find out how lazy they are, and then stuff comes up missing, and you know where it went. That's what we always found on the farm. Goddamn colored field hands—and wetbacks too—they ain't worth a shit when it comes to working, 'specially the coloreds. And they ain't got good sense neither. They broke Daddy's plow once 'cause they didn't know what they was doing. And then when you asked them what happened, the first thing you know, they was back-talking you and raising Cain."

Bill pulled out his cigarettes and offered one to Jimmy. "Smoke?"

"Yeah. I'll try one of yours," Jimmy said, taking one. Bill lit it for him, and Jimmy took a slow and steady drag, sucking the smoke deep into his lungs to add to his dizziness.

"Say, you need any help at the garage now?" Bill asked.

"Nah. Noah's all I need right now. He's not real swift and kind of lazy—"

"How come you keep him then?"

"Oh, I don't know. He's a good colored, far as they go. And he always worked for Daddy, and he does do what you tell him to, you know, without any back talk. And he handles any coloreds that come in—that's the big thing. I'll be goddamned if I'm gonna wait on them."

"So what's next, Jimmy?" Bill asked.

Jimmy looked away. "I'll call you guys."

THREE

Nineteen-oh-seven, Ron thought. *Somewhere east of Washington not long after the turn of the century.*

The house was quiet. Wilma and the children were still asleep. He poured a cup of coffee in the kitchen, went into his office, and sat on the rolling swivel chair at his big oak desk, which once was his father's. Bookcases, mostly empty, lined one wall. A dozen cardboard boxes awaited his attention. A recliner, armchair, and floor lamp invited him to sit down and read.

He had intended to check his e-mail, but instead let his mind slip into surfing—exploring the mazes and tunnels of the search engines, following aimless curiosity. He had had no intention of looking for his great-grandfather, but his subconscious was guiding his fingers.

He sipped his coffee and typed "lynchings" in the search field. Three hundred and sixty-one thousand results came up. *Whoa,* he thought. *Too much.*

Refining his search to "lynchings by year" brought statistics compiled by the Tuskegee Institute in Alabama between 1882 and 1968. The numbers made his stomach tighten. A total of 4,742 lynchings were recorded; 3,445 black victims and 1,297 white. The worst decade had been the 1890s when 1,111 blacks were killed. Fifty-eight were killed in 1907. Thankfully, each succeeding decade showed a gradual decline until the 1960s when the last lynching was recorded. Eight Southern states accounted for more than three-quarters of the lynchings of blacks. Maryland had "only" twenty-two during that period, and most states in the Midwest and West exceeded Maryland's total. Connecticut, Massachusetts, and New Hampshire had none.

Unable to find names of victims listed by location and date, Ron decided to examine photographic records. The location and date of the lynching and the name of the victim were often noted on photos. Maybe he would find his great-grandfather hanging from some tree on the Internet. He typed "lynchings photographs postcards," and found numerous pages with photos of hangings, shootings, burnings, and mutilations of black men. Mobs, large and small, gathered to witness the self-righteous events. For an hour he slogged through the horrific pictures, but found none that occurred in Maryland around 1907.

Wilma came in, and Ron quickly clicked over to e-mail, not wanting her to know he was looking for Thomas. She hugged him from behind and went into the kitchen to get some coffee.

Returning to his search, he found a site selling a book titled *100 Years of Lynchings* by an author named Ralph Ginzburg. According to the site, Ginzburg's book contained selected articles from a wide range of newspapers. *Maybe his story is in there*, Ron thought. He ordered the book.

His mind drifted from the lynching to the graffiti, then to the Ku Klux Klan. When he typed "KKK," more than two million results came up. He perused the KKK Web site and then drew a box on a piece of paper and made two lists, one headed "for" and one "against." The KKK was against interracial dating and marriage, Jews, homosexuals, women's liberation, Communists, the federal government, and immigration. They were for white Christianity, white power, school prayer, racial segregation, and white Americans taking back America. *No surprises here*, he thought. But it gave him satisfaction just to have organized and catalogued the information.

He went into the kitchen for coffee and found Wilma sitting on a stool at the island, engrossed in the newspaper. Marty and Rosalie were still in bed.

"What are you looking at in there?" she asked.

"Oh, just fooling around, surfing. I checked out the Klan Web site. It's big. Did you know that Lincoln was against blacks voting or holding office, or marrying whites? He said it in one of the Lincoln-Douglas debates. I couldn't believe it. But then I found the same quote on the National Park Service site. It's true. He was against slavery, but he wasn't for racial equality."

"That's the way things were back then."

"Yeah. He was a politician who was trying to get votes. And you know what else? The KKK site made me think how those graffiti morons mixed their swastikas with KKKs. But can you imagine what Hitler would have done with pointy-headed guys running around wearing masks and dresses to disguise their identity, instead of proper German uniforms? They would have been the first to get the gas."

"You mean wearing hoods and robes. But weren't the Nazis and KKK both against blacks and Jews?"

"Yes, but Hitler wanted to *kill* us all—us and the Jews. The KKK just wants to keep us separate and *subservient*."

On the way back to the computer, his mind continued to work. *Where did you live, great-grandfather?*

He typed "Maryland death records" and found the state's archive of Vital Records—adoption, birth, death, divorce, marriage, probate records, U.S. census info, tax rolls, and wills.

They might have a copy of Thomas Phillips's will, if he had completed one prior to his death. Maybe he owned land and paid taxes on it. He might have been a tenant farmer or sharecropper living on a landlord's property.

"Land Records" was on the menu of links, where transfers of property, rents, debts, and evictions of tenant farmers were kept, as was "Maryland Newspapers." *I might be able to find a newspaper description of the lynching there. But most of the information is on microfilm in the state archives. I might find Thomas there, but I'll have to take a Saturday and go to Annapolis.*

Ron had seen enough for one morning. He went upstairs and put on his running shoes. Back downstairs, he stretched, shouted good-bye to Wilma, started his stopwatch, and headed out the side door of the garage. The outside air was already hot and humid—so unlike the Bay Area. He only wanted a short run—he had too much to do—but he had to run.

Ever since they'd moved in, he'd wanted to find out where the path into the woods behind the house led. Taking it, he jogged awkwardly down into a shallow ravine, slipping and sliding as he went. He leapt across a small stream, and charged up the other side like a wide receiver passing a linebacker, his muscles rippling.

He was still amazed at how green the broadleaf forest was. The trees were mostly oak and maple, many with trunks two or three feet across. Honeysuckle, ferns, and poison ivy encroached on the path. A gray squirrel darted up a tree at his approach.

At the top of the hill, the path joined a straight paved trail. To the right was the bicycle bridge over Blake Station Road, the two-lane road he took to work. A cluster of old houses encircled the bridge, surrounded by subdivisions full of large new homes. *Anachronisms*, he thought as he looked at the old homes. *Are the occupants too?*

He turned the other way and ran past his subdivision, and then through a small wood. Beyond the wood, spindly trees rose from untended fields. On a hill to his left, in a stand of spreading oaks, stood a large old two-story brick house with double chimneys on the gable ends and a long porch on one side. Eight horses grazed in a meadow surrounded by a white fence, and soon he was avoiding clumps of horse manure on the trail.

To the left he saw a path into a woods and wondered where it might lead, but he ran past. Today he was more interested in seeing where the paved trail went.

A white, middle-aged jogger passed him going the other way,

surprisingly heavy for a runner, and they exchanged greetings. Two bicycles overtook him from behind, the first rider shouting a warning as they passed. "On your left!"

"Look out for the manure!" Ron warned back.

Emerging from the woods, he came to a bicycle bridge over another paved two-lane road and stopped at the center of the bridge. He clicked off his stopwatch at nine minutes and twelve seconds—just under one mile at his average of nine point seven minutes per mile.

Surveying the area, he saw another group of old houses surrounding this bridge—bungalows and two-story farmhouses with steep metal roofs, most with wrap-around porches and garages to the rear. Down the road to the left was a mammoth oak tree with a trunk six feet in diameter, knees supporting its base. Limbs as thick as tree trunks reached out over the road. He wondered how he'd failed to notice it when he had driven past before. The name of the road was Big Oak, and at once he realized why. *Man*, he thought. *It must have been here when people were using horses and wagons—or before there was a road— before people even came.*

Beneath the spreading tree was an old convenience store with three cars parked in its gravel lot. He could not imagine how the place could stay in business. Between the store and the bridge was a garage with two open overhead doors. A small road turned off beside the garage, paralleling the bicycle trail and crossing railroad tracks. Behind the garage sat the remains of a long building with a loading dock, large loading doors, and a caved-in roof. The old warehouse was gradually succumbing to the advances of brush and saplings. *I'm looking into the past*, he thought.

He restarted his stopwatch and retraced his route back to the present. By the time he reached home, his watch showed eighteen minutes and thirty-eight seconds, and his skin was glistening.

He showered and shaved. As he finished, he gazed at his mug with satisfaction—broad nose, moderately thick lips, and confident brown eyes—and then turned sideways and admired his swimmer's shoulders, respectable pecs, and flat stomach. He walked into the bedroom nude, and began to make the bed, stretching the bottom sheet tight and forming hospital corners with the top one.

Wilma came in, saw him, and glanced downward. "You better cover that thing up before you get in trouble."

He smiled lewdly and walked toward her. "But I like to get in trouble."

"Oh, you do, do you? Well—"

The doorbell rang downstairs, and she looked at him helplessly. "I better see who's there."

"Don't be long."

From upstairs, he heard her call "Marty! Jeff's here," and then heard the phone ring twice. Since Wilma didn't shout for anyone to pick up, he knew it was for her. After waiting in silence for several minutes, he gave up, dressed, and walked downstairs where he found her chatting away on the phone. He went out to mow the lawn, felt the humidity again, and realized that the shower had been a mistake. Marty and his friend were shooting baskets on the wheel-around hoop by the driveway. As he walked toward the garage, the ball bounced his way. He took a shot and missed, but was drawn into their game.

"Air ball," Marty said.

"Yeah, yeah."

The white neighbor from three houses down the street walked up and put out his hand. *Shit*, Ron thought, *another friendly white boy.*

"I'm Jeff's dad, Mike Hoffman." He was about forty years old, average height, tanned skin. Mike had stocky legs, a soft belly, and thinning brown hair. He wore a University of Maryland T-shirt hanging out over baggy old shorts. On his feet were dilapidated, low-cut basketball shoes with no socks.

Ron smiled, thrust out his hand, and squeezed hard. "Ron Watkins, Marty's dad. Nice to meet you. So you just moved in too?"

"Yeah, a week or so before you did," Mike said.

Ron was puzzled. *Why had they decided to live in this neighborhood instead of moving out like other whites?*

"So where do you work?" Mike asked.

Oh Christ, Ron thought. *Here we go: the white competition game.* "IRS, downtown."

"Great, our own friendly neighborhood auditor. Now every time I buy a car I'll have to look over my shoulder because you'll wonder where I got the money."

"I love to do audits. You can find out a lot about people that way. But I don't do them anymore. I let other people do them for me. I just give them a name and address and tell them where to go. By the way, what's your address?"

"Uh—I just moved in. I can't remember."

"Sure."

"So you're a CPA?"

"That's right."

"A bean counter."

"That's me."

The ball bounced toward Mike, and he took a few steps back and shot a three-pointer. Swish.

Marty grabbed the ball and passed it to his dad, who launched a shot. It bounced off the backboard and glanced off the hoop. Marty looked disappointed.

Ron decided to play the white game: "And what do you do, Mike?"

"I'm a meeting planner for an association in DC." The ball bounced Mike's way, and he drove in a few steps and shot a fade-away jumper. Again the ball went in without touching the rim.

"Wow," Marty said.

Jeff threw the ball to Ron. He carefully sighted a set shot and lofted it in the direction of the hoop. The twang of ball on metal was followed by Marty's "Aw, Dad." Jeff hid a smile with his hand.

"Where'd you learn to play ball?" Ron asked.

"Oh, I played high school ball in a small town north of Baltimore and then at University of Maryland at College Park. But I was only third-string at Maryland."

"At Maryland? That's still great," Ron said. "Everybody always thought I must've played basketball because I'm tall, but I couldn't shoot. My sports were swimming and diving, and a little boxing."

"Ever take a dive?"

"I get it," Ron said, laughing. "Yes I did. But just off the high board—not in the ring."

Mike drove sideways past Ron and made a lazy hook.

"Man," Marty said to Jeff, giving him the ball. "Doesn't he ever miss?"

"Sure, sometimes." Jeff dribbled twice and sank an awkward hook himself.

Ron took the ball, dribbled away from the backboard, and looked at Mike. "Okay, come on." He moved a step toward Mike, who tensed and raised his arms. Ron drove right at the defender, cut to the hoop, leaped high, and laid it in smoothly over Mike's outstretched arms.

"There!" he said, smiling at Marty and picking up the ball.

"Yay, Dad!" called Marty. "Now can Jeff and I shoot?"

"Yeah, yeah." He passed it to Marty and started chatting with Mike. "So where'd you guys move from?"

"Oh, about three miles from here. We had a sixties house with no basement, our first house. After we built up some equity in it, we decided to buy a new one. We needed more room for the boys."

"Why'd you move here?"

"We liked the development. The houses back up to the woods, and there's a community pool and playgrounds and the bike trail behind us. Mary grew up around here, and we wanted to stay close to her parents and family, and my family lives up the road in Baltimore."

"Were there any blacks where you used to live?" Ron was jolted by his own directness, but sometimes curiosity got the better of him.

"No—none, but some were moving in near there."

"And you don't mind having all these people of color in the neighborhood?"

"Hell no, man," Mike said, smiling. "Some of my best friends are black."

Ron forced a chuckle. "Go on."

"I tell you, there are so many people of color in DC and Baltimore—blacks, Asians, Indians, Middle Easterners, and Hispanics—and we knew so many at Maryland that we got used to it. Pretty soon it felt strange to be around only white people—so strange, in fact, that lots of times Mary would say, 'Where are the brothers?'"

White liberals, he silently sighed. "Well. I'm looking forward to meeting Mary."

"Sure. You gotta watch out, though. She has this amazing auditory memory. It seems like she remembers almost everything she hears. It's kind of like a photographic memory."

"Now that could be dangerous."

"Just be careful what you say," he said with a grin.

"Thanks for warning me."

The ball bounced his way, and he sent a three-pointer sailing toward the basket but missed.

"So what do you do for recreation?" Mike asked.

"You mean besides giving names and addresses of neighbors to my auditors?"

"Yeah, besides that."

"Not much. I run and swim, and go to the movies and museums and amusement parks with Wilma and the kids, you know, family stuff. And I guess eventually we'll join a church. Do you go to church?"

"You bet," Mike said. "Regularly. Every Christmas and Easter."

Ron laughed. "So what do you and Mary do for fun?"

"Well, this is horse country, and Mary rides in a horse club once a month, and we both go to the track a couple times a year. And she loves storytelling. She can tell a story that lasts an hour and holds you the whole way—I'm not kidding. She loves to go to the library and tell stories to the children."

"This storytelling, it must tie into her ability to remember things she hears."

"I'm sure it does."

Now the ball bounced Mike's way, and he took a long jump shot and missed.

"Uh-oh. You're slipping. Maybe we should play again after the boys are done," Ron said. "So what else do you guys do?"

"What else do locals do? Well, we like to watch the fireworks on the Mall on the Fourth, and go boating on the bay, and eat crabs and drink beer, and go to the mountains or the shore in the summer, and get together with family. Oh, and I'm a local history nut. That's about it."

"Local history, huh? I'm interested in that."

"I'll have to give you a tour of the area sometime, show you the historical sites."

"Great. When can we go?" *Gotta find out what he knows*, Ron thought.

"Hold your horses, man. We gotta check with the women, don't we?"

"Wilma won't want to go."

"Yeah, but she keeps your to-do list, doesn't she?"

"Yeah, but if we surprise her when she just gets up, we can blow right by her."

Mike laughed. "We can try. Say, did you see that racist graffiti on the highway?"

"Sure did. Great people you got around here. Friends of yours?"

"Nope. They just seem to come out of the ground once in a while, usually in the spring, and then disappear. I wouldn't worry about them."

"Easy for you to say. You're white."

FOUR

Wilma had hand-delivered invitations a week earlier, and the neighbors had received her warmly. But since no one RSVPed anymore, it was difficult to know how many would come. Now, after a day of work, preparations were nearly complete. She and seven-year-old Rosalie were making hot and spicy crab dip and fresh avocado-onion dip to go with corn chips and crackers when Ron walked in. Wilma was mixing ingredients in a stainless steel bowl, while Rosalie was standing on a footstool to reach the countertop and grate an onion. She was light-skinned, about four feet tall, but not slender like the rest of her family. Wilma wore a floral-print caftan. Rosalie's hair was in cornrows with braids.

Seeing his daughter's eyes water, Ron said, "Aw, quit your crying."

"Oh, Dad," she groaned.

Wilma and Rosalie had filled trays with hot sausages, cheese spears, chicken wings, smoked salmon, crackers, and sourdough bread. Oyster stew steamed on the stove. Ham and turkey were warming in the oven, and a dish of cheese enchiladas with chili pepper sauce waited in the microwave. Sweet potato pie, brownies, grapes, and a lemon-frosted yellow cake sat on the bar.

Ron had donned a Hawaiian shirt and white slacks for the occasion. To help set up for the party, he pushed back the furniture in the great room, rolled up the Oriental rug on the oak floor for dancing, and finished vacuuming. Then he iced down the beer and wine on the deck, set up the bar with assorted liquors, and put a mix of jazz, reggae, funk, and R&B in the CD changer. Marty took chips, popcorn, and soft drinks to the playroom, and flipped on video games on one TV and cartoons on the other.

They had planned the party for the early evening, six o'clock, so that parents could bring their children. The kids would be downstairs with Marty and Rosalie, who were quite responsible. Ron and Wilma knew that the children would make frequent visits upstairs to check on their parents.

~

Guests started trickling in; Ron greeted them at the door, while Wilma finished putting out the food. The first to arrive were the principal of a nearby middle school, Melvin Hayden, and his wife Harriet, a human resources manager. They were light-skinned African-Americans. Melvin wore a white sport shirt and brown slacks, and Harriet a flowered blouse and gray pants. Ron chatted with them briefly. He asked Melvin how many white children went to the area schools. Melvin replied that two-thirds of the county's residents were black now, and only about ten percent of the students in the school system were white. Ron said that it seemed like the end of racial integration. Melvin agreed that it was true in some areas, but that it didn't matter. Overall, the schools were good, although many parents did feel compelled to send their children to private schools. Both of their children had attended the county schools and done well at the University of Maryland.

Next was a couple that Ron didn't know but greeted warmly.

"I'm Sam Pierce, Ron. This is my wife Cherise, son Jeremy, and baby Saundra."

"How old are the kids?" Ron asked Cherise.

"Jeremy's five," Cherise said, "and Saundra's two months."

"We live in the third house on the left," Sam said. Both were tall and lean with dark brown skin and short hairstyles. Sam was in his mid-thirties and Cherise a few years younger. He wore creased khaki slacks and a yellow golf shirt. Cherise had on green plaid pants and a loose white blouse. She carried baby Saundra close to her body in a multicolored sling.

"You use that Hispanic lawn service, don't you?" Ron asked.

"Sure do. They're a lifesaver. I'm an attorney—do civil and criminal and wills and such—and keep evening and Saturday hours, when people can see me. So it's hard for me to find time to do the lawn." He handed Ron a business card. "If you ever need any legal work, give me a call. I handle about everything but taxes and divorces."

"Well, I don't think we need a divorce lawyer yet, Sam. So far Wilma and I are getting along pretty well, although she says I drive her crazy sometimes." They laughed. "And I work for the IRS, so I hope I don't need a lawyer for my taxes."

Following the Pierces were the Randolphs. Donna came first. She wore a short halter-top print dress with spaghetti straps over sandals. She had golden tan skin. John was husky and a shade darker and wore long khaki cargo shorts and a light blue shirt. Philip, five, was chunky and dressed in shorts and a Spiderman T-shirt. John was a career Air Force officer working in information technology. His speech was clipped and businesslike. Donna was a paralegal.

The Graffs came next. Arno was average height, dark. He wore his hair in short locks and twists and was dressed in tan shorts and a checkered T-shirt. He managed a shift at a printing plant. Judy was white and statuesque, several inches taller than Arno, with long brown hair braided down the middle of her back. She worked as a horticulturist at a nursery. Ron had already met Arno.

"Hi Arno," Ron said. "This must be Judy."

"Sure is," Arno replied.

"And who's this young fellow?"

"This is Robert," Judy said. "He's eight. Say hi to Mr. Watkins, Robert." Robert was light-skinned, reflecting his mixed heritage.

"Hi, Mr. Watkins."

Ron invited Robert to join the children in the basement, and took Arno and Judy back to the great room to meet the others. The bell rang again. Ron hurried back to encounter a woman with cocoa-colored skin wearing a low-cut leopard-print sundress that didn't hide the full breasts underneath. Her long locks of black hair were pulled to one side.

"Oh, Mr. Watkins," she said holding out her hand. "Tabatha Mance. So nice to meet you." Her eyes glanced down, around and up, taking in his shoulders and chest before landing on his face. He took her hand and gave it a firm shake. "I've seen you playing basketball with your son, Mr. Watkins. Now I finally get to meet you." She gave his hand a little squeeze and held it a bit too long.

"Call me Ron," he said, smiling.

Her husband stepped forward and shook Ron's hand. "Alfred Mance," he announced. He was dark, broad, and muscular with a large head, thick neck, short hair, and a kind of sneer on his mouth. His eyebrows were knitted into a permanent frown, and he looked about forty years old. He kept glancing around the room as they shook hands, and Ron could feel power in his grip.

"Have you been in the neighborhood long?"

"'Bout a year and a half," Alfred said. "We moved in from the District. I got a liquor store there, but it got held up twice, and the drug dealers set up a crack house two blocks from our house, and so we moved out—moved here."

"Do you like it here?"

"Yeah, man—nice houses, low crime. And it's ours, too. It's black and getting blacker all the time. The racist honkies keep moving out, and we keep moving in. They afraid of us. It used to be theirs out here. But it gonna be ours, man. All ours. We taking over here."

"You know we have white neighbors on our street who chose to live here."

"They won't be here long."

"Not if you show them your gun collection and your knives, Sugar Pie," Tabatha added.

"You keep guns?" Ron asked.

"Fuck yeah, man," he whispered a little too loudly, and at the same time curled his hands into fists. "We gotta protect ourselves. Be ready the next time they come at us."

"Who?"

"The rednecks. Who do you think?"

"The rednecks are going to come after us? In the twenty-first century?"

"Where you been, man? This is still redneck country, you better believe it. You saw that racist shit they wrote on that wall. They here, man, and some day they'll come for us."

"But all white folks aren't rednecks."

The muscles tightened around his eyes. "They all part of the system, man. They all want to keep us in our place. We still don't get nothing 'less we take it, same as always. Why, up until a few years ago this was all tobacca plantations around here—working for the massuh, bending and planting and pulling the weeds. We all used to be slaves—chopping stalks, spearing them on sticks, hanging them in barns. Right here. It was just like Mississippi, 'cept it was tobacca instead of cotton. Yes, suh, no, suh. Tell me what to do next, suh. But not no more. Why, it weren't forty years ago they wouldn't even let us buy a house out here. Now we can. Now we taking over, man."

"But don't you think we need to learn to live together—you know, like in Martin's dream?" He deepened his voice and began to imitate King. "I have a dream that one day little black boys and black girls will be able to join hands with little white boys and white girls as sisters and brothers—"

Alfred didn't let him finish. "Oh, you prob'ly think it cool to have white neighbors, like you finally as good as they are. Fuck that shit, man. They can kiss my ass, man, for all I care. And this deal about Arno marrying a white woman—I don't go with that. What, black women ain't good enough for him? When so many need a man? He's being disloyal to black women and the race, man —like he wants to be white 'stead of black. I don't buy that shit."

Ron directed them back to the kitchen, hoping that Alfred wouldn't make these comments in front of Arno and Judy.

~

Later, Wilma and several of the women were gathered around the kitchen island sampling hors d'oeuvres and sipping drinks. *They're really diving into the crab dip*, Wilma thought. *I should've made more.*

"We moved here two years ago," Donna Randolph said, "but we never know how long we'll be in one place. John's in the Air Force. He works at Andrews Air Force Base in computers."

"It must be tough moving all the time," Cherise Pierce said. Her baby moved in the sling, and Cherise looked down attentively. "Sam works long hours in his law practice, but at least we stay in one place."

"I don't mind much. I don't have much trouble getting paralegal jobs, and I find change stimulating," said Donna. "Pretty soon, though, I'll be going on maternity leave."

Cherise looked up excitedly. "Girl, when? You don't show yet."

"In January. It's a girl."

Baby Saundra let out a weak cry and went back to sleep. In the background, Ella was singing, "How High The Moon" and the men were laughing on the other side of the room. Outside the great room windows, dusk was gathering.

"Mm, mm, mm," Tabatha cooed with a tinge of sadness. You're blessed, honey. Alfred and I haven't been so lucky. You have a little boy too, don't you?"

"Yes. Philip," Donna said. "He's five."

"Oh, mine is too," Cherise said. "His name's Jeremy. He's downstairs with the other children."

"So's Philip," Donna said. "Maybe they'll be friends."

"Arno and I met at the nursery," Judy said. "Back in the rhododendrons and azaleas. He kept looking and looking, but never would buy. Then suddenly he asked me out."

Tabatha said, "Honey, he wasn't looking at the plants, now was he?" Everyone laughed.

Cherise told how she met Sam in Baltimore when he was in law school and she was an RN working in the emergency room. "He came in with an attack of appendicitis, I diagnosed it, and it was love at first sight. What about you, Wilma? Where did you and Ron meet?"

Wilma visualized a handsome young man sitting at a large wood table in a room with high ceilings and rows of book stacks. "We met at the library at San Francisco State. He was studying his accounting and I was studying my English lit. But he wasn't keeping his eyes on his book—he was watching me instead—and I looked up and bam—eye contact! He whispered 'Hello' to me, and I whispered 'Hello' back, and that's how it all began. Before we knew it, we were commuting to school together from Oakland, and soon after that, we were dating."

"A commuter courtship. How romantic," Cherise said.

"So you lived in Oakland?" Donna asked.

"Yes. My mom taught school there, and my dad was a welder at the shipyard. Ron's dad was a pharmacist near us, and we always used to buy our prescriptions from him, but Ron and I never bumped into each other in Oakland."

"Oh, that's funny. You had to go to San Francisco to meet," Cherise laughed.

"Are your parents still with you?" Donna asked Wilma.

"Our dads have passed, but our mothers are alive."

Cherise glanced over to the glass cabinet filled with miniature black ballet dancers, boys fishing, a woman holding a baby, men playing instruments, and children playing. "I love your figurines, Wilma," she said. Wilma thanked her.

The timer on the oven buzzed, and Wilma took out the ham and set it on the counter.

"Need any help?" Judy asked.

"Oh, no, thanks.

Donna broached the recent vandalism. "Did you see what those Klanners wrote on that wall?"

Wilma frowned. "Ron told me about it. It's disgusting. I wouldn't let the kids see it."

~

Ron opened the door and smiled. "Mike! Glad you could come."

"For a while we weren't sure we had the right night. We kept looking down the street and didn't see any cars or people, and we didn't want to be the first to arrive, and we thought it started at six o'clock."

Ron laughed. "Six o'clock CP time, man! That was your mistake. We colored people never arrive at a party on time. And who's this lovely lady—Mrs. Hoffman?"

"Yep. This is Mary." She was average height, in her late thirties, rounded but fit in her white gaucho pants. She was tan and freckled, with wavy, reddish-brown shoulder-length hair. Ron and Mary exchanged greetings. Jeff and Jason ran downstairs to see Marty and Rosalie.

"I bet they keep you busy," Ron said to Mary.

She smiled. "Oh yes. But I work outside the home too. I'm a research associate at the Museum of Natural History downtown—an anthropologist."

"And a storyteller too, Mike says."

"Oh yes. I love to tell stories, especially to kids."

"Oh that ham smells good, and those rolls. Did she just bake them?" Mike said, looking hungrily toward the source of the odors.

"Probably just took them out of the oven," Ron said. He became nervous as Alfred approached. Ron introduced them all.

"Alfred and I already met when we were working on our yards," Mike said. "We had a good time talking about local history."

"Yes, sir," Alfred said. "Talked about the mansions on the old plantations. They's one on top of every hill."

"Really?" Ron asked.

"That's about right," Mike said. "That's where the planters lived."

"You mean, the slave masters," Alfred said.

"Well, that's what they were before emancipation."

"And what they tried to be after 'mancipation, too—'cept the slaves left. They weren't about to keep slaving for their masters no more."

"Yes, but when it looked like there wouldn't be enough hands to work the fields, the planters started breaking up the plantations into small farms, and they got freed slaves to work the farms for a share of the crop."

"Sharecroppas," Alfred hissed.

"Yes, or they rented the farms."

"To tenant farmers!"

Mary looked impatient. Ron took her aside. "What's the matter? Not interested in plantations?"

"Save me, Ron. Where's Wilma?" He pointed her to the great room, and then stayed with Mike and Alfred to referee, if necessary.

" … And the masters fooled the croppas into thinking that if they worked for a share of the crop, they was free, and if they worked hard, some day they'd get enough money to buy they own farm. Then the masters charged them for the house and farm animals and lent them money for seed and fertilizer and food and clothes, and at the end of the year when they settled up, the farmers never had nothing to show for it."

Mike's head bobbed up and down in agreement. "Yep, and in a lot of ways it was better than slavery for the white owners. For one thing, they didn't have to take care of the old folks."

"Sheeit. They's a white myth. Slave masters never took care of old folks. Most of them let old folks starve and die—they weren't worth nothing—just like old mules."

Ron smiled nervously. Tinder and flint. Hope this doesn't escalate and ruin the party. "That's interesting!" he said, jumping in. Mike and Alfred ignored him.

"And most of the time the croppas ended up in debt to their masters and couldn't leave the farm till they paid off their debt. They never could get ahead. They was slaves to debt."

"Peons," Mike said.

"Yessir! And if they tried to walk away from the debt, they'd go to jail."

"But a lot of them did get ahead and bought their own farms."

"Not many. They's another white man's myth," Alfred said, spitting out the word 'white.' "If black farmers got too far ahead, the whites'd burn them out, drive them out, or lynch them." Now he was jabbing at Mike with his finger.

"That happened. But I think some of the farmers were at least able to pay off their debts and leave the farm for jobs that paid wages."

"Colored folk wages," Alfred said.

"Yeah. I guess they usually did get less than white workers."

"Believe it!"

"There!" Ron said. "You agree. But I want to know how you guys know so much about history."

"I don't know much," Mike said. "I'm just interested. I keep reading up on it and touring old mansions and so on. It's a hobby with me."

"What about you, Alfred?"

"Don't need to read about it. Been there, man. My family's from here. We was slaves first. And my granddaddy was a tenant farmer. Some of my cousins was sharecroppas, and some still worked tobacca here up to a few years ago when the state started paying farmers not to grow it."

"Did you ever work tobacco?" Mike asked Alfred.

"Sheeit. I've planted it, weeded it, wormed it, chopped it, speared it, hung it, sorted it, stacked it—ev'ything. Believe it!"

"I can't say I have," Ron said, shaking his head. "My family's been out west for a hundred years."

"Your folk went west. Mine went to DC. I fought my way up and scratched together my own business where I'm the boss. No one tells me what to do."

"Except the government," Mike said.

"You right there—Mr., uh … Mike."

By nine o'clock the group was content and well-fed. Ron turned the music to hip-hop and the booming thump, thump, thump of the bass guitar came from the speakers. Conversation grew thinner, laughter louder, and dancing began. Tabatha led the way, pulling Alfred onto the floor and shaking her booty at every man in the room. Several couples followed, and the great room came alive with sound and with limbs swaying in exuberant, sensuous motion. Physical joy overcame thought and inhibition. Beads of sweat appeared, and cheeks grew shiny. Only the Haydens remained seated, sipping drinks and enjoying watching the younger couples. Partners changed and couples mingled. Mike and Mary joined them. When Mary began dancing with Alfred, in what once would have been shocking, illicit race-mixing, Alfred seemed hesitant and carefully averted his eyes.

A reggae track came on, and the neighbors lined up to do a dance known as the Booty Call. Individuals became a group. Eyes looked ahead as feet moved and bodies turned in concert. No need to look down, everyone knew the step. The Haydens joined in the line dancing, and even Mike and Mary knew the sequence of movements.

At around ten guests began leaving—parents to take children home for bed, and the childless following their lead. Ron and Wilma went to the door to wish everyone a good night on the way out.

The Mances left last. Alfred and Ron extended fists and traded a gentle pound. "Enjoyed the paar-tay, bro."

"Be easy on Mike when you're doing yard work, man. He's not a bad guy."

"For a white man, you mean? But I gotta educate that boy—before he moves away."

"Don't mind him," Tabatha said. "He's just mad at the world. But I love him anyway."

She took Ron's hand again and said with a come-on smile, "I hope to be seeing a lot more of you around the 'hood, Ron."

"Oh, I'm sure you will."

FIVE

They all part of the system, man. They all want to keep us in our place. Ron was replaying Alfred's words as he collected dishes from the party. Images passed through his brain—the bartender in 1995 who refused to serve him, the occasional hateful looks of whites, times when he was just invisible to them, racial taunts, taxi drivers who looked at him and kept on going, the cop who pulled him over for no reason other than "driving while black." And he'd had it easy.

Segregation and lynchings were in the past, but white power still dominated government and business, using a few dark faces to support their claims of integration. Racial discrimination continued to plague the country—in jobs, housing, education, lending, justice, and politics. And whites fled blacks at every opportunity, to keep their lives pure and exclusive.

He remembered asking his father, a pharmacist, how to get ahead in a white-run world.

"I'll give you this advice," he had said. "Learn more, work harder, be pleasant, and play ball with them. That's the best you can do."

"But how much can you trust them? In the end, will they always put their race first?"

"I don't know, Ron. You've just got to be wary. You don't trust people unless you get to know them well. Then you have to take a chance … but you've still got to be careful."

He remembered how hard he had studied for his CPA exam, and how he always had fought to be better prepared than his colleagues at work, to always be the one they turned to for answers. He had greeted whites with a smile and believed that his friendliness had helped break barriers. Thus far, his dad's advice had been effective.

But now there was Thomas. If his children ever learned about the lynching, he could not allow them to grow up thinking that their great-great-grandfather was some kind of criminal. He might as well tell Wilma what he was going to do. He walked into the kitchen where she was loading the dishwasher and put the dishes he'd collected on the counter.

"I decided to look into this Thomas lynching," he said abruptly.

"Oh, Ron. Why? You said you had enough on your mind."

"I know, and that's true. It's not like I *want* to do it. You know how I feel about the subject. But I have to see if I can prove he was innocent and didn't commit any crime prior to the lynching."

"But your mother said he didn't do anything wrong."

"I know, but I need hard evidence."

"You can't trust your mother?"

"I need evidence to show to Marty and Rosy if it ever comes out that their great-great-grandfather was lynched."

He reminded her about Marty and the conversation about Emmett Till. "Marty's only a kid, and already, in his mind, someone has planted the seed that black people are bad and white people are good. Black people are presumed guilty until they're proven innocent. That's why I have to prove that Thomas was innocent."

"Oh, Ron. Why don't you leave it alone? You're just going to get worked up, and then everything else will suffer."

"I've got to know what happened. It's part of my past, too. My roots and our children's roots. I don't want our family's reputation disgraced by lies. I can't have that. And I don't want suspicions and innuendos undermining me at work, either. 'He's just like all those inner-city blacks. You know his great-grandfather was a murderer, don't you?'"

"But how would anyone find out about it? It was so long ago."

"Maybe they wouldn't find out. But maybe they would. These things happen. People do find out about things like this."

"And what if you find out that Thomas *did* do something bad? What then?"

"Well, I would want to know that, too."

"And if you find out he did nothing wrong? What will you do then?"

"Nothing, unless the children ask about it. I don't want to poison their minds against white people. But I don't know. Maybe I will tell them about it, when they're a lot older. I guess some day they should know."

"Ron. Forget it. It's water over the dam."

"Now you sound like a white person. 'I didn't lynch anybody. My family didn't either. I'm not to blame. It's ancient history.'"

"It's just going to make you mad, and fill you up with hate. Just leave it alone."

"At least I would have the personal satisfaction of knowing that Thomas was innocent, the knowledge that we're descended from a person we can all be proud of."

"You know, some people might not want you poking around in the past, claiming their relatives were murderers."

Ron stiffened. "Don't worry about me. I'll be careful." He saw her look of concern. "You know I will, baby."

~

Later that week, one evening after work, Ron drove under the bicycle bridge on Big Oak Road, past Big Oak Crossing Road and the garage on the corner, and pulled into the gravel lot of the old store. Wilma had asked him to pick up bread, cheese, and lunch meat on the way home. He thought the old general store might have these items. He also was curious about the place's owners. *How long have they been in business, and how do they survive?* He got out of his car, looking up at the massive oak tree. He felt minuscule and powerless, and wondered what the tree had witnessed over the years.

The two overhead doors of the garage were open, and above them was a large sign, CLAY OIL AND LUBE. Half a dozen cars were parked in the lot. A late-model car was up on a hydraulic lift, and a short, middle-aged black man was working on its wheels. Behind two empty concrete islands—tombstones for gas pumps—someone who seemed to be the car's owner talked to a white man holding a clipboard, dressed in work clothes and a motor-oil-logo cap.

Ron walked past the garage and noticed that the store had a side door, toward the rear, facing the garage, with a screen door reinforced by an old metal bread sign. *Door for coloreds*, he thought. He climbed three steps to the front porch. A sign over the front door read CLAY GROCERY, and large windows on both sides of the door were decorated with a variety of signs. COLD BEER AND WINE and MARYLAND LOTTO. PRODUCE and MEAT were lettered neatly on the window glass.

He went in and wandered through the store. Two white people were buying lottery tickets. The back wall of the store held soft drink fountains and freezers full of beer, soda, and dairy items. Three aisles of shelves displayed the usual food and drug items, and a low freezer case contained ice cream. Empty coffee pots sat on a counter next to the checkout. *No produce*, he observed, *and the meat is packaged cold cuts.*

He picked up a loaf of spongy wheat bread, a package of American cheese slices, and some turkey salami. He walked to the counter, put down the food, and waited for the salesclerk to complete the lottery transactions. The clerk was a white woman in her late twenties with suntanned arms emerging from a sleeveless white T-shirt, a tanned face with stringy blond hair hanging to her shoulders. Her slender body filled a tight pair of jeans. Ron noticed a small tattoo on her shoulder and her nipples pointing through the shirt. She saw him looking and glanced into his face, studying him. "Be with you in a minute."

The customers left, and he felt a twinge of anxiety at being alone with a white woman, the same feeling he had whenever he was alone with one on an elevator. Emmett Till jumped to mind again, murdered and mutilated in Mississippi in 1955 supposedly for whistling at a white woman in a country store.

"Will that be all?" the woman asked, inspecting his starched white dress shirt, stylish tie—loosened at the top—and gray dress pants.

Will that be all? What else are you offering? he thought. He smiled and said, "That's all."

She punched the prices into the register and gave him the total. He handed her some bills, looking her over again. "That sure is a big tree out there. How old do you think it is?"

"Ain't that something? They say it's over three hundred years old. Some people from the state came and measured it, and that's what they said. I don't suppose they could know that for sure unless they cut it down and counted the rings, which they would never do, 'cause it's our tree. Been on our farm as far back as we have records. And it's why they call this part of town Big Oak, and this road Big Oak Road." She counted out his change, and he put it into his pocket.

"Makes sense. How long has your family been here?"

"Since the seventeen hundreds, I know that. The farm used to be over a thousand acres, but that was back when the family was rich. Now we gotta make do with this store and garage. Oh well. That's life."

"How many acres do you have now?"

"Just seven, and the five on the other side of the road is mostly swampy. Can't build on it."

She seemed to be in no hurry, slowly reaching under the counter for a plastic bag.

"What was in the building behind the store?"

"Oh, the family used to sell feed, seed, and fertilizer."

"Really."

"And people used to catch the train for Baltimore and southern Maryland at the crossing. That's why we built the store here, with all those people coming and going."

"When did you build it?"

"1899."

"Interesting."

"Then in 1907 they put in the trolley line from Washington to Baltimore and people started building houses here and working every day in the city. That's when the store really started hopping."

The screen door slammed, and the man with the clipboard came in. He went to the soda machine in the back, filled a cup with crushed ice, and leaned against the wall, chewing ice and appraising Ron.

"Where do you live?" the woman asked. She finished bagging his items, tore off the receipt, and placed it in the bag.

"In John's Woods subdivision, off Spring Hill Road."

"Oh, I know where that is. Real pretty in there. Big houses."

"We like it. We're new here."

"Where did you move from?"

"Oakland, California."

"Long way. What brought you here?"

"A government job."

"Must be a good one to come all that way."

"Not bad."

"What's your name, anyway?"

"Ron. Ron Watkins. What's yours?"

"Annie Clay. Me and my brother Jimmy own this place. That's him back there."

Ron glanced back at the man by the soft drink machine, who stared back at him with no expression. Ron felt his muscles stiffen. He turned back to Annie and picked up his groceries.

"Nice to meet you, Miss Clay."

"You come back now," she said, glancing at his chest, then up into his eyes. "We'll treat you right."

She's coming on to me. No doubt about it. His breathing quickened, and he felt the heat of arousal rush through him. "I sure will. Have a nice day." He turned and left.

～

Jimmy was smoldering. "Well, bitch," he said, striding toward her. "Why didn't you just tear off your clothes and let that coon have you right here on the floor, in front of me and God and everybody, huh?"

"I'll do whatever I want to, Jimmy Clay. You ain't my lord and master. You can just mind your own business."

"And let you get it on with a jungle bunny, all dressed up like that in a shirt and tie like he was president or something. I'll not have you acting that way. You read your Bible, Sister. You'll go to hell if you keep this up."

She turned away. "Don't you throw Scripture at me, and don't act like my father. You're not my father, Jimmy Clay."

Jimmy grabbed her shoulder and spun her back toward him. "I'll tie you up in the basement and feed you bread and water till you learn."

She looked up into his eyes. "And who would run the store? You? Why, you'd starve to death trying to run this store."

"Oh yeah? Ever since you took them college courses, you know everything, don't you?"

"I know you couldn't run this store. You can't add two and two, and you wouldn't know what to get, or how much to get, or what to pay, or … or what. You couldn't keep the books. You're a grease monkey, Jimmy. All you know how to do is change oil and grease a car—not like that Mr. Watkins. Now there's a man. I wouldn't mind having that man."

"Why, you whore. I'm warning you." He pushed her hard against the wall. "You stay away from that black monkey, if you know what's good for you."

"Oh, you scare me *so* much."

～

Later that night, Jimmy sat on the screened porch of his and Annie's two-story farmhouse in the woods. He watched the headlights of Bill's dark blue Ford Crown Victoria and Dan's green Ford F250 pickup as they came down the long driveway and parked on the circle in front of the house next to his white Chevy Silverado pickup and white Cadillac DeVille. The trucks were late model and the sedans more than a decade old.

The three men sat in the dark on the porch drinking beer and smoking cigarettes. The glow of the burning ends brightened in the dark when they took a drag, and the odor of the smoke fought the sweet, damp smell of the woods. Their T-shirt sleeves were rolled over their shoulders. Each man had a tattoo of a four-link chain across one bicep. A German shepherd lay on the porch floor, looking into the woods.

The one-story porch stretched across the front of the house. A kitchen wing was appended to the rear of the home, and a shed attached to that kitchen contained the bathroom, added when the plumbing was moved indoors in the twenties. Chimneys climbed each gable end, a reminder of life before central heat, and a standing-seam tin roof kept out rain. The clapboard siding thirsted for paint, and several boards bowed and writhed in rebellion. Close by stood an icehouse and smokehouse. A carriage house, which Jimmy often promised to clean out but never did, was stuffed to uselessness with antiquated, broken farm implements. The roof of a chicken coop sagged badly, weakened by termites. The stone foundation walls of a long-gone barn lay wrapped in vines, full of rabbit warrens and groundhog burrows.

Jimmy, still nervous that the police might have traced the graffiti to him, listened carefully for intruders coming through the woods. *Can't hear nothin' but bugs*, he thought, responding to the night chorus of scraping katydids, trilling tree frogs, and buzzing cicadas.

Feeling warm from the beer, he revisited the rage he'd felt at the store earlier. "Goddamned uppity niggers, coming in here acting like they own the country, wearing their white shirts and ties, and dressing up in suits, and driving their big black SUVs."

"Yeah," Bill said.

"Buying them big, fancy houses, moving in their little black monkeys, coming into the stores and bars and restaurants and movies.

They're the problem. They don't know how to act. Don't know what it's like. They don't know their place."

"They may be rich, but they're still niggers," Dan said.

Jimmy took a deep drag on his cigarette and blew a long stream of smoke into the night. "Hand me another beer, Dan."

"Yeah, Jimmy." Dan opened the cooler, twisted the cap off a bottle and handed it to Jimmy. "They act like they own this country."

"They just keep coming, too," Jimmy said. "Thousands of them."

"We oughta send 'em back to the District," Bill said.

"Or Africa," Dan said, "where they came from."

Jimmy shook his head. "Too many of them now. As fast as they can throw up them plastic boxes, here comes another bunch of them. They keep moving in everywhere." He stubbed out his cigarette and pulled out another. "I just hope my daddy and granddaddy and great granddaddy ain't up there looking down. They'd cry if they saw all them niggers living all over their farm. Shit! Hey Bill, gimme a light." His eyes narrowed, and he saw the farm as it was before, fields and fences and woods and farm buildings. *Damn them all anyway—developers, banks, county. Damn all of them.*

"Sure thing, Jimmy," Bill said, handing him his lit cigarette. Jimmy held the fire against his own tube of tobacco, puffed a few times, and handed it back.

"We gotta do something about them, put them down. Put them in their place, show them who's boss," Jimmy said. "Got to do something."

"You better do something about Annie, too," Dan said. "She's gone wild."

"She's lost her way," Jimmy said. "The devil's in her. She don't understand—don't have no self-respect. She don't understand she's in the superior race. She don't care about keeping the white race pure and supreme. God Almighty, that's all we need—for her to go mixing it up and having a litter of little tan nigger babies crawling all over around here. Mommy and Daddy would die all over again if that happened. They'd be glad they're already dead."

"She's too pretty," Bill said. "That's the problem."

"Yes, she is," Dan said.

"Too pretty for either of you two, that's for sure."

"Well, you better get her married off to someone, before she picks her one of them jungle bunnies," Dan said.

Jimmy sat up straight and looked sharply at each of his companions in turn. "She ain't gettin' married—no time soon at least—and she ain't having no children either. I'll see to that."

Dan and Bill stiffened at Jimmy's serious tone.

"What do you want us to do, Jimmy?" Bill asked.

"I want you boys to keep an eye on this Ron Watkins. I don't like the look of him, and I don't like the way he was acting around Annie. Find out where he lives in that John's Woods tract, and what he does in his spare time. That's one we gotta watch—like hawks."

SIX

The next week, Ron came home from work to find a package in the day's mail. He removed the brown wrapper and found a paperback inside: *100 Years of Lynchings*, by Ralph Ginzburg. The cover showed a silhouette of the United States map, dripping with blood. Ron took it into his office to read.

The book's copyright date was 1962. Hundreds of newspaper articles—mostly from big-city newspapers throughout the Northeast and South—described lynching incidents from around America. Most took place in the South, many motivated by a desire to protect the virtue of white women. Ron could barely bring himself to read the horrific accounts. The murders described had exacted extralegal justice for a black man raping, attacking, kissing, speaking to, insulting, writing to, or accidentally jostling a white woman. Some mobs tortured and murdered blacks for stealing meat or chickens, or, in one case, three mules. This was justice? Vigilante justice, with no fair trials, no testimony from black witnesses, and a punishment that did not fit the crime.

The articles were dated chronologically, from 1880 to 1961. Ron thumbed through, looking for 1907 articles. There were two dispatches from 1906, both from the *New York Tribune*. One reported that in Louisiana, thirty whites had hanged a Negro accused of killing a white man's cow. The second reported that in Tennessee, a mob took from jail and lynched a Negro who had been convicted of rape but had been granted an appeal by the U.S. Supreme Court.

From there, the articles skipped ahead to 1910. A northern newspaper reported the hanging in Arkansas of "Judge Jones," a Negro, for alleged improper conduct with a young white woman. In that same year, a southern paper reported that a Texas mob had hunted down and killed fifteen Negroes for no known cause. Ron kept shaking his head, his upper lip curled in revulsion. Another item described Florida blacks fleeing for their lives after four men were hung and shot to avenge the murder of a schoolgirl. An Alabama county recorded its first lynching when a woman in a mining camp gave birth to a child "of doubtful color"; the woman denied charges of miscegenation for several days, then declared that a Negro had assaulted her and was father of the child. The sheriff had apprehended the man and was leading him to jail when a mob seized him and shot him "to pieces." In a geographic reversal, a southern newspaper report from 1911 recorded a Pennsylvania mob seizing a black accused murderer from a hospital bed and burning him alive.

The stories went on and on, but Ron wanted only those from Maryland. He searched the pages and encountered several surprises—lynchings in Omaha, Duluth, and Chicago. Eventually, he found one in Maryland. The *New York Times* reported the lynching of a George Armwood, age twenty-four, on October 18, 1933 in Princess Anne on the south end of the Eastern Shore. A "frenzied mob of three thousand men, women, and children overpowered fifty state troopers," smashed through three doors, "tore from a prison cell a Negro prisoner accused of attacking an aged white woman, and lynched him in front of the home of a judge" to shouts of "Let him swing." Then they ripped off the dead man's clothes, let him hang nude "for some minutes, cut down the body, dragged it through the main thoroughfares for more than half a mile and tossed it on a burning pyre." *In 1933*, Ron thought. A week later, the *New York Herald-Tribune* reported that at the coroner's inquest, "each of twenty-one witnesses testified that they did not recognize a single member of the lynching mob. 'I could not recognize any of them; they were strangers,' the sheriff stated."

He read on. In 1935, a Louisiana mob broke into a jail and shot to death "a Negro whose conviction for murder was reversed … by the Louisiana Supreme Court on grounds that his trial was unfair." *Lots of stories, each one horrifying*, Ron thought, *but what was my great-grandfather's story?*

~

The following Saturday morning, Ron's doorbell rang. He answered the door in shorts and a Raiders T-shirt. It was Mike.

"Hey, my man," Ron said. "What's up?"

"I was wondering if you'd like to come with me and look at some of those historical sites in the area, like we talked about."

"Yeah, I'd like that. When did you want to go?"

"What are you doing right now?"

Ron blinked. He wasn't prepared for such an abrupt change of plans. "Right now? You're kidding. I was gonna go to the home center and pick up some things."

"Oh, this'll be a lot more interesting than the home center."

"You're crazy. What could be more interesting than the home center? You're a man, aren't you?"

"Yes. A real beer-drinking, b-ball-loving man."

"Well I guess the home center could wait if you're really desperate to do this thing. You are, aren't you?"

Mike smirked.

Ron wondered how Mike was getting out of his Saturday chores. "So what's Mary doing today, memorizing books on tape?"

"That's good. No, actually, she's going to take care of the kids, so you and I can play."

Ron told Wilma where he was going and that he would be back in a few hours. He said goodbye to Marty and Rosalie, who were in their pajamas watching cartoons on TV, and the men left in Mike's ancient black BMW two-seat coupe.

Over the next four hours, Mike showed him plantation houses from the eighteenth and nineteenth centuries, barns with slats on the sides for air-drying tobacco, old schools for white children, and schools for black children built in the twenties with seed money from Julius Rosenwald, the president of Sears and Roebuck. Traffic was light and the weather was pleasant. Ron rested his arm out the window and felt the cool morning air.

They drove under the big oak and passed Clay Grocery and looked at the old right-of-way of the interurban trolley line that ran from Washington to Baltimore to Annapolis, which now was the paved bike trail.

"That's where I run," said Ron, and he told Mike about meeting Annie at Clay Grocery and seeing her brother Jimmy look at him from the back of the store.

"Oooo. Watch out for her, Ron."

"Why? Do you know her?"

"No. But I bought some milk and cheese in there once, and she almost scared the pants off me with her sexy talk."

"Well, I'm glad you kept your pants on!"

"Yeah. And Mary told me that from what she heard, Jimmy is a real lowlife."

"He didn't look like someone I wanted to know."

Mike told him more about the trolley line. "It carried passengers from 1908 until 1935," Mike said. "Then automobiles killed it. The tracks sat there abandoned until a few years ago when they built this bike trail. You can tell there was a trolley line by the names of the roads around here. Blake Station Road, Harvey Station Road, Meadville Station Road—they were all trolley stops."

Ron pointed out the window. "I noticed the groups of old houses where the trail crossed roads. I wondered why they were built there."

"Yeah, people liked to build where they could catch a trolley to

Baltimore or DC to work or shop. There's one community on the trolley line developed and built in the twenties by wealthy blacks for black residents."

"I bet they had to ride in the back of the car," Ron said.

"Or in the back car when there was more than one. Yes. 'Fraid so. The Jim Crow transportation law was enacted here in 1906, a year after they passed a similar law in Alabama, and ten years after the U.S. Supreme Court ruled that separate but equal railway accommodations for whites and blacks in Louisiana was constitutional."

"Plessy v. Ferguson," Ron said.

"Yep. In DC, blacks could ride up front. But out here, in 1906, a Howard University professor, who was black, was arrested and jailed for riding in the front of a trolley car. He appealed, but the court found for the trolley company. They left him in the clink. This was long before Rosa Parks."

Ron frowned. "Yes, but the case in 1906 didn't start a civil rights movement."

"No, I guess not," Mike said.

They rode past woods and rolling pastures with horses and cows between lines of old homes and entrances to new subdivisions.

"There must have been plenty of lynching back then. Black people were afraid to cause too much trouble," Ron said.

Mike grabbed the stick and downshifted up a steep hill. "Maybe. Do you know that in 1905, the planters tried to get a Maryland constitutional amendment passed to disfranchise black voters?"

"Really?"

"White men who could vote before the Fifteenth Amendment went into effect, and their male descendents, were eligible to vote—that was the grandfather clause—but anyone else would have to pass a reading test, according to the proposed amendment. Since most blacks couldn't read, it would keep them from voting."

"What happened?"

"The governor opposed it, so the legislature, which was dominated by the rural counties, submitted it directly to the people. But the immigrants in Baltimore were afraid that they would lose their voting rights too because so many of them couldn't read and write either. So they joined with the blacks, and many rural people joined them, and the amendment lost. In fact, it lost in most of the counties."

"Thank goodness the brothers had some allies." Ron decided to bring up the subject of lynching again—he had Thomas on his mind. "Say, Mike, let me ask you a question. You're really up on local history, so let me ask you this: Have you ever heard of any lynchings around here?"

Mike thought for a second. "I know there were some down on the Eastern Shore, and at least one in Annapolis."

"Oh yeah? When was that?"

He pulled up to a red light. "1906, I think. Henry Davis—I think that was his name. They said he assaulted a woman. They caught him and put him in the Annapolis jail. Then the woman identified him and he confessed, and the lynch mob took him from the jail and hung him and shot him about a hundred times."

"God. It happened all the time back then, didn't it?"

"Yep. Why are you interested in lynchings?"

He looked at Mike. *Can I bring it up now? Can I trust him?*

"Mike, if I tell you something, can you keep it to yourself? I mean, it's okay to tell Mary, but I'm not interested in the whole world knowing about it."

"Shoot."

"Well, the reason I'm interested in the topic is because my great-grandfather was lynched somewhere near here."

The traffic started moving and Mike shifted into gear. "What?" he asked incredulously. "You're kidding."

"Nope. I want to find out how it happened. And I'm looking for some hard evidence that he was innocent, like my mother said he was."

"Jeez. Do you know when it happened?"

"1907. Somewhere between Washington and Annapolis."

"God. That … kind of brings all this home, doesn't it?"

"Yeah. Makes it personal."

"So why did you tell me?"

"I was just thinking that with your interest in history, you might come across some information on it. And I was hoping that if you did, you'd pass it on to me."

"I sure will, Ron. What was his name?"

"Thomas Phillips. I went digging through the Internet trying to find him, but I came up empty. I searched lynchings, lynchings by year, and lynchings by state, and I looked up lynching photos and postcards, and the KKK, but I couldn't find anything on him. I think I'll have to go to Annapolis and look into the death records."

"Maybe I can go with you."

"Great."

"I'll take a look on the Internet too, when I get a chance. Maybe I'll get lucky."

Trust white people, but be wary, Ron thought, remembering his father's advice.

~

It was a week later—another Saturday morning. Jimmy watched Dan pull in front of the garage in his green pickup truck. Dan motioned for Jimmy to come to the truck. Noah was under a car draining oil. Dan spoke softly so that Noah wouldn't hear. "He went running at seven-fifteen, and he's coming this way on the bike trail."

"Good. Where'd you see him?"

"Well, I drove past his house to see if they were up yet, but the drapes were closed. So I parked on the shoulder out on Spring Hill Road, about a hundred yards from the bike bridge. I could watch his house from there. Then about seven-fifteen I saw him come out the side door of the garage and run into his backyard toward the bike trail.

So I drove closer to the bridge and waited to see if he crossed it, but he didn't. Then I drove up to where I could get to the trail. I looked down the trail and saw him running toward Big Oak, so I got back in, went under the bridge, and came over on Mayville Road and Big Oak. He ought to be here in a few minutes."

"Good. You better get going, so he doesn't see your truck."

"Yeah."

"See if you can find out how often he runs, and what time of day, and where."

Dan nodded and drove away.

~

Ron was running early to escape the heat of the day. He could do yard work and errands later. He was taking easy strides down the bike trail toward Big Oak. He thought about work for a while. Things were going well. His subordinates and supervisor were competent, diligent and accepting, and he hadn't had to deal with any major personnel problems yet.

Getting his head out of his job and into his home life always took a while on a Saturday morning. Today, however, the shift came abruptly on the wings of an insect. A horsefly darted out of the woods and attacked—buzzing, circling, hitting his arms, neck, and head. It somehow worked its way under his t-shirt, and he grabbed and shook the back of the garment. He sprinted and flailed his arms wildly. Finally he stopped, let the bug land, and smashed it as it was biting him. *Death to flies*, he thought. He resumed his run, passing the overgrown field. He saw the big old house on the hill, and wondered who lived there. It certainly had a commanding view.

When he came to the path into the deep woods, he decided to see where it went. Lunging awkwardly down a steep grade onto the trail and lifting his feet higher than normal to avoid tripping, he ducked under branches and crossed a stream with two leaps. The air in the hardwood forest was cool and refreshing, and the ground was carpeted with ferns and moss. He only hoped there were no more kamikaze insects.

Twice he stopped on a long downhill grade to pick his way through thorny bushes invading the trail. He ran by a large swampy area where sharpened tree trunks jutted from the water and spied a jumbled mound of sticks at the water's edge. *Beavers*, he thought.

Down the trail and around a bend he saw distant buildings—an old two-story house with worn paint and a rusty roof next to some ramshackle sheds and a garage too small for cars. The stream wandered past, well below the house.

Ron hoped he would not encounter guard dogs. They were a common problem when running through rural areas and unknown neighborhoods. People kept rottweilers, pit bulls, and other aggressive dogs, usually letting them run free.

The trail split, and Ron decided to turn to the right, away from the old house. He knew he was trespassing, and was somewhat fearful of whomever might live there. He came to the stream and leapt back across, stepping on a large stone in the middle. He continued, looking back twice to see if he was being followed.

A ways beyond, he came to a hill. At the top he was surprised to find the big oak tree and old store. Deciding to buy some bottled water, he clicked off his stopwatch, and went to the side door. He wanted to hear the sound of the spring stretching and the screen door banging behind him. He saw Annie's brother, Jimmy, standing by the short black man, the two watching him approach.

"Go ahead and bring that Chevy in," he heard Jimmy tell the black man.

Inside, he went to the upright cooler, glanced at the beer and soda, grabbed a plastic bottle of water, and took it to the counter. Annie was sitting on a stool, again wearing tight jeans and sleeveless T-shirt. Ron took in her exposed bra straps, bare midriff, and a gold navel piercing.

As he approached, she looked him all over, appraising his muscles and assessing his manliness through his thin running shorts. "My, my, Mr. Watkins, you're all wet."

"I've been out for a run."

She gave him a little smile. "Well, you need a cold shower and a massage now, don't you?"

"That would be nice, but I still have a long way to go. Say, I ran down off the bike trail into the woods just now and came to an old house. Do you know who lives there?"

"That's where me and Jimmy live. If you lived there, you'd be home by now."

He laughed. "I saw that sign too. What makes you think I'd want to live with Jimmy?"

"I know what you mean." The screen door slammed behind them "That'll be a dollar."

He looked down at the counter, reached into the small pocket inside the elastic waistband of his shorts, and pulled out a sweat-dampened bill. "Hope you don't mind."

"Money's money, I guess."

"Thanks a lot." He headed for the front door.

Outside, he could hear Jimmy ask her, "What'd he say to you?"

"Nothing. Just bought his water and left."

After restarting his watch, he ran down Big Oak Road replaying Annie's suggestive words and fantasizing about illicit sex in an old farmhouse. Beyond the store, he saw a private gravel drive on the left with a mailbox out front. Crossing over, he looked down the driveway and saw three signs guarding it: NO TRESPASSING, BEWARE OF DOG, and farther down, KEEP OUT. WE MEAN IT. Glancing at the mailbox, he read the name of the owners: CLAY. As he continued his run, he envisioned a dog leaping through a doorway toward his naked body. *No thanks, Annie. You can keep your hot sex—even in my dreams.*

He ran past the entrance to Big Oak Station, a new subdivision. Beyond that was a gravel driveway with brick columns on either side supporting black wrought-iron gates. A brass sign on the column read

OAK VIEW FARM. To one side was a black mailbox with a galloping horse on top.

Ron turned left onto Owens Farm Road, left onto Spring Hill Road, left again at Blake Station Circle, and sprinted to his driveway. He turned off his stopwatch at forty-nine minutes twelve seconds, and did a quick calculation. *Just over five miles*, he thought.

As he came into the great room, Wilma looked up from her newspaper. "How was your run?"

"Good. Interesting. I went off the bike path down through the woods past a swamp and found an old house. I'm lucky I didn't get my leg chewed off by a dog or my butt splattered with buckshot!"

"Oh Ronnie, why do you do things like that?"

"So I took another path, and it came out at that country store at that big oak tree over on Big Oak Road, you know, near the road that crosses the railroad tracks, and I went in to buy a bottle of water and talked to that woman in there. She told me that the old house is where she and her brother live. He came in the store when I was leaving. Man, he looks like a redneck if I ever saw one."

"Uh-oh."

"Then I ran by where their driveway comes out to Big Oak Road, and it has a million threatening signs."

"Well, signs never bothered you before."

"Not when there's one. But that many does. I think I'll stay away from that place. Of course, I didn't get close enough to see what architectural style the house was, and I didn't get to see what kind of dog they have, so I may want to—"

"Ron!"

SEVEN

M ike sat at his computer in swimming trunks and a Baltimore Ravens T-shirt. He was searching for Ron's great-grandfather Thomas. His queries led him to a document entitled "The Lynching Century: African-Americans who Died in Racial Violence in the United States, Names of the Dead, Dates of Death, Places of Death, 1865–1965," from the Tuskegee Institute Lynching Inventory. The list included about twenty-four hundred out of an estimated six thousand black lynching victims. Even better, the site provided sortable data: names of victims alphabetically with place and date of death, names and places chronologically, and names, locations, and dates chronologically by state.

Mike chose to look first by state. It listed twenty-two black men lynched in Maryland from the 1870s until1930, and thirteen around the year 1907, but no Thomas Phillips. Still, he thought the names might be useful in their investigation, so he printed the list and slipped it into his notebook. He wanted to show it to Ron. It certainly showed that lynchings were common in Maryland around 1907.

Thirteen black men lynched from 1894 to 1911 in Maryland

Stephen Williams	Upper Marlboro	October 20, 1894
Jacob Henson	Ellicott City	May 27, 1895
James Bown	Frederick	November 17, 1895
William Anderson	Princess Anne	June 9, 1897
Wright Smith	Annapolis	October 2, 1898
Garfield King	Salisbury	May 26, 1898
Lewis Harris	Belair	March 26, 1900
Edward Watson	Pocomoke City	June 14, 1906
Henry Davis	Annapolis	December 21, 1906
James Reed	Crisfield	July 28, 1907
William Burns	Cumberland	October 5, 1907
William Ramsay	Rosedale	March 8, 1909
King Davis	Brooklyn	December 25, 1911

His wife called from the next room. "Mike? Are you ready?" Her voice sounded tired. The whole family was in bathing suits and she was gathering up towels.

"Just a minute," he said, starting to shut down the computer.

"Come on, Dad," whined Jeff. "The pool closes at eight o'clock and it's six-thirty already."

"Hurry up!" screamed Jason.

Mike set the security system and deadbolted the front door. The Hoffmans piled into their tan Oldsmobile minivan and pulled away.

~

It was dinnertime on Friday night and the crowd at the pool was light. As Mary signed them in, Mike noticed Ron doing laps in the far lane. He marveled at Ron's athleticism, watching his powerful crawl, strong flutter kick, quick turn, and smooth underwater glide. He saw Wilma sitting at a table in the shade, reading a book. He led his procession in her direction. Marty and Rosalie were throwing a ball back and forth in shallow water nearby.

"How are you doing?" he asked Wilma.

"Just fine. Do you want to join us?"

"Sure," Mike said.

Mary greeted Wilma and put her bag and towels by the table. Jason was pulling on her hand and asking if they could go in. Mary agreed and led him toward the shallow part of the pool. Jeff left to play with Marty and Rosalie.

Sitting in a white plastic chair at the table, Mike could hear the sounds of splashing and laughter coming from the kiddie pool. Gazing at the pool, he could see Ron doing his laps.

"Ron sure is a powerful swimmer," Mike said to Wilma. "When do you think he'll finish?"

"It won't be long. You're not going in?"

"Oh, pretty soon. I just wanted to catch him when he gets out."

"Mary's quiet today," Wilma said.

"Yeah. She's a little moody sometimes. Today's one of her quiet days. Tired, I guess. What are you reading?"

She held it up for him to see.

"*The Known World*. Edward P. Jones," Mike said. "I've heard of that. Is it good?"

"I'm enjoying it. It won the Pulitzer Prize and was a National Book Award finalist. It's about black slaveowners in Virginia."

"That's different."

Ron emerged gracefully from the side of the pool and walked over. "Hey, Mike," he said, beaming. "Great pool, huh?"

"Sure is. Say, I wanted to tell you. I went on the computer and tried to find your great-granddaddy, but I ran into a dead end, just like you did. I did find a list of names of black people lynched in Maryland around that time, but Thomas Phillips wasn't on it."

"Well, you tried." He picked up his towel and began drying off—rubbing his head, patting his face and chest, pulling it behind his back, and drying each leg.

"But it wasn't a complete list. Not even half the victims were on it. We'll just have to keep looking."

Wilma eyed Ron. "You have Mike working on this now?"

Ron smiled impishly. "He volunteered. It fits in with his history hobby."

"Well, don't let him work you too hard, Mike. I'm not wild about him doing it at all. I don't know what he'll do if he finds out how it happened, except get mad."

"I understand his curiosity," Mike said. "I'd sure want to know what happened if it were my great-grandfather."

Ron sat down. Wilma was between him and Mike. "So, what are you doing tomorrow, Mike?"

"Not much. Why?"

"What do you say we go to the Maryland Archives in Annapolis, see what we can dig up?"

"Sounds like fun to me."

Wilma shook her head. "Oh my. Don't say I didn't warn you."

Mike saw Ron look at the pool again. "I'm going back in," Ron said. "My body needs more punishment." He walked around to the lap lanes, jumped in, and started thrashing toward the other end.

~

Marriage certificate and death certificate, Ron thought as he picked up Mike. *Let's see what we can find.*

They drove east on Route 50 in Ron's white Ford Taurus sedan. The Saturday morning traffic was fairly heavy. Some cars were turning off at the malls. Others were loaded with bikes, surfboards, and fishing gear—heading for the beach on the Eastern Shore, avoiding the Friday night Bay Bridge backup.

"You've got a nice car, Ron," Mike said.

"You mean, for a plain vanilla American-made sedan."

"Well, yes. But I guess it's important for an IRS man to drive a car that doesn't attract a lot of attention."

"Yeah, that's one reason I drive it. But it's a real deceptive car, too."

"How's that?"

"You'd be surprised at how much power the thing has. In fact," Ron said grinning, "that's what I call her: *White Power.*"

"Oh, no!" Mike said, protesting Ron's humor. "And how much power does White Power have?"

"Plenty. For once, I get to sit in the driver's seat, put the pedal down, and pass all these other people—black and white."

"That's how you get ahead, I get it. But how come I never see you drive more than nine miles over the speed limit?"

Turning off the highway, they drove past the Navy–Marine Corps Memorial Stadium. Ron nearly missed the turn, and had to brake hard. He glanced at his rearview mirror, and was relieved that the blue car behind him had not been riding his bumper. He pulled into the lot at the archives. After parking, Ron noticed that the blue car had followed them in.

He and Mike walked into the newly constructed brick building. After showing identification and signing in, they received chains with desk numbers, a numbered block of wood to put in place of microfilm they might remove from a file cabinet, and a plastic card to insert in the copy machine to record the number of copies they made. Closed containers were not permitted in the search room, so Ron left his briefcase in a locker.

The search room had high ceilings, library tables, desks with computers and microfilm readers, and a few book stacks. Glass walls enclosed microform shelves and more readers. A large locked room contained records accessible only to the librarians.

The two men found their assigned tables and waited in line to speak with a librarian. She showed them how to use the computer, fill out forms to obtain records, and retrieve microfilm. Some newspapers were at other locations, such as the law library across the street.

Since they knew for certain that Thomas Phillips was dead and had been married, they decided to split the task: Ron would search death records, Mike marriage records.

Under *Vital Records*, Ron clicked on *Death, 1801–1910*, and found the accession numbers for 1907. Then he went to the reference room, found the film for January, and put it on a reader in the microfilm room. The first death certificate came up. It was a printed form, the top of which was filled out by "Nearest Friend" and the bottom by the physician or coroner. He scrolled to Anne Arundel County, the county that included Annapolis, found the names listed alphabetically, and slowed when he neared the Ps. There was no Phillips. He increased the speed of his cranking and continued through the hundreds of records until he reached Patuxent County, the next county to the west, where he lived. Again he slowed near the P's. Again, no Phillips. These were the only counties between Washington and Annapolis. He laboriously cranked backward, removed the film, and returned to the file cabinet to retrieve February.

This time he tried a reader with power advance. *What a difference,* he thought. He sped through to Anne Arundel County, passed the Ps, and scrolled backward to look for the name. No Phillips. He pushed the advance button, and the film whirred quickly forward. He missed Patuxent County entirely and had to go back, but again, no Phillips. *Back to the file cabinet for March.* He sat down at the reader and went back to work …

"Got it," Mike said, sitting beside him.

Ron looked up, startled. "What?"

"His marriage certificate. He was married in 1893, and it gives the name of the church. I'll make you a copy of it."

"That was quick!"

"No problem, man. You just gotta know what you're doing, that's all."

Ron groaned.

"I only had to look on two films—one for Anne Arundel County and one for Patuxent County," Mike explained.

He made the copy, returned, and handed it to Ron.

"Date of Issuing License—July 9, 1893; Name of Person Married—Phillips, Thomas; Residence—Ptx. County; Age—20; Color—Col; Related or Not—No; Degree of Relationship—(blank); Names of Persons Married—Thomas Phillips–Rebecca Booth; Date of Marrying—1893 July 8th; Place of Marriage—Hawkins A.M.E. Chapel; Name of Minister—Joseph B. Taylor; Date of Filing License—1893 July 10; Name of Applicant for License—Thomas Phillips."

"Great, Mike."

"How's it going with your search?"

"Kind of slow. I'm into February."

Mike offered to help, and they began searching alternating months. They worked for almost an hour and a half and were nearing the end of the year when Ron gasped. "My God. Here it is."

They read it silently: "Certificate of Death. Thomas Phillips. Died at—Big Oak, Ptx County, Maryland; Date—Dec 27, 1907; Age—34; Male; Colerd; Birthplace—Ptx County; Occupation—farmer; Where Residing if not at place of death—nr. Spring Hill Farm; Married to—Rebecca Booth; Father's Name—Henry Phillips; Mother's Maiden Name—Johnson; Name of Person Giving Information—on hearsay; Cause of Death: Primary—Kil'd by unknown mob; Cause of Death: Immediate—shot and lynched; Signature—R. L. Eaton Coroner, PTX. County."

"Shot and lynched at Big Oak," Ron said. "Shit. That's where we live!" Ron was shaking. *There it is,* he thought. *Killed by an unknown mob. Shit. And nothing about what they accused him of. Just that they killed him. In the most brutal way. Damn it.* "We're done here."

They drove to a trendy bar in a nearby strip mall, not saying much, and ordered hamburgers, fries, and beers.

"I can't believe it, Mike. Killed by an unknown mob. That's

bullshit, man." His fists were clenched. "They knew who did it. And there's nothing about what they accused him of. They just killed him—brutally. And justice was served. Fuck."

"It's really shitty."

"And at Big Oak. Shot and lynched at Big Oak," Ron said. "But what does that include? There are a whole lot of old houses around there—some where the trolley crossed Big Oak Road, some down the road, some back off the road, some on that Big Oak Crossing Road."

"I know," Mike said. "I'm not sure where exactly Big Oak is. It's not incorporated, and the road is several miles long. I've seen it marked on maps, but I'm not sure it's always in the same place."

"And where's this Spring Hill Farm?"

"I don't know where that is either, but we do know where Spring Hill Road is."

Ron slowly shook his head in disbelief. "It's where we live, man. We drive on Spring Hill Road every day."

"So what do you want to do now?" Mike asked.

"I wanna drive my car, Mike, and put the pedal down."

EIGHT

Shot and lynched at Big Oak, Ron thought again as they drove back. Then he interrupted the silence in the car. "Mike, I want to find out where Big Oak is. I mean I know where the tree is and the roads and the subdivision, but where exactly was he lynched? And I want to find out where Spring Hill Farm is and this Hawkins A.M.E. Chapel where they were married, if it's still around."

"Uh-huh. I think Hawkins Chapel is. I've heard of it, but I'm not sure where it is. Mary might know. Or I bet we can find out at the historical society. It's open this afternoon."

"Where is it?"

"Not too far from where we live, actually. I've been there several times, looking up information on mansions and railroads and stuff."

"You can take the lead, then—asking questions. Let's do it. Do you have time?"

"I guess. And you know … I was thinking … we maybe shouldn't approach this subject head-on. We should kind of, you know, ease into it, so whoever we talk to doesn't know exactly where we're coming from."

"Or going to. Yeah, I was thinking that too. Lynching is kind of an inflammatory topic. It might make them clam up."

They pulled into the driveway of an eighteenth-century mansion and went into the Patuxent County Historical Society, located in the mansion's basement. Two big reading tables and a dozen chairs occupied the center of the room. At one end were library stacks, file cabinets, microfilm cabinets, map cabinets with narrow horizontal drawers, a copy machine, and a microfilm reader. Stacks of newspapers and maps lay about, evidence of work in progress. The basement had a musty odor—book mold mixed with magazine paste, glue, copy toner, and dust. Only the soft conversation of staff and volunteers broke the silence. Two white women sat at the tables putting mailing labels on newsletters. One had gray hair, pinned up in the back. The other, who was younger, had salt-and-pepper hair to her shoulders. The younger one wore tan slacks and a white button-up shirt. Both women looked up when the men entered. Mike smiled and greeted them.

The younger woman rose. "Oh, Mr.—uh—Mr. Hoffman, is it?"

"Good recall, Mrs. Jamison," Mike said.

"We haven't seen you in a while. Who's your friend?"

"This is Ron Watkins. He's new to the area, and he's interested in learning some of our history, so I told him he had to meet our local historians."

Mrs. Jamison thrust her hand toward Ron, who gave it a gentle shake. "Nice to meet you, Mr. Watkins."

"Good to meet you, Mrs. Jamison, is it?"

"Yes, that's right. How can we help you today?"

Mike took the lead. "Well, I was telling Ron about all the mansions and plantations around here, and he was kind of interested in seeing where they were."

"We have some maps you might like to see. What period are you interested in?"

"Do you have one from the turn of the century, around 1900?"

"We have maps from about 1880 and from just before the Civil War. The maps before 1900 have the locations of the houses shown with the names of the owners, and many of these were on plantations. After 1900, the maps just show dots for houses, without the names of the owners."

She opened a large flat drawer, removed the 1880 map of "Mayville—15th District," and placed it on the table. She showed them the roads, pointing with her index finger. Ron noticed that her nails were trimmed short and had clear polish. "Here's Route 450, the old Annapolis Road from Washington. It was a one-lane dirt road back then."

Ron saw that Mike looked perplexed. "Where's Route 3-301?" Mike asked.

"Here," she said, pointing. "It was just a dirt farm road running between the tobacco fields."

"Oh. And where's the trolley line?"

"It wasn't built until 1908, or at least that's when it opened."

"Oh, that's right. And what are some things we would recognize?"

She looked down at the map, carefully moving it so she could see better, and began pointing out some important mansions—all on the National Register of Historic Places. "Well, here's where we are, at Gabriel Mansion. Over here is Baruch Plantation House, and up here is Samuel Mansion."

"They're all kind of along Route 450, aren't they?" Mike asked.

"Yes. It's the old road from Washington to Annapolis."

"I'm trying to figure out where we live," Ron said.

"We're over on Blake Station Circle off Spring Hill Road," Mike added.

"I'm not quite sure where that is," Mrs. Jamison confessed. "Maybe Mrs. Schmidt would know. She's our real historian. Let me see if she's busy."

She left for a moment and returned accompanied by a white woman in her early forties dressed in a gray skirt and white blouse, hair tied back in a bun, her angular face wearing an engaging smile. "Nice to see you again, Mr. Hoffman," she said to Mike. "And you are Mr. Watson?"

"Watkins," Ron said.

"Mr. Watkins. How do you do? I'm Mrs. Schmidt. How may I help you?"

Ron smiled. "Oh, I just moved into the county, and I'm interested in learning about the history. Mrs. Jamison was showing us where some of the mansions and plantations were, and I was asking what farm or plantation was near where Mike and I live. We live on Blake Station Circle, off Spring Hill Road."

"That would be Spring Hill Farm." She pointed to the map, moving her finger to guide them. "It extended in this whole area on both sides of Big Oak Road westward, to well past Spring Hill Road and between the Mayville Road and Owens Farm Road."

Ron nodded, hiding the excitement he felt at locating the farm where his great-grandfather was living at the time of his murder. "Interesting. And I see Big Oak Road, but where exactly is Big Oak? Is it a town?"

"No. It's just a neighborhood—a group of houses near that big oak tree and the store—near the intersection of Big Oak Road and Big Oak Crossing Road."

"Near the big oak," Ron repeated. "Well, that makes sense."

Mike changed the subject. "What crops did they grow on Spring Hill Farm?"

"Most of the farms here grew corn and oats and hay for the animals," she said, directing her words to both Mike and Ron. "And tobacco and wheat were the main cash crops. But when tobacco declined and moved more to Virginia and North Carolina, farmers here began to grow more wheat, especially in the northern part of the county. Then farmers in the Midwest started shipping wheat into Baltimore by rail, and wheat production in the county declined. Agriculture declined overall and farmers started growing more fruits and vegetables and producing more meat and dairy to sell in Baltimore and Washington. I expect Spring Hill Farm followed the general pattern."

"Is there a plantation house there?" Ron asked.

"Yes, it's still there. Spring Hill Farm House—built in 1764 and still in good condition, with very few changes made. It's been designated as a county historic site for preservation."

"Where is it?"

"It's on the hill by Big Oak Road, but you can't see it from the road. It's up behind that woods along the road, kind of across from the old grocery store."

Ron smiled. "Oh. I think I may have seen it from the bike trail when I was running. It's brick and has two chimneys on each end and a long porch on one side and big trees around it, doesn't it? And it's surrounded by a meadow with horses in it?"

"That sounds like the one," Mrs. Schmidt said.

"Who lives there now?" Mike asked.

"A Carlson family. They're a young family. They're in the historical society. I think he's involved in some high-tech gene research company. They wanted a historic house with enough land to raise horses, but reasonably close to BWI airport, where his company is located. They've done some very tasteful period renovations on the house."

Ron glanced at Mike. "Who built the house originally?"

"Major William Clay. He was an officer in the French and Indian War and married an heir to the Wilmington estate, part of the land given by Lord Baltimore. You can see the family name right here on the map."

"Clay," Mike said. "That's the name on that old grocery store and oil-and-lube by the big oak tree. Do some of his descendants own those businesses?"

She wrinkled her brow quizzically and gave a quick nod. "Yes, I think Major Clay was their grandfather, six or seven generations removed."

Ron tilted his head back, looked down on her, and thought, *I wonder if a Clay had anything to do with the lynching.* "Huh," he said. "And how old is the store?"

He thought she looked intimidated, curious about the pointed nature of their questions. "1899, I believe. It's in the inventory of historic buildings, but it's been modified somewhat since it was built."

It was there when they lynched him, Ron thought.

"But Colonel Jeremiah Clay started the store. He was a colonel in the Civil War, I believe. His family also lived in Spring Hill Farm House."

"And when was the service station built?" Mike asked.

"Oh, that came much later. Sometime in the forties, I believe."

Ron pointed at the map. "I noticed that there's another old house in the woods, right about here, between the Spring Hill Farm House and the store. Who built that?"

"I'm not sure. It may have belonged to a family that sold their farm to the Clays, or it may be one of the farmhouses the Clay family built after Emancipation, when they split Spring Hill into smaller farms to rent to tenant farmers or sharecroppers."

Ron folded his arms and looked at the floor. "Fascinating. And these tenants were former slaves?"

Mrs. Schmidt nodded. "Yes, or freedmen. Before the Civil War, African-Americans in Maryland amounted to over a quarter of the population, and almost half were already free. But, of course, this county was quite different from most of the state. Almost sixty percent of our county population was black back then, and over ninety percent of black people here were slaves. In the district south of us, nearly three-quarters of the population were slaves."

Ron looked puzzled. "Why was this county different?"

"It's because we grew tobacco here. It's a very labor-intensive crop, all year round. On the Eastern Shore and in northern and western Maryland, the planters needed labor primarily to plant and harvest grains and didn't want to support slaves for the entire year. It was more economical to hire field hands on a seasonal basis."

"That's what I understand," Mike said. "But why did the tobacco farmers split up their farms after Emancipation?"

"It was the new order. The planters needed labor, and they got it by renting the small farms, houses, equipment, and farm animals to tenant farmers in exchange for half-to-three-quarters of the crop, depending on what the tenant rented. But the system also gave the black farmers independence and responsibility, and the freedom to do their work the way they thought best without being under an overseer."

"I wonder how the landowners and tenants got along back then?" Ron said, thinking, *Did the landowners cheat the tenants and make things hard for them? Did they threaten them with violence to keep them in their place?*

"Generally, they got along quite well," Mrs. Schmidt said. "They needed each other to survive economically. And they lived right next to each other throughout the county. Blacks and whites were neighbors. They visited each other sometimes, and their children played together. Of course, they had separate schools and churches."

Ron seized on the word "churches" and waved his hand over the map. "Are there any of the old African-American churches left around here?"

"Oh, yes. African-American churches, schools, all sorts of things. We did a survey of them and published it in book form. I think you'd find it interesting. We sell them in the gift shop."

"Great," Ron said.

Mike pursued a specific answer. "Yes, but speaking of churches, do you know where the Hawkins A.M.E. Chapel is or was? I think it's near where we live."

Mrs. Schmidt gave them a mystified look, as if to ask, *what are you two after?* "Why, yes. It's on Owens Farm Road in Hawkinstown."

Ron sensed that she wanted to get back to what she had been doing, so he warmly thanked her and Mrs. Jamison. Mike echoed his gratitude, and they departed into the gift shop where they each bought the African-American survey book, plus a more general survey of historic sites in the county. Ron also bought copies of maps, one from 1860 and another from 1880.

As they headed out of the parking lot, Ron said, "Do you see that dark blue Ford over there? I'd swear I saw it back at the archives in Annapolis."

"What? You're not getting paranoid on me now, are you?"

"Nah." Ron let the thought go.

"Glad of that."

"What a day," Ron said. "We learned a hell of a lot."

"You said it."

"My God," Ron said. "We *live* on the Spring Hill Farm, where my great-grandfather lived when he was killed. And he was lynched in Big Oak—maybe on the big tree itself."

"Could be," Mike said.

"And to think that that redneck Jimmy Clay and his sister Annie live in a house that was probably occupied by tenant farmers."

"Fascinating."

"But what a comedown it is for the Clay family. Their heirs live in a house where former slaves of the family lived. Who knows, maybe Thomas and his family lived there."

~

Mary'll be interested in what we learned, Mike thought. She was cooking dinner when Mike came home. He told her how they learned where Ron's great-grandfather was married, lived, and was lynched.

"We live on Spring Hill Farm, where he lived," she said, staring at green beans in a pan.

Mike nodded. "Yep."

"Hawkins A.M.E. Chapel is only a couple miles from here," Mary announced. "And Big Oak is right around the corner."

Mike was puzzled. "How do you know that?"

"Oh, they're on this historical survey I bought a copy of—the chapel and Spring Hill Farm House. It's on the bookshelf in the living room."

"Oh well," Mike said. "Now we have two copies. I bought another one today."

"That's a good way to support the historical society," she said, smiling.

"I think that Clay's grocery is on the survey, too."

"I've heard some things about those Clays, too," Mary said. "I heard that she goes after anything in pants and usually gets in them, and that Jimmy, he's as mean as can be—mean to her, too."

"I know. You told me."

"I saw her once with an awful black eye, and they say he gave it to her. You'd think he was her husband instead of her brother, as jealous as he gets."

"Really." Mike visualized the sexy blond with a black eye.

"Yeah, and people say she's afraid to leave him, 'cause she thinks he'll come after her," she said. "Please tell Ron to stay away from him, and her, too, for that matter." Mike was baffled by her concerned look and the urgency in her voice. "And you stay away too, darling."

"Why? You don't trust me?"

Mary smiled. "I trust that you might act like a fool around a woman like that."

"Me? I'm a one-woman man, Mary, you know that. So where'd you hear all this about the Clays?"

"Word gets around."

~

That same afternoon, while Noah cleaned up the lube bays, Jimmy sat behind the counter in the garage office, drinking a beer, looking through a news magazine a customer had left behind, and waiting for Bill. Country music drifted out of an old radio on a shelf behind his chair. A faded calendar, showing a blond wearing a cowboy hat and little else, decorated the wall behind him. The bottom of the calendar was dated December 1991.

Jimmy watched Bill unfold himself from his blue sedan and walk in. "Hey, Bill," he said, his voice low and steady, his eyes challenging. "What's going on? What did Mr. Jungle Bunny do today?"

"I ain't real sure what he did. He and a white guy from down the street went to Annapolis to some kind of a liberry near the Navy stadium."

"Was there a sign in front of it?"

"Yeah. It said Maryland Archives." Bill pronounced the last syllable with a soft ch-, as in the wild onion.

"Ar-chives?" Jimmy repeated, squinting. "Oh, *archives*," he said. "Yeah. I seen that place. What'd they do there?"

"They went in and stayed a couple of hours," Bill said.

Jimmy leaned toward him. *What was goin' on there?* "Did you go in?"

Bill shrugged and splayed his hands in self-defense. "No, I couldn't."

"How come?"

"I went to the door, but there was some girl sitting at a desk and people filling out papers there."

Jimmy cocked his head to the side. "So?"

"Well, there was a guard sitting across from the girl," Bill pleaded, "and it looked like people was showing him their driver's licenses, and I didn't want to do that, so I stayed out in the parking lot. What else could I do?"

"Uh-huh. Wonder what the hell they were doing in there." Jimmy's eyes locked onto Bill's. "And what was that spook doing with a white guy?"

Bill grew irritated and looked down. "Hell, I don't know. You think I can read minds or something?"

"Sometimes I think you ain't even got a mind."

"Well, thank you," Bill said in sing-song.

Jimmy took a long swig of beer. "So what'd they do then?"

"They came out, the coon looking like he'd seen a ghost or something, and then they went to a bar for a while."

"Yeah?" Jimmy seethed with curiosity.

"And then they drove back here, to that Gabriel Mansion on the highway there and went down in the basement for a while."

"What? The basement?" Jimmy shook his head in puzzlement.

"Yeah, there was a sign pointing to the basement that said 'Historical Society.' I guess that's where they went."

Jimmy pulled out a smoke and lit up, all the while shaking his head. "Well now, that's interesting. Instead of laying around the pool or playing golf, these guys go to a library and a his-to-ric-al society. What kind of queers would spend a Saturday like that?"

"I don't know," Bill said.

"Well, all I gotta say is, good going, Bill." Jimmy nodded his head and brought his lower jaw forward. "You done good today. I want you to keep watching them guys. I want to know what they're up to."

Bill left, and Jimmy went into the store. It was deserted except for Annie, who sat on a stool adding numbers on a calculator. Jimmy grabbed a beef stick from a display, tore off the plastic wrapper, and took a bite.

"What're you doing?" she asked. "Don't you come in here and start eating again."

"Damn you, sister. It's just a beef stick."

"I work hard in here, Jimmy, and I can't have you coming in here eating up my profits like that any time you want."

Shit, thought Jimmy. "I own this place too, remember?"

"You do, and you'll run it into the ground just like you're doing with the lube business. Noah does all the work. All you do is sit around and tell him what to do—do this and do that—you never do nothing!"

"That ain't true."

"All you do is come in here and eat up my profits and spend money on beer for your sorry-ass friends! You have no idea how little money we make here. Why, if it weren't for the beer and lottery tickets bringing people in, we wouldn't sell nothing. We throw away half the milk we buy! The distributor won't stop here any more. And you keep eating up the profits. You just can't keep coming in here eating whatever you want. You can't!"

"There you go again. Over a fucking beef stick!"

"You can't even be nice to your customers. Face it, Jimmy. The people who drive in here are gonna be black, most of them. If you want their business, you gotta be nice to them, treat them right."

"Fucking coons."

"See, that's what I mean! And when black people come in here, you just stand back there and give them that cold stare of yours. You'll drive them away from the store. I want you to stay out of here, Jimmy!"

"I'll come in here whenever I want. Someone's got to watch you. You don't know how to behave with these coons. One of these days one of them'll shove you behind the counter, throw you down, and put it to you."

"You're crazy, Jimmy! They're our customers. We need them. We'll starve without them. What are we gonna do, Jimmy? You tell me. You run your lube business into the ground and then eat up my profits and scare people away, and kill this one off too, and then what'll we do? We'll have to sell out, that's what. And then we won't have nothing! There won't be nothing left, Jimmy. It'll be all gone. We'll have to sell out and move."

"We're never gonna leave here. We're never gonna let them get it."

"We'll just starve, then, I suppose. But not me. I'll move out and leave you, Jimmy."

He glared. "In a fucking pine box, maybe. That's how you'll leave."

NINE

On Sunday morning Ron cut and trimmed his lawn and set up the sprinkler.

As soon as the sprinkler was on, Rosalie was dancing under it with Marty right behind, both in bathing suits. Ron knew they had been lying in wait. "You'll get grass clippings on your feet," he warned half-heartedly.

They ignored him. Rosalie began performing a wild dance, tossing her head and flailing her arms, bending at the knees and waist as she hopped around in a circle under the droplets. Marty watched in amusement with his hands on his hips.

"Looking good, little girl," Ron said.

Suddenly she slipped on the wet grass and fell hard. Ron ran into the spray and gave her a hand, while Marty happily brushed clippings off her backside.

"And now you know more about how water reduces friction," Ron said.

"What?" Marty asked.

"Water makes things slippery."

"Oh."

"But that was a great dance, Rosie. I liked it." She looked up and smiled.

Glancing down the street, Ron saw Alfred working on his lawn. He told the kids not to wear out the grass, and walked over to say hello.

"Hey, if you need a break on the lawn, how 'bout letting me see your gun collection?"

"Okay my man, but if you tells anyone about it, I'll have to kill you." Alfred spoke with a lopsided grin, his small eyes drilling into Ron's.

Ron returned the smile. "Trust me."

"And there are two questions you can't ask me—'Where'd you get that?' and 'You got a permit for that?'"

"No problem. Won't even cross my mind."

Inside, Ron asked, "Where's Tabatha?"

"Out spending my money. Ain't that what women do?"

The Mance house had dark hardwood floors and mahogany-stained banisters going up to the second floor. In the living room, Ron noticed a large picture of Malcolm X on the wall.

"So which Malcolm do you like better, the young Black Muslim who liked violence and separation from whites, or the older one, the Sunni Muslim who renounced racism?"

"I don't know much about Sunnis, but I know the real Malcolm was the young one. Said nonviolence is the 'philosophy of the fool,' and whites are devils who'll do anything to keep us down. Mothafucking honkies needs to stay in their world, and we in ours—otherwise there'll be blood in the streets, and that's that."

Ron smirked. "I don't see horns and tails growing out of all those white people."

"They're there. You just ain't seen them. I noticed you been spending a lot of time with that Mike. I don't trust that boy. What's he got you doing for him?"

Ron smiled and shook his head. "It's the other way around. I have him helping me try to find where one of my relatives lived around here a long time ago. It's been quite a hunt, and Mike's a pretty good detective."

Alfred remained wary. "You just watch him, and don't trust him. He'll show his white skin sooner or later."

They went into the family room. Over the fireplace was a wood and glass case containing a rifle with a wood stock and engraved brass on the receiver around the trigger and hammer. "It's a Winchester Repeater, like the Buffalo Soldiers used," Alfred said. "It's a reproduction, but it shoots." He pointed to another case that displayed a U.S. Cavalry saber. "You could cut a man's head off with that. It's sharp as a razor."

"Do you shave with it?"

Alfred smiled. "When my razor gets dull."

Ron asked him about a framed photograph of buildings on fire.

"That was DC in '68 after they shot King. About Seventh or Eighth Street Northwest—where they just built that new convention center. Burn, baby, burn."

Alfred opened the door leading to his basement, but Ron stopped again, this time in front of a photo of a black soldier standing by a grass hut. "Who's that?"

"That's my daddy in the Nam. He got killed over there when I was six."

Ron shook his head. "Too bad, man. I see he was a sergeant."

"Yeah. Fucker got shot in a tunnel during that Tet offensive in '68. That's when it started to get rough for Mom and us kids. Goddamned white man's war anyway—just like all the rest. The whites started it and then they sent black boys over to die for their country. They started a draft, then let all them white college kids out. Shee-it. Then they had all that integration and equality stuff in the service, but when the black boys come home it was the same old shit, just like after all them other wars. Nam. What a waste. We didn't have nothing against those yellow gooks, anyway. Hell, they was colored too. We should've been fighting whitey, not them."

Ron nodded. *It was a shitty war*, he thought. "Is his name on the wall?"

"You better believe it is. James W. Mance. On that black, black wall. I've been down there lots of times to curse him for getting killed and leaving us like that, and to curse the goddamned white government for sending him to die."

"So where'd you grow up?"

"In the District. We lived in the projects. There was dealers and junkies and shootings and whores all around us. Gangs too."

Ron visualized the DC slum and a gang of seventies-era black men. "Were you in one?"

"Shit yeah. Everyone needed protection."

"Did you get in any fights?"

"It was a war zone, bro! I had buddies killed, and I cut some guys up pretty bad myself. You had to show you weren't afraid. If you were tough enough, they might leave you alone. Or they might just shoot you if you got in their way. So you had to have friends to watch your back and guns and knives to protect yourself."

"Tough."

"Damn straight."

The basement walls and ceiling were drywall, and the floor was carpeted. On one wall was a big-screen TV. Behind a bar with stools was a counter with a sink. Above the sink were shelves stocked with liquors; under it sat a small refrigerator for beer and ice. At the other end of the room was a pool table. The walls were decorated with photographs of great black boxers—Jack Johnson, Joe Louis, Jersey Joe Walcott, Sugar Ray Robinson, Archie Moore, Floyd Patterson, Joe Frazier, George Foreman, Muhammad Ali, and Sugar Ray Leonard.

Ron gazed at the images, impressed. "Great photos," he said. "Great fighters."

Alfred led Ron over to a corner, where a barbell and other weights were scattered. The equipment waited silently for a chance to test someone's strength.

"How much do you have on there?"

"Three hundred fifty pounds."

"Can you lift it?"

Alfred snorted derisively. He spread his legs, bent at the waist, and grasped the bar. With one motion and a grunt, he raised it to shoulder height. There he held it for a moment while he moved one leg in front of the other and bent his knees slightly. Then, with another grunt, he thrust the bar over his head and brought his feet parallel. After a few seconds, he brought the bar down smoothly onto the concrete floor.

"Well, that's not bad," Ron said, hiding his amazement. But he wanted to challenge Alfred further. "Can you bench-press that much?"

"Yeah," was Alfred's cool reply.

"With or without help?"

"Who's gonna help me, Tabatha?"

"I'd like to see you press it."

"Don't think I can do it, do you?" He walked over and lifted the barbell onto the rack. Laying down on the bench, he took the bar, and with a grunt, pulled it down to his chest. He thrust his arms upward. He held it a few seconds, then lowered the weight back to the rack with a clang.

Ron was amazed. "Now I'm impressed."

Alfred got up as if nothing had happened. "Come on back here, now, Ron." He walked over to a plain steel door set in concrete walls and punched a code into a security panel. The door unlocked and Alfred opened it, flipping on a light inside.

It's an arsenal, Ron thought. "What's in here?"

"Just part of the collection." He began handing Ron a stream of weapons, one by one. His collection included nearly every rifle, machine gun, shotgun, and pistol used by the military since World War I. Alfred described the weight, range, and other specifications for each, from an ancient Browning Automatic Rifle to a Vietnam-era M16 rifle, and the even shorter version carried by American soldiers in Iraq.

"Do they all still shoot?"

"Yessir. They're cleaned, zeroed in, and good to go. I test them all at the rifle range, so I *know* they're ready. You never know when you're gonna need them."

"Are they loaded?"

"No, but I got the ammo for them."

"But don't you have any other pistols?"

Alfred replied that he and Tabatha kept their own in their nightstands, "just in case."

"You two don't fight, do you?" Ron visualized them crouching behind the furniture, taking potshots at each other.

"Hell no. And we have a password, in case we run into each other in the dark."

"Oh yeah? What is it?"

"Fo'get it, man."

Alfred took Ron back up to see his knife collection, which included Bowie knives, nine and twelve inches long; a sixteen-inch double-edged dagger; two five-inch double-edged throwing knives with Velcro sheaths; two six-inch switchblades, spring-loaded to leap straight into a victim; and two eighteen-inch machetes with leather sheaths.

"Nice," Ron said.

"You want to go to the range with me sometime and try out some of my guns?"

"Yeah, sometime, maybe. But I'm kind of busy right now with the kids and all."

~

At home, he told Wilma about Alfred's weapons, swearing her to secrecy.

"Is he dangerous?" she asked.

"Not to black folk, unless we try to rob him, and probably not to white folk either, unless they attack him. But if they do, they better look out. He's armed to the teeth, and he really hates white people."

"Love one another. That's what Jesus said."

"I know. But let me tell you, if push comes to shove, I want Alfred on my side."

~

Later that afternoon, Ron opened up the book he had bought at the historical society. He found "Hawkins A.M.E. Chapel" in the index—where Thomas Phillips was married to Rebecca Booth in 1893.

He turned to the page indicated, and saw a picture of a small rectangular building with white lap siding, sloped roof, and three evenly-spaced rectangular windows on the side. The front door opened into a vestibule, a miniature version of the chapel building. The book described the church in detail. *Hawkins African Methodist Episcopal Chapel was constructed in 1889 by the black community of Hawkinstown on the south side of the Baltimore and Potomac spur to Washington. One acre of land from the John Whitlaw tract was sold to George W. Hawkins, Stanley Moore, Henry Phillips, and Samuel Smith for a church and burial ground for colored persons.*

Ron checked the printout from the marriage license records: Henry Phillips. *That's Thomas's father! Could that also be where they buried Thomas after the lynching?*

He resumed reading: ... *The town and chapel were named after George W. Hawkins, a graduate of Howard University Law School and a Washington real estate developer. Some members of the community worked on the railroad and some in the saw mill, but most worked on area farms as field hands, sharecroppers, or tenant farmers. A few commuted on the train to work in Washington ....*

Ron thought to himself. *I have to see it. It's four o'clock on Sunday. Probably no one will be there. The services will be over, if they still hold services there.*

He thought of the African-American churches in the area—great edifices with sanctuaries seating thousands, offices, schools, gymnasiums, and chapels. Who would go to a tiny church like Hawkins?

～

"Be back in a while, honey," he shouted out the back door to Wilma, who was planting some flowers in the backyard while Marty and Rosalie played outside.

He hopped in his Ford and turned down Spring Hill Road, made a right onto Owens Farm Road, which followed the railroad, then crossed Big Oak Road. He passed a group of old houses and came to the chapel. He pulled into the parking lot. A sign read "Historic Hawkins A.M.E. Chapel—Built 1889."

Someone is caring for this building, Ron thought. Fresh white paint gleamed, the landscaping was neat, and the grass was recently mowed. Small print on the sign explained that the county owned and maintained the property.

Ron looked through a window. Six dark wood pews about eight feet long sat on one side of an aisle, and five on the other. A small stove took the space of one pew. The floors were dark varnished wood, and the walls, ceiling, and rafters were painted white. At the front of the church he could see the door to the vestibule, and at the rear sat a small lectern, altar, and a dark wood cross on the wall.

In his mind's eye he saw his great-grandfather standing beside Rebecca Booth while a preacher read them their vows. Ron's great-great-grandparents and friends and relatives sat in rapt attention, rhythmically punctuating pauses in the minister's words with praise:

" … Thomas and Rebecca love Jesus—"

"Yes, Lord."

"They take each other till death do them part—"

"Uh-huh."

"They will live righteously—"

"Yes, Lord."

"And obey God's laws—"

"Yes."

"They will go to Jesus and enter the promised land—"

"Praise Jesus."

"They will live together as one—"

"Yes, Lord."

"And be together forever and ever—"

"Praise the Lord."

"A-men."

"A-men."

He could imagine the voices rising in a joyful hymn to celebrate the great event, and he saw smiles, tears, and hugs as the couple came down the aisle. He saw it all. These were his people. He was home.

The vision faded, and he walked around the building, finding the burial ground, where scores of gravestones stood in ordered rows. He wandered among them. Most were less than a foot high and only an inch or two thick—some rectangular, some rounded on top, others with curves, a few rising to a point, some with names chiseled on top, but most inscribed on the face. He tried to read names as he went, but many of the markers were weathered, the names illegible. A few stones looked fairly new.

He found a white stone with a curved top. He was able to make out the name Henry Phillips and the date of death, 1917. But he could not read the date of birth. On the stone next to it—done in the same style—he read the faint inscription: Esther Phillips, 1847–1921. He examined the surrounding stones but could find no other Phillipses. To the left, about ten feet away, he noticed a plain block, a foot wide and six inches high and thick. Unlike the other stones, which all had inscriptions, though often undecipherable, this stone had none. Its surface was smooth but weathered. Ron stared at it, transfixed. He could not turn his gaze. *Why is there nothing carved into this marker? This person was buried with no name. Is this great-grandfather's grave? Would parents not chisel the name of a lynched son on a headstone? Perhaps his parents would not boldly inscribe the name of their son on his headstone to memorialize him for future generations after he had been accused of an atrocity. They might think an inscription would bring violence to them. They might think it would bring vandals to destroy the grave or unearth the body and leave it in the woods for animals to consume, to end his peaceful rest in the earth. Perhaps they dared not take the chance of calling attention to him.*

The more he thought, the more certain he became. He could feel the knowledge, the certainty, rising from the earth up through his legs, filling his body and bursting into his brain. *Yes. This is the unmarked grave of great-grandfather, buried anonymously. This is where he lies—dismembered, shot, burned though he may be—this is where he now lies in peace, beneath my feet.*

His eyes filled with tears. He kneeled to the ground. "God bless you, great-grandfather," he said quietly.

~

Ron pulled into the driveway and went into his house. "I found where he is buried," he told Wilma.

"Your great-grandfather?"

"Yes."

"My goodness. Where?"

"In a graveyard by a tiny A.M.E. church about two miles from here. His parents are buried there too."

"Did you find his name on a tombstone?"

"No, the stone was unmarked, the way a lynching victim's stone would be. But it was close to where Henry and Esther Phillips were buried. Henry Phillips was the name on Thomas Phillips' death certificate. And they were the right generation to be his parents. I had a feeling—a very strong feeling—that Thomas was there. I—I'm certain it's his grave."

"Could be, sweetie."

TEN

The next Saturday, Ron remembered that he needed an oil change. No big name oil-and-lube franchises were close by, and he wanted to see what he could learn about the Clays, so he drove over.

The black man who worked for the Clays was on the roof of the store spreading tar on the metal flashing around the brick chimney when Ron pulled up. Jimmy Clay came out of the office with a clipboard in his hand. Ron approached him.

"Good morning," Ron said. He was a head taller than Jimmy Clay.

"What do you need?" Jimmy asked brusquely.

Ron stiffened. "An oil change and lube."

"Just a minute." Jimmy looked up and yelled to the black man on the roof. "Customer!" He handed Ron the clipboard and returned to the office.

Ron bristled. He was sure that Jimmy had called to his black employee because he didn't want to wait on a man of color. Ron wanted to walk away, take his business elsewhere. There was no reason why he had to accept such blatant racism. But he took a deep breath, exhaled, and decided to overlook the slight, since he wanted to learn more about the Clays.

The black man came down the ladder, walked over to Ron, and took the clipboard. He was just over five feet tall, dark with a wiry build and thinning gray hair. His forehead was permanently creased with wrinkles, and Ron guessed he was in his late sixties.

"Help you?" the man asked.

"Yes. I need an oil change and lube job."

"Oil filter?" he asked in a flat voice, filling out the order form without a smile.

"Yeah."

"Clean it out, check your fluids, do the windows?"

"Sure."

He took down Ron's name and address and said, "Go ahead and pull it in."

The man guided him onto the lift tracks. After Ron got out, he told him, "You can wait in the office if you want."

"Mind if I hang out here and watch you work?"

"Don't matter to me."

He raised the car on the lift, while Ron leaned against the wall a few steps away.

"I just like to talk instead of sitting around."

"Uh-huh."

Ron glanced idly at the stuff along the walls—cases of oil, filters, windshield wipers, containers of grease.

"Do you keep pretty busy down here?"

"Yassuh. Sometimes. We got our regular customers, and new ones, too."

"That's good … Say, I was kind of curious about why your boss Jimmy got you to take my order instead of doing it himself."

"Don't know." He unscrewed the plug and oil started draining into the pan.

"He doesn't seem to care for black people."

"I couldn't say about that." The man took a grease gun and started applying lube to the wheels and joints. Ron followed him around the car to facilitate conversation.

"Does he ever do any of the work?"

"Yassuh, when we get busy."

"So where do you live?"

Noah looked at him suspiciously. "Why do you want to know?"

"I'm just making conversation."

"I live down in Hawkinstown."

"Near that old church?"

"Yassuh."

"I went by there on Sunday. I'm kind of interested in local history. I took a walk in the graveyard."

He looked up at Ron. "Why are you interested in that old graveyard? You ain't even from here, are you?"

"No, we just moved here from the West Coast. I just like to know a little bit about where I live."

"You live in one of them new houses off Spring Hill Road, don't you?"

"Yes. How did you know that?"

"I heard Miss Annie tell Mr. Jimmy that's where you live."

"Oh … Say, do you have a bathroom here?"

"Out back. It's open."

Ron walked around to the rear of the building. There were two doors. One said "Men," the other "Women." But Ron could see other words through the paint: under the word "Men" he could see "Colored," and through "Women," "White." *Times change*, he said to himself. *But I still get to use the colored restroom.* He opened the door and looked around. *And it's still filthy.*

When he returned, the man was lowering the lift.

"Done?"

"No, suh. I gots lots to do."

"What's your name?"

"Noah Johnson."

Johnson, Ron thought. *He might be related to my great-great-grandmother.* "I'm Ron Watkins. Nice to meet you. So has your family been around here long?"

"Yassuh—for as long as anyone knows."

"During slavery?"

"That's what they say."

An old tractor trailer carrying a load of logs turned onto Big Oak Road and roared through its gears past them and the store, spewing diesel exhaust under the canopy of the big oak.

Whew, that stinks, Ron thought. Then he continued grilling Noah. "Did your family work on Spring Hill Farm?"

"Yassuh. How do you know about Spring Hill Farm?"

"I went to the historical society in Gabriel Mansion, and the woman there said this whole area was part of Spring Hill Farm."

Noah replaced the oil filter, inspected the air filter, and started checking fluids. Ron walked to the front of his car to continue their chat.

"So how long have you worked for Jimmy Clay?"

"'Bout all my life, for him and his daddy, Mr. Clay. Jimmy's daddy and I used to play together when we was kids, and my daddy and I worked in his tobacca fields and helped stock shelves in the store. But then the price of tobacca went down, and Mr. Clay, he couldn't seem to make a go of it no more, 'specially with his drinking. He did like his bourbon, but he got real mean when he drank, and it seemed like he drank more and more. He rented out some of his fields, but didn't get much money for them. And then my daddy and I helped him out here at the station."

"Did this used to be a gas station?"

"Yassuh. We used to pump gas for people and fix cars, too, before cars got them computers in them. Mr. Clay and my daddy knew a lot about cars. Mr. Jimmy never took much interest."

"Why did they close the gas station?"

"Too many other stations, and Mr. Clay, he couldn't afford to put in the new pumps they wanted when people decided they didn't need full service no more and wanted to use credit cards."

"What happened to Mr. Clay?"

"Oh, he and Mrs. Clay was killed in a car wreck about five years ago. Mr. Clay was drinking. My daddy died before them. I worked for Mr. Clay before he was killed, and I been working for Mr. Jimmy ever since."

Ron shook his head. "That's sad about his parents. How do you like working for Jimmy?"

"Jus' fine."

Noah began vacuuming the interior of the car, interrupting their conversation. He finished, and while he was winding up the vacuum cord, Ron resumed. "So do you do anything here besides oil changes and lube jobs?"

"Not much. But sometimes I go with Mr. Jimmy to the market or Wal-Mart to get stuff for the store. And I help keep up the store and the house."

"What house?"

"The one they live in down in the woods."

"Does that take much work?"

"Man, you got a lot of questions. Yassuh. It's an old house and kind of rundown."

"Sorry, I just thought you might like some conversation."

"Oh, I do, I do. It gets kind of quiet around here sometimes."

"I bet it does. So tell me, when their parents died, didn't Jimmy and his sister get some money?"

"Oh, they got some, I think." Noah was washing the car's windows now, inside and out.

"So who used to live in the old house? Surely not the whole Clay family."

"Oh, yassuh. But they lived in the big house on the hill for hunderds of years, and tenants lived in the house in the woods."

"Tenant farmers?"

"Yassuh. Then no one lived there for I don't know how many years, till Mr. Clay had to sell the big house, and he and Mrs. Clay and Mr. Jimmy and Miss Annie moved down into the woods. Mr. Jimmy and Miss Annie was jus' little kids then."

"Oh, I see what you mean." Ron watched a car on Big Oak Road slow down at the store and continue on. "What was the house in the woods like when they moved in?"

"Well, it was pretty well falling down when they moved in. It had vines growing all over it. I had to tear them off. Mr. Clay said he was gonna fix the house up good when they moved in, and he did have some new wiring put in, and a new bathroom and kitchen, and a furnace. They had me fix the steps and roof and windows, get the squirrels out of the attic, and fix the eaves. But it's all I can do to keep that old house from coming down on them even now. I keep tarring that old metal roof every time it rains. And that house got termites too."

Ron shook his head. "Sounds like it would have been cheaper for them to tear the house down and build a new one."

"Yassuh."

"Why didn't they?"

"Don't know. Mr. Clay and Mr. Jimmy, they liked their privacy, always did. I think Mr. Clay wanted to keep a part of the old place jus' the way it was. You can take the car out now. Pay in the store."

"This is for you," Ron said, slipping him a five-dollar bill.

"Thank you, suh."

Ron went to the front door of the store, and noticed Jimmy coming out the side door, walking toward the service station. Inside, he found Annie in one of the aisles, squatting in her tight blue jeans, restocking shelves.

"Be right with you."

He watched her place a few more cans on the shelf. She rose, smoothing her blouse over her breasts, and glided toward him, looking him up and down once again. As she went behind the counter, she slowly ran a hand over her buttocks. "And how are *you* today, Mr. Watkins? You're getting to be a regular customer. Did Noah take good care of you? Is there any way I can be of service to you?" She gazed into his brown eyes, and slowly licked her upper lip.

Ron swallowed and thought, *Oh my God.* "He did a good job, Miss Clay."

"Call me Annie."

"Okay, Annie," he said, handing her a credit card. "What do I owe you?"

"Full service? Oil, filter, lube, and clean?"

"Yes, ma'am."

"Anything else for you today?" she asked, embracing him with her eyes. "Anything to eat?"

"Not today."

"Well, that'll be twenty-nine dollars plus tax. Thirty dollars forty-five cents total." The store had an old-fashioned credit-card machine, a manual slide that used carbon-paper slips. She worked the bar over the form to imprint his card. Ron signed the slip and handed it back, and she gave him the carbon. "Thanks, Mr. Watkins. Next time, you come visit with me while Noah does your car. Promise me you will?"

"I'll do that."

~

Out in the garage, Noah was pouring Ron's oil into a waste barrel when Jimmy approached him.

"What did you two talk about?" *Gotta watch this guy Watkins,* Jimmy thought.

"Nothing much. He axed if this used to be a gas station. I told him yes. He axed where I live, and I told him Hawkinstown. Axed about the church graveyard down there and said he walked around in there."

"What? Now why did he do that?"

"He didn't say."

Jimmy scowled. "I don't like that guy. He's up to something. We need to keep an eye on him."

"Right, boss."

"What else did he ask? Did he ask anything about Annie?"

"Nothing 'bout her. Axed how long I been working for you. I told him me and my daddy always worked for you and your daddy."

~

The following Saturday, Ron and Mike headed for Annapolis again. Ron gunned his Taurus down the narrow, winding road toward Route 50.

He glanced at Mike's attire and thought, *Oh, no.* "I see you dressed up today. White shorts, old running shoes, and your very best 'Maryland is for Crabs' T-shirt."

"And I see you got on your khaki pants and knit golf shirt, like you're ready to meet some chicks—like that Annie. Man, you like to live dangerously, don't you? You know, Mary says Annie Clay goes after anything in pants and usually gets into them, too."

"Oh yeah?"

"Yeah, and Mary also said that Jimmy's mean and very jealous of anybody Annie goes after. Mary said you should stay away from the Clays."

"Oh, I'm a big boy, Mike. I don't scare easily."

Ron turned down the ramp onto the interstate and accelerated into traffic. The sky was gray, but no rain was predicted.

Mike started dogging him. "You know they used to lynch black men for looking sideways at white girls. I'd be careful if I were you. Whites were always afraid that blacks would rape their girls and give them brown grandchildren."

Ron shook his head. "Well, they got that backward!"

Mike looked surprised. "What do you mean?"

"Aw, come on, Mike. We blacks were always afraid whites would rape *our* girls and give *us* brown grandchildren." Ron jabbed his own arm with his forefinger. "Look at my skin. Now, does that look black to you?"

"No. It's brown."

"That's right. And do you know how it got to be brown when we all started out black?"

"I suppose it was mostly from white planters screwing black slaves."

"Huh-uh. *Raping* black slaves, Mike. When you look around and see all the different shades of browns and tans and yellows, just remember that most of those shades came from white men raping black women. Slaves and maids and nursemaids and cleaning women."

Mike tried to lighten the conversation. "So, how much black blood do you have to have to be a member?"

Ron chuckled. "Of what, the black race?"

"Yeah."

"You tell me. You white people decide that. I think you started out saying one-quarter, and then it was one-eighth. Last I heard it was one drop. It doesn't matter if most of your ancestors are white. If one of them is black, you're black."

"But some people are calling themselves mixed-race if they're black and white."

"Sure, until you white people call them black."

"And you black people call them high yellow."

"Ha. But let me tell you this, if you look too white, you might need a DNA test to get into the black race."

Mike laughed. "But all light-skinned black people have to do to get into the white race is to lie, and fool white people."

"That's right. A lot of you pure white folks don't even know you're black. White folks are easy to fool."

They turned off Route 50 toward downtown Annapolis. This time they headed to the law library at the Court of Appeals. At the front desk, Ron asked where they could find the archives of the *Baltimore Courier*. The librarian led them to the microfilm files and readers, admonishing the pair to leave any films they pulled on top of the cabinets for easier reshelving. Ron thanked her.

Ron quickly found the film for December 1907. Mike took out the one for January 1908. They put the spools on the pins. Ron pushed the automatic scroll button and delved into the December issues, and Mike did the same with January.

Think I'll start at the end, Ron thought. *That's when the lynching was.* He found the December 28 issue and scanned the headlines on each page. He found crime news on page eight, but there was nothing about a lynching. He continued perusing each page to the end. *Damn*, he thought. *Where is it?* Then it occurred to him that while the lynching may have occurred on December 27, the story may not have been reported until later. He continued on to December 29, finding crime news on page ten.

My God, he thought. *Here it is.*

NEGRO LYNCHED IN MAYVILLE

Farmer Attacked Planter's Daughter

MAYVILLE, MARYLAND. DECEMBER 27—*Thomas Phillips, a negro farmer, age 34, was lynched at Big Oak last night by a mob of men who took him from his house.*

Late yesterday afternoon, following a disagreement over his account, the negro attacked Mrs. Agnes Strickland in Clay Grocery at Big Oak where she keeps books. Mrs. Strickland's brother, John Clay, rescued her before she was hurt or defiled. The negro ran across the road down a wagon path leading to his house. Phillips owned the farm adjacent to Spring Hill Farm, which is owned by Jeremiah Clay, father of Mrs. Strickland and John Clay.

Word of the incident spread rapidly throughout the countryside and by ten o'clock at night, a mob of some 150 men, mostly on horseback, gathered at the store. Members of the mob wore feed sacks over their heads with holes cut for their eyes. The mob rode to the negro's house carrying torches and rifles and fired fusillades through the windows before breaking into the house. The negro was found cowering with his family in the basement of the house. In front of his wife and children, he confessed to attacking Mrs. Strickland and was taken from the house. He attempted to escape and was shot in front of the house with more than a hundred bullets. The mob dragged the body behind a horse to Big Oak Road and hanged it from a limb of the big oak tree in front of Clay Grocery.

Mr. and Mrs. Jeremiah Clay and Mr. and Mrs. Strickland were at home asleep during the entire disturbance.

The following afternoon, the sheriff dispersed a crowd at the site, cut down the body, and attempted to find witnesses to the lynching. Owing to the darkness at the time of the lynching and the head coverings worn by the participants, no member of the mob could be identified.

R. L. Eaton, county coroner, arrived in the afternoon, pronounced the negro dead by a mob of unknown persons, and completed the death certificate.

Ron felt the sap running out of him. He was suddenly weak, exhausted. "Mike," he whispered from his seat, too upset to stand. "Look at this."

"Did you find it?"

"Yes. It's right here."

He printed two copies and gave one to Mike. They read the story carefully.

Soon Ron regained his energy. "Shit!" he barked, jumping to his feet. "They lynched him for attacking her. But what did he actually do to her?"

"I don't know," Mike said. "I guess he went after her, and her brother stopped him."

"But he didn't actually hurt her!" Ron said. "It says her brother rescued her *before* she was 'hurt or defiled.'"

"You're right."

Ron crossed his arms and shook his head. "Thomas didn't hurt her. He probably didn't even touch her. And for that they took him from his family and lynched him!"

"And there was no trial," Mike said. "No witnesses, no judge, no jury."

"Of course not. There were never any witnesses to lynchings. It was vigilante justice."

"I know there were some black witnesses. His family, for instance."

"But blacks were prohibited by law from testifying against whites," Ron said. "Black testimony against whites was inadmissible."

"Oh yeah."

Ron began pacing. "It said he confessed in front of his family to attacking that woman. Now why would he confess?" he asked rhetorically. "Because they probably beat it out of him."

"But why would they have wanted a confession at all?"

"So they could say they were justified in lynching him!"

"I guess so."

"Vigilante justice," Ron said.

"Yeah," Mike said. "And what does it mean, her brother rescued her before she was defiled? Are they saying he tried to sexually assault her after an argument?"

Ron shook his head. "That doesn't make any sense. Sexually assault her in front of her brother? That's just bullshit. There was no sexual assault."

"The instigators of the lynching must have just made it up."

Ron wagged his head up and down like a wooden doll. "Yeah—to stir people up, to get them to join in the lynching."

"They couldn't have just said they were having an argument over money," Mike said.

"Shit. Another white woman nearly defiled and another black man lynched."

"But we'll never know exactly what happened because there was no trial and no witnesses."

"We'll see," Ron said. "We'll see."

When his composure returned, Ron looked through the remaining

December issues to see if there were any followup stories, and Mike looked forward in January. They failed to find any—the lynching hadn't gotten much attention.

When they finished, they removed the spools, put them back in their boxes, and laid them on top of the cabinet for the librarian, as she had requested. They thanked her on the way out.

~

In the car going back, Mike had more questions. "Is that it? The end of the search? I mean, you have a pretty good idea of how it happened and who did it."

"The Clays did it, I'm sure of that. But I'd sure like to know more about how it happened and what exactly that argument was about. Did they kill him because of that dispute, or did they want him dead for some other reason?"

"Maybe they just wanted to kill a colored man to keep the others in line."

"Maybe," Ron said. "But I can't stop looking just because of what it says in the paper. No. We aren't done yet. For one thing, the paper said Thomas owned the farm. But now the Clays own it. How did *that* happen? Something doesn't add up."

ELEVEN

Late that day, as dusk became dark in the woods, the dark blue Ford eased down the gravel driveway and stopped next to Jimmy's white Cadillac DeVille. Jimmy's pickup and Annie's red Camaro sat nearby, parked with their back wheels toward to the house. Lights were on in the living room and kitchen. Bill walked up the steps and knocked on the frame of the screen door. Annie answered, dressed in her uniform of tight blue jeans and a blouse with the top two buttons undone. Her face was made up, and her straight blond hair fell gently to her shoulders.

"Jimmy here?" Bill asked.

"Just a minute," she said, making him wait outside. "Jimmy!"

Jimmy came to the door. He looked at Annie with disgust. He invited Bill in with a nod, barking at Annie, "Why didn't you let him in?"

"He's your friend, not mine." She walked out with a small purse dangling from her shoulder. Jimmy didn't bother asking where she was going or when she would be back.

He and Bill walked back to the kitchen. Jimmy opened the refrigerator and handed Bill a beer. "Find out anything?"

"Yeah. They went to Annapolis again. But this time they went to a courthouse across from the archives."

"You know, I called that archives place and asked them what people do there, and the girl said that some people come to look at historical records, but most of them come in to look up their relatives. You know, that genology crap."

"Huh."

"So what relatives was he looking up?"

"No clue. I thought he was from California."

"Yeah. So why's he looking up relatives in Maryland?"

"Ya got me."

Jimmy took a swig of beer. "What'd they do at that courthouse?"

"They went inside and went into a liberry there. I followed them in and went back into the stacks and pretended to look for things. The liberrian asked me twice if she could help me, but I told her no thanks, I was just looking."

"Weren't none of her business what you were doing."

"Right. And then they looked at microfilms for over an hour. I couldn't believe it. I just kept looking at law books."

"Hmmph," Jimmy snorted with a grin, thinking of Bill reading law books.

"Then they printed something out, and I could hear them talking about some lynching back then."

"Lynching!" Jimmy spat.

"Yeah, and when they left, they put the microfilms they was using on top of the file cabinet, and I grabbed the one the nigger was looking at and slipped it in my shirt."

"You got it?"

"Yeah, right here. *Baltimore Courier*. December 1907."

"1907! Shit! That's when they lynched that fucking coon that used to live in this house!"

"Well, shit. But we don't know that's what they were looking at in the newspaper."

"And it's just an accident that he's around here all the time, you numbnuts, talking to Annie, talking to Noah, looking at gravestones, and going to archives, looking at old newspapers—from the month and year of the lynching?"

"You're right, Jimmy. It can't be no coincident."

～

Wilma was reading, and Rosalie and Mike's son Jason were playing a computer game when Ron walked in.

Rosalie ran up and hugged his waist. "Daddy!" she said, and Ron felt himself melt.

"You two having a good time?"

"Yeah. He's good." She ran back to the computer.

Ron took Wilma aside and told her about the newspaper account of the lynching.

"That's horrible, Ron. But you knew it would end like this, didn't you?"

"I guess."

"It's time to forget about it. Just be glad we live in the twenty-first century."

"But I still don't think he attacked her, sexually or otherwise, because Mother said he didn't do anything wrong. There's gotta be more to it than that."

"Oh Ron. So what if there is? So what if the lynching was even more evil than you thought it was. It won't change a thing for you to find out. Just stop. It won't get you anywhere."

"I can't stop now—not until I know what really happened, and prove he was innocent!"

～

After the trip to the law library in Annapolis, Mike felt rejuvenated. He came through his front door shouting. "Mary! Let's go for a walk! We better hurry, the sun is getting low. Maybe we'll see the beaver."

"Okay," she said. "Run down to the Watkins' and see if you can get the kids away from their friends, or tell them where we're going. I'll get some bread for the ducks."

He bounced out the door and up the street. Unsurprisingly, no one wanted to join them, but Wilma said she would keep an eye on the children. *Oh well,* he thought. *We'll have a nice walk anyway.*

He and Mary walked to the end of the cul-de-sac and took the paved path, which wandered for a few hundred yards through woods behind the houses to a small lake. On their walk, they talked about Ron's discovery.

"He was pretty mad," Mike said.

"He deserves to be," Mary replied thoughtfully, "but I hope he doesn't stay that way. That was a long time ago, and there's nothing that can be done about it now."

"I know. But he says he's not satisfied. He thinks the whites made up this attack thing, and may have killed Thomas for some other reason. He wants to find out what it was."

"I—I think he should be careful. You tell him that, honey. He seems to be getting pulled in closer to Jimmy Clay, and Jimmy is a nasty, nasty man."

"I already told him what you said, but I'll tell him again," Mike said, puzzled anew by her insistence.

~

Ron turned on his stopwatch and plodded into the woods. He slowed to a walk going up the hill to the bike path. It was Monday morning and he was tired, but he needed to run. As he moved along the path and began to think about the weekend's discoveries, he was soon moving at a quicker than normal pace. *After Thomas ran home, someone must have saddled a horse and ridden out to invite people to the lynching party. I can see them arriving on horseback, putting on their feed sacks, lighting their torches, and riding down the driveway to the house. Then they shot out the windows, broke into the house, and found the family cowering in the basement. Shit! Then they probably beat a confession out of him in front of his family and took him outside. It said he tried to escape. That was to give them an excuse to shoot him. And they* all *shot him, so no one could know who killed him and no one person could be held responsible. Cowards! Then they dragged his bloody carcass down the dirt road and hung it up, so all the colored folk would know what would happen to them if they attacked a white person or stepped out of line in any way. I can see it now—photographers, hundreds of sightseers. The sheriff asked for witnesses, but there were none. There never were. And then the coroner pronounced him dead.*

Ron's feet gripped asphalt as he flew past the overgrown fields around Spring Hill Farm House, built in 1764 by Major William Clay, grandfather, six or seven generations removed, of Annie and Jimmy Clay, who had lived there as children. Then he came to the path that led to the house where the Clays lived now. He had promised Wilma that he would stay away from the house and its redneck owner. But having learned that this was the location where his great-grandfather had lived and died, he had to see it again.

He turned off the bike trail and bolted down the bank into the woods toward the house, stopping for a moment to pick up a short, stout stick for protection. He crossed the stream, rounded a bend, and strode downhill through the forest. He moved past the swamp with the beaver lodge, and around another bend until he saw the buildings—the broken-down shed and icehouse and garage, and the two-story house where it had happened. He stopped and stared, hoping to see visions or hear sounds from the past. But the house was still. He turned onto the path to the right, away from the house. He re-crossed the stream, and went up to the road, gazing with new eyes at the store and the gigantic oak tree. Then he ran home. His run took forty-seven minutes and twenty-three seconds.

~

"Gosh. I wonder how our parents will get along with the Mances," Mary said. She and Mike were planning a crab feast for neighbors and family. Crabs were so expensive that they were inviting only those neighbors within a few doors in either direction. Within those parameters, they didn't want to exclude anyone.

"I don't know," Mike said. "But we had to invite them. They're our next-door neighbors, and we have to live with them. We don't live with our parents."

"Yes, I know."

"Your dad might enjoy talking local history with Alfred."

"Maybe," Mary said. "But they come from such different backgrounds. They're just a few generations away from being slave and master."

"Well, everybody has to change sometime, and we have to give your parents the chance. Throw them into the crucible and see what comes out. Get them to make some exceptions and maybe see things in a new way."

"It won't be dull, that's for sure."

"Especially if Tabatha gives your dad the eye," Mike said.

"*Your* dad might enjoy that too. Make him feel like a young stud again."

~

The newspaper account said Thomas owned the farm, Ron thought, *but now the Clays own it. How did that happen?*

On the computer, he accessed the official county Web site to find out more about real estate records. The county had on file all deeds and all public records connected to real estate in the county. The information was public, but had to be obtained by self-guided research; the law prohibited clerks from providing assistance or performing title searches. The office was open from eight-thirty to four-thirty, Monday through Friday. That was about it. No deeds were available online, so he would have to go to the office in the county seat. He called to confirm the Web site's information. Ron decided to take Friday off, which was a glorious Washington summer tradition anyway.

At eight-fifteen on Friday, he found a long line waiting to get into the deed office. The line quickly diffused into interior rooms when staff opened the door. He smiled at the woman at the information desk. "Can you tell me how to find a deed to a property?"

"What's the name of the owner?"

"Which one, the current one or the one at the time the property was transferred?"

She frowned. "When did the transfer take place?"

"I'd say in 1907 or 1908."

"You don't know?"

"Well, I'm not positive."

"Oh," she said in a judgmental tone. "Well, you can try searching back from the current owner, if you know who it is, but we can't help you with that. You might be better off hiring an attorney to do it, if it's important."

"I think I'd like to try it myself."

"You can do that. You start by entering the current owner's name in one of the computers in that room." She pointed to an adjoining room, and turned back to her own computer.

"Thanks."

Ten computers lined the walls of the room, all occupied. A queue of five people waited. In the center of the room was a long, counter-height table with books stacked down the middle and more on shelves underneath. Those in line glanced around the room at the computers, looking for signs that users were preparing to leave. The game appeared to be first come, first served. He wondered if he might have to race competitors around the center table to take possession of a vacant machine.

After nearly an hour, one became available. Although he didn't know what to do when he got there, he quickly claimed it. Unable to even bring up a menu, he looked around helplessly. A young woman—next in line—asked, impatiently, "Do you need some help?"

"Yes."

She showed him how to get the deed references—the date of the transfer, grantor, or seller (party of the first part), name of grantee or recipient (party of the second part), the liber (book number) and folio (page number) of the previous transfer, and any exceptions to the transfer (portions of the property conveyed to others)—and directed him toward the deed room.

"Great, but how do I find the deeds of the previous owners?"

"That's what the liber and folio refer to."

"So I just get the names and numbers from each deed and look up them up in the deed books?"

"C'rect."

He thanked her and headed into the deed room. The young woman quickly took his seat, removed a legal pad from her briefcase, and began typing rapidly.

The deed room contained another long table. The top of this one sloped upward so that people could place a book on it and easily read it from a standing position. Underneath it were shelves full of large, heavy books, each identified with a number. Numbered stacks surrounded the table, and along one wall were several copy machines.

Ron looked through the stacks and found the book numbered L. 15376. He took it to the table, and opened it to page 294. There it was—the first deed, anyway—recording conveyance of the property from James C. Clay, Jr., deceased, to James C. Clay III and Annie M. Clay on June 19, 2000. The deed gave the liber and folio number of the deed conveying the land to James C. Clay in 1994, as well as a physical description of the property—location of stakes, acreage, and buildings included. On the next page was a similar deed for different property. *Must be the store*, Ron thought.

He started a list on a sheet of lined paper—date recorded, grantor, recipient, liber, folio, and exceptions. Then back and forth to the stacks he went, carrying the heavy books, looking up the deed references, tracking the property back in time, filling in his list, and noting the exceptions.

In 2000 Jimmy and Annie received five acres, more or less, from their father's estate. Before that, the land had passed through consecutive generations of Clays from 1908, when Jeremiah Clay, great-great-grandfather of Jimmy and Annie, bought the land at Thomas Phillips' estate auction—after Thomas was lynched. Thomas had purchased the property in 1904 from Milton Smith, who had purchased it a few days earlier from Harley Archer, who in turn had purchased it in 1899 from Jeremiah Clay. *There has to be a story there*, Ron thought as he examined his chart.

By the time Jimmy and Annie received the land from their father's estate, thirty-two of the thirty-seven acres that Thomas had owned had been sold to people outside of the family.

One search complete, Ron then traced ownership of the store property, which followed an identical pattern, except that it always remained in Jeremiah Clay's hands and was never owned by Harley Archer, Milton Smith, or Thomas Phillips. The tract on which the store was situated shrank from ten acres to two in 1961.

Ron drove home mulling more questions. *An auction. How is it that Jeremiah Clay bought Thomas's land at an estate auction after Thomas was lynched?* He wondered whether the land was auctioned to pay off some debt. *And this thing with Milton Smith.* He was curious about why there were two transaction dates so close together, and he did not understand what had made Jeremiah Clay sell land to Harley Archer in 1899, only to buy it back again in 1908, and why later on Jeremiah had sold three acres in six one-half acre parcels.

By the time he arrived home in the late afternoon, all the transactions had begun to run together in his mind. He was glad he had taken good notes.

"Daddy!"

"Rosy!" He picked his daughter up, instantly forgetting land transfers and deed books for a while.

TWELVE

Just after seven the next morning, Ron came out of his garage. He saw a green pickup truck parked on the shoulder of Spring Hill Road. It looked vaguely familiar. *Maybe somebody catches a ride there,* he thought.

He stretched for a few minutes. The truck was still there. He clicked his watch and headed into the woods, up the hill, and onto the bike trail toward Big Oak. The morning was cooler than normal, and Ron was invigorated. It felt good to stretch and work his muscles as he sped along.

His mind was at the office. It amazed him how he could turn off his search for the truth about Thomas and completely immerse himself in meetings, reports, e-mails, calls, budgets, and deadlines. The pesky questions about Thomas lay dormant, coming to mind only at odd moments, and then seeming more like dream than reality.

He came to the field and looked past the grazing horses toward the brick mansion. From the other side of the path, he heard the rumble of machinery. Looking to the right in the early morning light, he saw a yellow loader attacking a mound of kudzu vines two hundred yards away. No, it was not a mound. The kudzu was engulfing and digesting a small building. He stopped and watched. Through the vines, the teeth of the loader's gaping steel mouth lifted off the structure's roof. Ron watched as a small brick chimney shook, teetered, and landed on the soft earth. A wall with two windows was exposed.

So small, Ron thought. *Who lived in a house that small? Tenants? Slaves?*

He tore himself away and ran down the path at a strong pace, veering down the hill toward Thomas's former house. This was part of his regular route now; he was drawn to it like a dying man revisiting his past. In some ways, he felt that he owned the house: it was bought and paid for with Thomas's blood and the suffering of his wife and children. He could imagine the family together—eating, sleeping, working, and praying within those walls—and could also visualize the violence and terror that came later. Ron stopped and urinated on the ground, marking his territory. Then, remembering the BEWARE OF DOG sign, he again picked up a stick before continuing toward the house.

He passed the swamp. As the decaying buildings appeared through the woods, he once more stopped and stared. This time, however, a large German shepherd came through the screen door on the porch. Growling, the dog leapt down the steps, and sped toward him. Ron sprinted back toward the woods as fast as he could, yet he still heard the throaty barking gaining on him.

The dog was nearly upon him when Ron saw the hill. He charged to the top, coming into the road in front of the store. Knowing the dog was about to attack him, feeling his fear change to anger, he turned and faced the beast. He raised the stick and stepped toward the animal. "Get away!" he roared.

The dog halted, but kept snarling and barking, its mouth like a steel bear trap, its teeth glistening, and its ears, fur, and tail raised. From side to side it paced, looking for an opening, an angle of attack. Each time the dog moved, Ron feigned attack, shook the stick overhead, and shouted, "Hey!" "Get away!" or "Beat it!"

Then he threw the stick at the dog, making it jump out of the way, ran up the store stairs, and went through the screen door. Panting, he wiped sweat from his brow, but still remembered to stop his watch.

"I see you met Fury," Annie said. "Most people try to stay away from him. Wonder what made him come after you."

"I don't know. I was coming down off the bike trail, and he came out of the woods at me."

"Well, that's funny. He's never done that before. He always stays down in the woods and guards the house."

"Not today, I guess."

She smiled, puzzled. "And he didn't bite you?"

"No. I turned and faced him down with a stick."

"Most people would've kept on running, and the dog would've bitten their butt. But you just turned on him and faced him down? Well, I've never seen anything like that before."

"Most dogs are cowardly, if you face them and go after them."

"Yeah, but most people don't try to find out if dogs are cowards."

"He was going to get me, and I got mad. What else could I do but fight?"

The animal was at the door now, nose on the screen, snarling and whining. Ron flinched, taking a step away. He then stepped toward Fury, raised his arm, and yelled, "Beat it!" This time, the dog held its ground.

"Well, Mr. Watkins, you made it in here, but how are you going to get out?" She hunched up a shoulder, rested her head on it, and raised her eyebrows coquettishly. "Looks to me like Fury and I got you trapped."

"Hmmph. Well, I'll just have to call 911. They'll save me. Here— let me borrow your phone."

Annie sighed. "Oh, and I thought we might be able to spend a little time together."

"Not today, Annie. Too much to do."

In a firm voice, she yelled a command through the screen. "Fury, go home." The dog turned at once and trotted across the road and into the woods.

"How did you do that?"

"It just took a little training. He's a very obedient dog."

"So if I practiced, I could learn to do that?"

"Maybe."

"But if I didn't say it right, he might go for my throat."

"Yep. How 'bout a cold drink on the house? Can't have you leaving here all hot and bothered."

"Thanks. Just water, please."

"Okay." She went to the cooler and took out a plastic bottle, stroking it with her fingertips a few times before giving it to him. "Here you are, Mr. Jogger-Dogfighter Watkins."

The spring twanged on the rear door, and Jimmy walked in. The screen door slammed behind him. "What's going on? What was Fury barking at?"

"Oh, nothing," Annie said. "He just seemed to take a dislike for Mr. Watkins here and came at him when he was running by the store."

"What was Fury doing up here?"

"I don't know," said Annie.

"You need to keep your dog tied up, Mr. Clay. One of these days he's going to bite someone, and then you'll have a lawsuit on your hands."

"It won't happen again," Jimmy said, his face contorted into a sneer. "No problem."

~

That night, Dan and Bill stopped by the garage at Jimmy's request. They found him sitting on a wooden stool, drinking beer from a bottle and smoking a cigarette. Noah had already cleaned up and left, and the big garage doors were closed.

"You know where it is," Jimmy told them.

They went to the old refrigerator by the office door, and each took out a beer. They twisted off their caps, and took beef sticks from a box on top of the fridge.

"So what'd you find out?" Jimmy asked Dan.

"Far as I can tell, he runs on Mondays, Wednesdays, and Saturdays starting between six-thirty and seven in the morning. Always goes the same way—out the back of the house, down the bike trail, past the store, and back around on Owens Farm Road. Except now I think he's started taking that path through the woods near your house. Today I was parked up the road on the other side of the bike trail, hidden behind some bushes, waiting for him, and what do you know, he came up out of the woods from your place instead, with the dog right behind him."

"I *knew* he was lying! Fury wouldn't have come after him unless he was down at the house. That lying, sneaky monkey. Who does he think he is trespassing on my property?" Jimmy took a swig of beer.

"Amazing," Bill said. "Don't have a lot of brains, does he? Wonder why Fury didn't bite him."

"I was out back taking a dump, and I heard Fury barking. Then I went in the store, and Annie said the nigger faced him down with a big stick."

"You're shitting me," Bill said. "Fury?"

Dan glowered. "He either got big fucking balls, or he's dumber 'n hell."

"She said he waved that stick at Fury and shouted 'Get away' and 'Get back' and such, and then backed his way to the porch, and then threw the stick at Fury and almost hit him—made him jump out of the way."

"Damn," Dan said. "He's a fucking contender."

"I can't believe the nerve of that coon!" Jimmy said. "'Ya need to keep your dog tied up,' he says. 'One day he'll bite someone,' he says. 'Then they'll sue you,' he says. He was threatening me—threatening to sue me!" Jimmy took another long swig of beer. "You know, used to be they'd string up a nigger for threatening a white man like that. Imagine! The gall of that spook."

"Unbelievable," Bill said.

"They used to shoot niggers for not getting off the sidewalk when a white man came along," Jimmy said, "or for touching a white woman, or even looking at one sideways. Now they can trespass on your property and back-talk you and lie in your face! Shit! What's this fucked-up world coming to?" He flicked the fire from his cigarette onto the concrete floor, and ground it out with the sole of his work boot; then he crushed the butt between his fingers, and flipped it into the coffee can on the floor. Finishing his beer, he tossed the empty into the cardboard case by the door, and went to the refrigerator for another.

"Ain't coming to no good, that's for sure," Bill said.

"Now they think they can come right up on your property and snoop around your house and all just like it was theirs. I can't believe it," Dan muttered. He took a bite of beef stick and sucked on his beer.

"Fucking nigger threatened to sue me. That's had me burning all day. The monkey's gonna take me to court if my dog bites him on my land. On my land! Fuckin' A, that makes me mad."

"Wasn't like your dog went on his land and bit him," Bill sympathized.

"Fuck no," Jimmy said.

"He'd prob'ly win, too, " Dan said, "with all the niggers they put on juries today. Hell, my cousin Ted wrecked his car and had to go to trial because they said he was drunk, and most of the people on the jury was niggers. He didn't have a chance."

"Yeah, and that's the kind of jury I'd get if that fucking Watkins sued me. They'd say it was my fault the dog bit him on my own land."

"You're right, Jimmy," Dan agreed.

"They'd prob'ly *give* him my land because my dog bit him on it!"

"Ain't that some shit," Bill said.

"It's all going too far," Jimmy said. "One day, we're gonna have to take back this country. Take it back from the niggers and spics and chinks and fucking A-rabs and Muslims."

"Get it back for us whites," Dan chimed in.

"Bring back Jim Crow," Bill said. "Put them all in their place."

"Get them back out of the schools and hotels and restaurants," Dan said.

"We need to start the war," Jimmy said.

"Get the guns," Dan said.

"Yeah," Bill said.

"Get everyone together, let the blood flow, and cleanse the nation," Jimmy said.

"And do it soon," Bill said, "while there's still more of us than them."

"You know, what I can't understand is why that spook is so interested in that lynching."

"Don't know," Dan said. "But we might have a problem. I think he recognized my truck this morning. He gave it a long, hard look before he went on his run."

"It don't matter," Jimmy said. "Don't matter a bit." Then he removed his cap and ran his hands over his close-cropped hair, displaying a swastika on the inside of each bicep. He looked at his watch. "Shit. I gotta get down to Wal-Mart and pick up some stuff for the store." He stood up and brought his heels together. His right arm shot out, and he barked "Heil Hitler!"

Bill and Dan jumped to their feet, matching his salute. "Heil Hitler!"

THIRTEEN

After his encounter with Fury, Ron burst into the house full of adrenaline, his muscles tense, fighting the dog again, this time in his mind, and this time smashing its skull with the stick. He showered, shaved, and dressed, ate a bowl of cereal and told Wilma the story, with a bit of relish.

"I told him he ought to keep his dog tied up so he won't get sued."

"Oh Ron," she said, shaking her head.

"That shut him up. Listen, I've gotta leave again, but I'll be back."

"Where are you going now?"

"I want to see if I can talk to some people who live down by that old chapel on Owens Farm Road."

"I wish you would finish with this thing. It's turning into an obsession."

"I'll finish."

"You already know what happened."

"Not everything."

Wilma sighed. "Well, we'll be at the pool."

"This morning?"

"It's not as crowded in the morning, and they want to swim. I was hoping you could help them. The pool closes in a few weeks, but I guess we can take them to an indoor pool later."

"Thanks."

"This afternoon, I'm taking them to a one o'clock movie with Jeff and Jason. Mary wants to get the kids out of her hair for a while. Don't forget about the crab feast. We're supposed to be there at four."

～

As he drove down the narrow, winding road toward the chapel, Ron noticed large trees running along only one side. *They must have widened it from one lane,* he reasoned. Turning onto Owens Farm Road, the railroad side of the roadway was still wooded. But the other side was lined with houses of various ages—old two-story farmhouses with wrap-around porches, one-and-a-half story bungalows, two-story neo-Colonials, and some small ranch houses that reminded him of the house he was raised in, except the California house had stucco walls and a tile roof instead of wood siding and asphalt shingles. There was also one particularly large and new neo-Colonial with big windows, vinyl siding, and a brick front.

Across Big Oak Road, he came to a sign reading "Hawkinstown." He passed Hawkins A.M.E. Chapel, and arrived at a cluster of small two-story houses lining both sides of the road. Most of these homes were narrow but deep, with gables and front porches facing the street, built on deep, skinny lots with large shade trees and garages in the rear. Chain-link fences surrounded a few yards to hold dogs—more living security systems.

Ron parked on the shoulder and took out his steno pad. He climbed out, walking past a flower garden on his way up some stairs to a screened porch. He knocked on the frame of the screen door and waited, then knocked louder. A curtain moved on a front window. After a while, the door opened wide enough for the head of a man to emerge. He was dark, with close-cropped white hair and a wrinkled face.

"Can I help you?"

"Hi, my name's Ron Watkins. I live over on Blake Station Circle off Spring Hill Road."

"Yes?"

"I'm interested in the history of the area, and I wondered if you know of anyone in the neighborhood who lived here a hundred years ago." Ron watched the man's left eyebrow go up.

"A hundred years ago? They'd be dead, wouldn't they?"

"I know that's a long time ago, and it's not very likely, but I just thought I'd ask."

"I don't know," the man said, eyeing Ron suspiciously.

"Well, do you know anyone who's lived here a long time?"

"No."

"How long have you lived here?"

"Why do you want to know?"

"Just interested," Ron said.

The door closed abruptly.

He went to another house, wondering whether people would be more receptive if he were selling siding or religion. The porch on this house had no screening, so he was able to make it all the way to the front door. He pushed the doorbell and heard a ding-dong inside. No one was home.

Across the street was a house with a fenced-in yard. Inside the fence, a rottweiler trotted over to investigate the intruder. Ron stayed clear, deciding that a second encounter with a canine this day might be pushing his luck. He bypassed that house, but stayed on the same side of the street.

At the next house, he saw a swing-set in the back yard. The door was answered by a light-skinned, full-bodied young woman in polyester warm-ups, running shoes, and a T-shirt. She was accompanied by a little boy who looked up at Ron quizzically.

"Yes?" she asked as she took in Ron's tan khakis, knit shirt, and handsome face. "Can I help you?"

"I hope so. My name's Ron Watkins. I live over on Blake Station Circle off of Spring Hill Road. I'm new in the area, and I'm interested in local history. Someone told me that this is a historically black neighborhood."

"Yes, that's what they told us when we bought the house."

"So you haven't lived here very long either?"

"No, just a few months."

"Have you met anyone whose family has lived here a long time?"

"You might try Mrs. Wrigley, two doors down. I think she's been here a long time."

"Thanks. What's your name?"

"Ms. Norris."

"Nice to meet you, Ms. Norris, and thanks a lot."

"No problem."

The sun was high now, and he began to feel the heat of the day. Two doors down, he walked through a neatly-kept yard to a house with a freshly-painted porch. He went up the stairs, rang the bell, and listened to a melody on chimes. He heard footsteps pause at the door and noticed a peephole. A short and slender brown-skinned woman wearing tan slacks and a flowered blouse opened the door part way, keeping a hand on the edge to push it shut if necessary. Ron guessed she was in her fifties.

"Yes?"

"Mrs. Wrigley?"

"Yes?"

"Good morning, ma'am. I just met Ms. Norris down the street, and she said you might be able to help me. My name's Ron Watkins. My wife and I live over on Blake Station Circle, off Spring Hill Road, and we're new here. I'm interested in learning some of the local history. My family originally came from around here, and Ms. Norris said your family has lived here a long time."

"Oh yes—since before the Civil War."

"Well, I think I may have some relatives in the Hawkins Chapel cemetery—Henry and Esther Phillips." He was unsure just how much to tell her.

"Hmm. I seem to recall they were among the founders of Hawkinstown and Hawkins Chapel."

"They were. I read that in a book the county historical society published. And I found their headstones in the cemetery."

"Yes. If I'm remembering my history, the Phillipses lived in the house right next to the chapel, the one with the big porch."

"Well, that's interesting."

She hesitated briefly. "Mr. Watkins, would you like to come in out of the heat for a while to talk? I need to close this door to keep in the air conditioning. My husband will be home in a few minutes, and he may be able to help you too."

"Why, thank you."

She led him into the living room, asking him if he would like something to drink. He asked for water. She left the room and returned with a glass of ice water. He noticed that she paused for a moment at the door, perhaps to be sure he was still in his chair. Her caution made him wonder if her husband really would be home soon.

"You have a lovely home here. I love the dark woodwork." A painting of the Last Supper hung above the sofa, with a brown-skinned Jesus and disciples. Another painting depicted a wooded glade with sun sifting through the trees.

"It's home. Now, what sorts of things are you interested in?"

"Well, do you know if the Phillipses have any relatives who still live around here?"

"No, not that I know of. I believe they all moved away."

"I know my side of the family did. We went to Chicago, then on to the West Coast, to Oakland, California."

"That's a long ways away."

"Yes ma'am. But now that we moved back, I thought I would try to learn more about my family. Do you know anyone who would know anything about them?"

"I would say my mother might, if she was still alive. But she and my father passed a few years ago. They were in a car crash. Some damn fool got drunk and crossed the line, hit them head-on."

"Oh, I'm sorry."

"Yes. I bet she could've told you a lot of stories about your family."

"Well, that's too bad. Do you know anyone else who might know about them?"

"My gram might, if she can remember."

"Your grandmother?"

"Yes. She's 105 years old."

"105?" Ron said excitedly.

"Yes, she was born in 1900. She lives down at Love of Jesus Nursing Home in Northeast. She *might* be able to remember. She used to live in this house."

She would have been seven years old when Thomas was lynched, he thought. "How is she?"

"Well, she has to be pushed in a wheelchair now, and her eyesight is poor. But her health is good, and she's still sharp mentally—no Alzheimer's or anything like that. I just don't know if she would be able to remember that far back."

"Mrs. Wrigley, do you think that I could go talk to her some time?"

"Why, I think she might enjoy that, Mr. Watkins. I happen to be going this afternoon, if you want to join me."

"Well, that'd be nice. I'd like to do that, if it's okay with you."

"My, yes. Why don't you meet me here at one o'clock, and you can follow me down."

"Thank you very much. I'll be here at one."

∼

After checking in at home and eating a sandwich, Ron headed back to Hawkinstown. He followed Mrs. Wrigley to the nursing home, a large red-brick building with a slate roof, concrete steps, and a new wheelchair ramp snaking up one side. They signed in at the desk in the lobby, and took the elevator to the fourth floor. Mrs. Wrigley led him to her grandmother's room.

"What's her name?" Ron asked.

"Mrs. Simmons."

"I think I remember some Simmonses in the cemetery."

"Oh yes. My grandfather—he passed about thirty years ago—and my parents."

Mrs. Simmons wasn't in her room. They looked for her in the day room at the end of the hall. Other residents, mostly black women in their eighties and nineties, sat along the walls. Many stared into space. One spoke quietly to herself. Some gathered around an old color television set. Some gently rocked their upper bodies, forward and backward, and four silently, methodically played cards at a table.

"There she is," Mrs. Wrigley said. They approached a chestnut-colored woman with thin white hair and deeply wrinkled skin. Mrs. Simmons sat in a wheelchair gazing vacantly toward the TV.

"Gram? It's Monique!" Mrs. Wrigley said. "How are you doing today?"

The old woman stirred from her reverie. "Is that you, child?" she asked in a weak voice.

"Yes, it's me, Monique! How are you today?"

"Well, I'm just fine, I guess. Not much to report." Mrs. Wrigley and Ron chuckled.

"You still have your sense of humor, I can report that."

"Well, child, there's no reason to be a sourpuss. Nobody likes a sourpuss."

Ron laughed out loud.

"Now who do you have with you today? It's not Walter, is it?" Her voice was getting stronger.

"No, Gram. I brought someone else today. This is Ron Watkins."

"Nice to meet you, Mrs. Simmons."

"Well, it's nice to meet someone new for a change. Do you live near Monique?"

"Yes ma'am. My wife and I live on a new street off Spring Hill Road."

"Oh, so you're married. That's bad luck for me, Mr. Watkins. I'm still trying to catch me a man, but it's not easy for a woman of my age."

"Oh, I don't know," Ron said. "But you may have to settle for a younger man."

"That's why I was interested in you, Mr. Watkins."

"Now, Gram, you always said we children shouldn't just throw ourselves at a man."

"Not if he's dumb and ugly. But for me, ugly don't matter, 'cause I can hardly see any more."

"You'll have to excuse my grandmother, Mr. Watkins, for her immodest and forward behavior."

"I'm just glad she can't see how ugly I am."

"Now, just why did you come to see me, Mr. Watkins? Are you sweet on Monique?"

"Mr. Watkins moved here from California, Gram. But long ago, when you were growing up, his family lived in Hawkinstown."

"My, my."

"I think I'm related to Henry and Esther Phillips."

"I remember those names. They used to live in the house next to the chapel. Henry was one of the founders of Hawkinstown. He worked on the railroad as a Pullman porter. Mrs. Phillips was a Johnson, I believe."

Ron flipped open his pad and began taking notes.

"Did they have many children?"

"Oh, that was so long ago. I know there were several at least, but they were a lot older than me. But I do remember there was some kind of trouble with one of them."

"What kind of trouble, Gram?"

"Awful trouble, honey. The wors' kind."

"What happened?" Mrs. Wrigley asked.

"Well, I don't remember it very well. I was just a child when it happened."

Ron and Mrs. Wrigley waited in silence, keenly focused.

"I remember the night it happened. It was just after Christmas, but it was one of those winter warm spells you get sometimes, when the air feels damp and spring-like and something feels strange and wrong. We had a small Christmas tree still up, decorated with strings of red berries and popcorn, I think, and Papa always put a paper star on top that he cut out with scissors. We children were playing when we heard a lot of horses galloping down the road and a lot of men shouting and hollering, angry-like. And they was white men."

"Mm, mm, mm," Mrs. Wrigley said.

"Mama made us go to the back of the house and lay down on the floor. We turned out all the lights, and Papa took out his shotgun and kneeled at the front window in the dark."

"You never told us about this, Gram."

"I don't think I remembered it, child."

"What happened then?" Mrs. Wrigley asked.

"Well, the noise kept up all night. We just laid there, scared out of our wits. Mama and Papa sneaked around the house, and I heard them whispering to each other. I know they was scared too. And they came and told us that if the white men came, no matter what, we was to run out the back of the house and into the woods to the railroad, but don't go on the tracks 'cause they might see us there, or a train might come along."

"Go on, Gram."

"Well, that's all that happened that night. We made it through till morning. Next morning, word spread pretty quick through the neighborhood that there had been a lynching down at Big Oak."

"Lord have mercy!" Mrs. Wrigley exclaimed.

"Word was that a Negro man was accused of attacking that Clay woman who ran the store at Big Oak, and that a mob came in the night with feed sacks over their heads and carrying torches, and they took the Negro man out of his house and shot him to pieces, and then hung his body by a rope from a limb of that big oak tree. Then a whole crowd of white people from all over the county was out looking at the body and taking pictures. Even some of the white kids from around the corner were up there gaping at the thing."

"Oh Lord, Lord, Lord."

"Then the white sheriff came to the door—I guess he was going to all the houses in town—and asked Papa and Mama if they had seen any of the riders the night before. Papa and Mama told him no, that it was dark out and we was all in bed asleep."

"Then what, Mrs. Simmons?"

"Well, late in the afternoon this wagon come down the road, and I looked down the street, and I saw some of the neighbor men lifting something heavy out of the wagon. It was wrapped in a blanket, but we all knew what it was. And I remember the Phillipses—" she paused in recognition—"your kin, Mr. Watkins, I remember seeing them walking down the road toward the wagon, and Mrs. Phillips was just a-wailing and crying with tears pouring down her face, and Mr. Phillips on her arm, trying to steady her."

"Damn," Ron said.

"Now don't you be cursing around an old woman like that, young man. I won't have that."

"Sorry, Mrs. Simmons, but that was my great-grandfather, Thomas Phillips, that they lynched that night at Big Oak."

"No," Mrs. Wrigley gasped.

"It don't matter none, Mr. Watkins. There's no excuse for profanity."

"You're right, Mrs. Simmons. I apologize. Please go on."

"Well, I remember them bringing out a wood box, and they put that body in the box, and Mr. and Mrs. Phillips looked in it, and they both started a-wailing and moaning again, and got weak in the knees, and fell down right there in the dirt road. Then the men nailed it shut quick. They didn't want no one looking at that body."

"Oh," Mrs. Wrigley said.

"And they was afraid to have a funeral for him, Mr. Watkins, considering what they said he did and how hot those white folks was. So the men went out back into the cemetery, and dug out a deep hole and put the box in, and everyone in the neighborhood and the man's wife and children gathered around the hole, and the preacher said words over it, and they covered it up quick and put an unmarked stone on it. Then they went out and dug some grass up and put it on the grave to try to make it look like it wasn't fresh."

"And then?" Ron asked.

"And that's all there was, young man. People never spoke about it. The man's wife and children came and lived with the Phillipses for a while, and we played with the children some, but they were kind of backward and didn't talk much. And then one day they were gone, and we never heard anything about them after that. Mr. Phillips kept working for the railroad, and he and Mrs. Phillips acted kind of sad a lot of the time, but no one ever spoke about it, and we almost forgot about it, like a bad dream. But we never did forget the sound of them horses, and the shouting and hollering of them white men. No, suh. We never did."

FOURTEEN

My crab feast's pièce de résistance, Mary thought as she poured ten egg yolks into the top of a double boiler. She added a cup of dry sherry, and began to whip the mixture with a manual beater. Aromas of bacon, clams, garlic, and sherry wafted from the pot on the stove.

Mike's mother, Dottie Hoffman, a slender woman with glasses and graying brown hair, and Lonnie, who was married to Mary's younger brother Randy, were sitting at the round kitchen table along with Mary's mother, Beth. Lonnie and Beth both had blond hair—Beth's in tight curls and Lonnie's curving smoothly to her shoulders. Lonnie and Dottie wore shorts and Beth wore capri pants with a matching knit shirt.

The kitchen in the Hoffmans' great room had ten-foot-high ceilings and large windows looking out onto a deck overlooking the woods beyond. Spices, celery stalks, rosemary, two fresh corncobs, some onion skins, and an empty can of clams cluttered the island bar, evidence that a masterpiece was in the works.

"I'm looking forward to meeting your neighbors," Dottie told Mary.

"I'm sure they're very nice people," Beth said.

"We're enjoying them," Mary said.

"Do you find that black neighbors tend to stay to themselves?" Beth asked. "I've always found that to be the case. They're rather hard to get to know."

"I haven't noticed that," Mary said, "but you do have to reach out a little to make friends with anyone. We've already become pretty close to one couple—the Watkins. You'll meet them today, Wilma and Ron." She stopped beating the eggs, turned the flame to low, and resumed stirring the chowder pot. "I don't know what I would have done today without Wilma. She took Jeff and Jason to the movies today with her kids. Got the boys out of my hair, thank goodness."

"Does she have boys or girls?" Beth asked.

"One of each. You'll meet them in a little while."

"You know how I feel about boys and girls of different races mixing like that."

"Yes, Mom, I know." She opened the refrigerator and took out a quart of whipping cream.

"That always worried me. Boys will be boys, and girls girls."

"Yes, Mom. And before we know it, you'll be holding brown great-grandchildren," Mary said as she poured the cream into a mixing bowl.

"Mary," Lonnie chided. "Be nice."

"Well, that's what she's worried about."

"Well … doesn't that worry you?" Lonnie asked.

"Not in the least. These are beautiful, intelligent people, and I wouldn't mind adding a little color to the family."

"You're such a radical," Lonnie said. "Ever since you had that black girlfriend in college."

Mary took out an electric beater and plugged it in. "I learned a lot from Danielle. She was witty and brilliant and cared a lot about people."

Dottie looked peeved. "I don't think Mary's a radical. I think she's right. I used to teach in Baltimore, and I soon found that white and black and brown are all beautiful. It's nastiness and hatefulness that are ugly."

"Thank you, Mother Hoffman," Mary said with a smile as she whipped the cream into clouds of froth.

"Frank and I really can't understand why you moved here," Beth said, "when everyone else is moving out."

"You mean white people."

"That's what we are," Lonnie said.

"I didn't want to move away from where I grew up and where you live. Why should I? Mike and I have no problem living with African-Americans."

Beth raised her hands head-high, palms up. "Yes, but what about property values? Frank says that they always go down when black people move in."

"It seems to me the property values have gone up here with all these big new homes," Dottie said.

"Frank says that as soon as we have a few murders and robberies and drug arrests, values will go down fast. Don't forget—he's been in real estate for many years."

"I just hope we don't get into a housing bubble like we had with the Internet," Dottie said to blank stares. "They say that's possible."

"What about the schools?" Lonnie said. "A lot of white people moved out because they want better schools for their children."

"Maybe they just didn't want their kids going to school with black kids," Dottie said.

"Any kid who works hard here can get into a good college," Mary said.

~

Ron noticed a few unfamiliar cars at the curb as he and Wilma walked down the street with the kids. Mike was in the driveway standing by two propane steamer pots, adjusting the flame on one.

"Ron! Glad you could make it," he shouted. "Hi, kids, Wilma."

Ron eyed his faded jeans, T-shirt, dirty old running shoes with no socks, and long white apron. The apron bore a cartoon of a blue crab on it and the inscription, "Get Crabby." *Typical Mike*, he thought.

"Hey Mike. Hot enough for you? You don't even need a steamer to steam crabs today."

"Right on, man. What you got there?"

"Ron has the potato salad," Wilma said, "and I have two pies."

"What kind?"

Wilma smiled. "Pecan. It's a recipe that came down through my family."

"Oh, I *love* pecan pie. I can't wait to sink my teeth into that."

"So what are you doing there, Mike?" Ron asked. Marty and Rosalie stood by, curiously surveying the paraphernalia.

"Well, I've been steaming some potatoes and onions and carrots until more people get here. And right now I'm gonna rinse a batch of these ugly critters in the wash pans before I drop them into the steamer and send them to their maker. Want a beer?" He nodded toward another washtub filled with ice and beers. "That's the beauty of the job. We have to do four batches of crabs, and each batch takes about a half an hour, and we get to drink one beer with each batch."

"Sounds civilized."

"I'm going in before you two get tanked," Wilma said. "Here, Ron. Give Marty that salad."

"Mary's in the kitchen finishing the chowder, Wilma. Go on in through the garage. You can meet our parents. Oh, and Rosalie and Marty, Jeff and Jason are in the back. Tell them they can come see the crabs now." Marty preceded his mother into the house, while Rosalie ran to the backyard to find Jeff and Jason.

"Oh, and I got some good single-malt in the garage too," Mike whispered to Ron, "and some paper cups to drink it in."

"All right! Time to paar-tay. So who all's coming today, bro?"

"Well, the neighbors, and my parents and Mary's parents, and her sister and brother-in-law, and her younger brother and his wife."

"Is that all your relatives who live around here?"

"Most of them. We had to count guests carefully to order the crabs. If I counted right, that's twenty adults, and about half a dozen kids. So, we needed, say, twelve dozen crabs. That's about two bushels of mediums if we take away the dead ones. That gives us about six for each person. Some people don't like crabs, or don't like the looks of them, and some just get tired picking, and some folks from Iowa and other non-Marylanders just don't know what to do with a crab, so Randy's grilling chicken and burgers and hot dogs for the lazy ones and the folks who don't know what to do with a crab. Do you like crabs?"

"Sure, but we're used to Dungeness crabs and big Alaskan king crabs."

"These blue crabs may take a little more work, but ooh, are they good. So … what did you find out today?"

Ron told him about meeting Mrs. Wrigley and the conversation with Mrs. Simmons in the nursing home.

"Wow," Mike said. "Who would ever have thought there would be a person alive today who remembered it? That's just amazing!"

"You said it. Well, I guess I better go give my hellos to everybody. I'll be back."

~

The conversation in the kitchen drifted to children, and Mary was folding the whipped cream into the steaming egg yolk-sherry mixture when Wilma, Marty, and Rosalie came in.

"Hi Mary," Wilma said. "Sure smells good in here."

"Wilma!" Mary said, a little nervous now that her black friend would meet her white relatives. *Here we go*, Mary thought. "Welcome! Come meet my mom, Beth Fletcher. And this is Mike's mother, Dottie Hoffman, and my sister-in-law, Lonnie." She pointed out the window with a wooden spoon and said, "And out back that's my dad, Frank, sitting with Mike's dad, Bob. And that's my younger brother Randy out there grilling chicken. That's everyone so far."

"Well, it's certainly nice to meet you all."

"I don't know what I would have done today if Wilma hadn't taken the kids to the movies," Mary said.

"No problem. We had a good time."

"How's the job hunt coming?"

"I have an interview at Mayville High next week."

"Where did you go to college?" Beth asked. It sounded to Mary like her mother was trying to find some flaw in Wilma's qualifications.

"Ron and I went to San Francisco State." Beth looked puzzled. "In California."

"Oh. What do you teach?"

"English and language arts. I really like to teach twentieth-century literature, and I'm fond of Shakespeare, but I can teach most subjects."

~

Ron walked into the kitchen and looked around. *Mike and Mary's relatives*, he thought. "Hi, everybody. I'm Ron Watkins." Then he inhaled deeply. "Oooh, Mary. Something smells good!"

Mary stood with her hands on her hips, wooden spoon jutting out from one hand. "Well, Ron! When Mike and I tried to come to your party on time, you said we were an hour early because we didn't know CP time. You said, 'We colored people never arrive at a party on time.'"

He grinned. "You remember that, huh?"

"Every word. So how come you're on time tonight?"

"Wilma made me do it. She said she was hungry. You can quote me on that."

Wilma smiled. "I told him Mike might need some help."

"So what are you cooking, Mary?" Ron asked.

"Eastern Shore clam chowder. I guarantee you've never had anything like it."

Mary made the introductions again for Ron. He then went into the backyard, where four picnic tables were covered with newspapers, wooden crab mallets, and large steak knives with thick wooden handles.

Randy was sweating profusely as he turned the chicken and sipped beer from a can. A second grill awaited hot dogs and hamburgers, and a cart between the grills held buns and condiments.

Jeff and Marty were playing keep-away from Jason and Rosalie with a small football. Ron reminded them about the spectacle out front. "Don't you want to see the crabs?"

"In a minute," said Jeff.

Ron approached the men for another round of introductions and handshakes.

Mary's dad asked him, "So, what do you do for a living?"

"I run an audit department for the IRS downtown. I'm a CPA. And what about you?"

"I'm in real estate. I buy and sell homes and commercial property for people. Done it for thirty years."

"How 'bout you, Randy?"

"I manage construction jobs. We build a lot of these McMansions around here."

"Beautiful homes," Ron said.

"We think so. Do you like sports? Football?"

"Sure. I'm a Raiders fan. But I'm really into participatory sports. I like to run and swim, and I play a little b-ball. I'm not very good, but it keeps me in shape."

Randy grinned. "Participatory sports are great. Right now, I participate in golf."

"Terrific. Well, I promised to help Mike with those crabs. I'll be back. Come on kids, let's see what Mr. Mike is up to." The boys dropped the ball and followed Ron around the house.

~

"Okay, kids," Mike said. "Let's see what these critters look like." They gathered around while he straightened the bent wires on the bushel basket until the lid was free. He dumped half of the seething mass of crawling crustaceans into the washtub, and re-fastened the lid to the basket.

"Help me throw the rinsed ones in this bucket, Ron. Grab them by their backs, and be careful they don't reach back and pinch you. If you find a dead one, throw it over onto the lawn."

Looks like fun, Ron thought. He started picking crabs out of the water, holding them away from him, watching them wave their claws. Only two showed no signs of life. Two others escaped over the rim of the washtub, and Ron had to retrieve them as they skittered sideways across the gently sloping concrete driveway.

"Oh man!" Marty shouted. "Look at those things."

"Watch out," Jeff told Rosalie. "They'll bite you."

Rosalie stepped back.

Neighbors began arriving now. First came the Haydens. Melvin was carrying a covered roaster pan.

"How are the Haydens today?" Mike asked.

"Just fine," Harriet said. "We brought you some corn on the cob."

"Wonderful. Just take it in through the garage and Mary'll show you where you can put it."

Mike carried the bucket of rinsed crabs over to the steamer and set it down. He slipped on a leather glove that extended well up his forearm, and took the lid off the pot, releasing a cloud of steam into the air. Ron helped him pick wriggling crabs out of the bucket and toss them into the pot, and Mike sprinkled them with seasoning from a shaker.

"What's that?" Ron asked.

"My own special mixture—paprika, cloves, garlic powder, and some other spices." He replaced the lid, and checked his watch. "Twenty minutes. Then they're ready."

"Did you see what they did with those crabs?" Marty said to Rosalie. "They threw them in that pot, and now they're cooking them alive!" Her eyes grew wide.

Ron watched as other neighbors began to drift in. Arno and Judy

Graff came with eight-year-old Robert. Judy was carrying grocery bags full of chips. Alfred and Tabatha Mance arrived with Sam and Cherise Pierce and their kids. Tabatha wore a flimsy yellow sundress above the top of which brimmed her ample bosom.

"Well, hello, Mr. Watkins," Tabatha cooed.

"Hello, Tabatha," Ron said, cooing back.

"And how are you today, Mr. Hoffman?"

"Fine as hair on a frog!" Mike said, glancing at her cleavage. "And greetings, Sam, Cherise."

Alfred stepped up to Ron, carrying a box. "Wha' do you say, bro? What's up, Mike?"

"What's in the box?" Mike asked.

"A little taste of the grape," Alfred replied.

"Chowder's on!" Lonnie broadcast from the garage entry door. "Come and get it. Best in the state! She just put in the whipped cream and egg yolks."

~

An hour later, mounds of crab shells covered the newspapers on the picnic tables. Mike was raking the remains into a plastic garbage bag to make room for the next batch, and collecting empty beer cans and bottles.

Ron watched as Alfred broke the claws off a crab, inserted the fingers of his left hand under the apron, placed the fingers of his right hand on top, and easily pried off the shell. He scraped out the mustard-colored fat, feathery gray gills, and intestines with a steak knife, and then he put his thumbs together and broke the shell in half revealing the white crab meat. He began pulling out meat with the knife and inserting it into his mouth, pausing occasionally to gulp some wine.

"So why did you move out of the District?" Frank asked him, punctuating the sentence by cracking a crab claw with his mallet.

"Goddamned crackheads wouldn't let us be," Alfred said. "Held up my store twice down there. Held a shotgun to my head once. And then some dealers set up a crack house right down the street from our house. Wasn't two blocks away. At one time it was a nice neighborhood, but no more. We could afford to get out, so we did."

"I tell you, Mr. Mance, these people just don't care about property."

"No, sir. They're no damned good. And the po-lice won't do nothing about them either. Makes it hard for a man to make a living, even if he does own property and has scratched all his life to get ahead."

"Maybe you should open a store out here," Frank said. "I know a couple of properties you could lease right now, in good locations too, and I know some people who could help you get together a business plan and put together some financing for you."

"I was thinking about that. Nothing keeping me in DC. I could sell out down there and start up out here, and maybe die in bed someday."

"Might be a good idea, Mr. Mance. This part of the county is growing fast, and most of the people are coming from DC and towns inside the Beltway. They'd probably like dealing with someone like themselves."

"You mean brothers buying from brothers."

"Yes."

"I think you're right about that. It might work out."

"If you're serious about it, we could make an appointment for next week. I think you'd like what you see."

"Let's do it," Alfred said.

~

Later, as he stood by the fence sipping scotch from a paper cup, Ron thought he would ask Alfred about Frank.

"So, are you going to do some business with Mary's dad?"

"That white motherfucker prob'ly thinks he gonna take some dumb-ass black for a ride and make himself a quick buck, just like they always took us for a ride. But he's got another think coming, 'cause this is one black man that ain't no fool. Yessir, he gonna find that out real fast. He don't know who he dealing with."

Ron pursed his lips and blew out some air. "You know, he might be trying to put together something that'll benefit both of you."

"I'll find that out soon enough, too. I didn't get where I'm at today being ripped off by honkies."

~

Ron was out front helping clean up when Mike asked him about their search for Thomas. "So where do we go next, big guy?"

"I don't know. I don't have the evidence I need, and I don't know where to get it either. I'm at a loss. The Internet, those lynching books, the death certificate and newspaper article—none of them had anything that supported his innocence. The land records raised some questions, but didn't give any answers. Even Mrs. Simmons, who was right there during the lynching, she didn't have any evidence that he was innocent. I don't know where to go now. Maybe there's something in his coffin, something buried down in there. Maybe I could dig it up some moonless night."

"And maybe you could get someone else to help you."

"What's the matter, Mike? Wimping out on me already?"

FIFTEEN

Jimmy watched the headlights through the window as the aged pickup slowly rounded the curve to the house. The bare light bulb by the porch door flickered slightly as a moth bounced against it in the darkness. The truck stopped in front of the porch, the motor cut off, and the driver's door opened. Noah stepped out and walked to the bottom of the steps. Jimmy stood inside the screen door at the top.

"Evening, Mr. Jimmy."

"What's up?"

"Don't mean to bother you, but I thought you might like to know that my wife heard from a neighbor that Mr. Watkins went knocking on doors in Hawkinstown today, axing if there was anybody around who lived there a hunderd years ago. He said his fam'ly was from here."

Jimmy scowled. "Yeah?"

"Well, then he went to see Mrs. Wrigley, and she took him in."

"Ain't she a widow?"

"Yassuh, and I'm surprised she let him in, but she did, and they was in there some time."

"What happened then?"

Noah told him that after lunch, Watkins and Mrs. Wrigley went to Love of Jesus Nursing Home and saw Mrs. Simmons, and that she told him all about the lynching of Thomas Phillips, who was his great-grandfather.

Jimmy blinked. "Well. I'll be damned. How'd you find out all that?"

"Mrs. Wrigley likes to talk, and word gets around town fast."

"Anything else?"

"No, suh, that's about all."

"Thanks for the news. You done good."

Noah drove off, and Jimmy pulled his cell phone out of the front pocket of his jeans. He dialed Bill and Dan and told them to come over.

Annie had gone out for the night, which pleased Jimmy, for once. Tonight he did not want her around.

~

In the musty, windowless basement, Jimmy watched the shadows of the three of them dance on the plaster walls and ceilings, projected by the wavering light of the propane lamp. They faced each other, sitting on old wooden chairs. On the wall, behind a long wooden altar, was a poster-sized enlargement of a photo of a black man's body riddled with bullets, covered with blood turned black, hanging by his neck from a low limb of a large oak tree. In the background of the photo, a crowd of white men, women, and children looked up at the body. The general store was visible behind the crowd.

A steel-gray cloth bearing a black swastika, about three feet square in size, hung on the wall next to the grisly poster. Other old framed images hung on the walls: a slave auction, a large black woman carrying a white baby, black field hands stooped over in a tobacco field, goose-stepping German stormtroopers, German Panzer VI Tiger tanks in Normandy, a gilt-framed picture of Adolph Hitler ranting into a microphone, a photo of Martin Luther King lying dead at the Memphis motel. On another wall was a painting of Major William Clay in his military uniform and a framed photograph of the Clays' great-great-grandfather, Lieutenant Colonel Jeremiah Clay, in his Confederate cavalry uniform, slouch hat, and droopy horseshoe moustache. A banner read "The Strong Man Is Mightiest Alone." Another read "Heil Hitler!" The number 88, symbolizing the eighth letter of the alphabet, HH, for "Heil Hitler," appeared numerous times on the walls in large characters and small. On another wall was a poster showing a Nazi seal, an eagle with angular spread wings holding in its talons a wreath encircling a swastika.

A silver frame encased a typewritten page of thin, yellowing paper. The paper read *In a bastardized and niggerized world, all the concepts of the humanly beautiful and sublime, as well as all ideas of an idealized future of our humanity, would be lost forever. Human culture and civilization on this continent are inseparably bound up with the presence of the Aryan. If he dies out or declines, the dark veils of an age without culture will again descend on this globe.*—Mein Kampf *by Adolf Hitler.*"

On the altar was an old boot with a bone protruding from it and a steel shackle gripping the bone. Other shackles lay beside it, plus a collection of leather whips, and a long, coiled, heavy rope with one end frayed, as if the twisted cords were sawed with a dull knife. The other end of the rope was tied in a noose. Photos of other lynchings were strewn on the table along with postcards of the Big Oak lynching. Several books rested on the altar, including a small black book without markings and an English translation of *Mein Kampf.*

"I took that film to the Mayville library and looked at it on one of them microfilm readers," Jimmy said, "and damned if it didn't have the newspaper story about the lynching right in the paper—the *Baltimore Courier,* December 27, 1907. It says that the Ne-gro, Thomas Phillips, attacked my great aunt Agnes—the daughter of Jeremiah Clay, my great-great-grandfather. He attacked her in the store. My great-grandfather pulled him off of her and kept him from raping her. Then lynch law took care of him. The mob came that night wearing hoods, so no one would know who they were. It says they pulled this here Ne-gro right out of this basement we're in right now, shot him over a hundred times in front of the porch, dragged his body up to the road, and hung it on the big oak for everyone to see, so all them niggers could take warning from it, and never again step over the line." He looked up at the poster of the lynching, and Bill and Dan did too.

"Justice," Bill said.

"But the other thing I wanted to tell you is that Noah came by." He told them about Ron knocking on doors and going to the nursing home.

"Damn! She's still alive, and she was here back then," Dan said. "Wonder how old she was then."

"I figure she was only seven when we lynched that boy, but she still might have seen something," Jimmy said.

"Sure could've," Bill said.

"But the big thing is that Watkins told the old woman that Thomas Phillips was his great-grandfather."

"Shit," Dan said.

In a moment of silence, Jimmy could hear rain falling outside.

"This is hallowed ground," he said.

"That's the truth," Bill said.

"But now this de-scen-dant has come back and dug it all up. He knows just what happened. And after talking to that old woman today, he might know a lot more than we know."

"So what's he gonna do?" Dan asked.

"Yeah, what's he after?"

"I know damned well what he's after," Jimmy said. He stared at the picture of the body hanging in front of the store. "That day he cut through the woods past the house, and Fury chased him, I had a talk with him. I won't ever forget what he said. He said that some day the dog would bite someone, and then I'd get sued. Sued. That's all them people think about—how to sue white people and get their money!"

"Oh, I get it," Dan said. "He's been digging up shit so he can sue you for being a part of that lynching."

"I bet it's part of this reparations shit they've been dreaming up," Bill said, "to trick us into giving them our money for nothing. You know how they been suing the railroads and insurance companies for all the money they say slaves made for them."

"That's what I think too," Jimmy said. "He's gonna try and get some smart lawyer to convince some jury that this property belongs to him because his relative got lynched here. He wants the house, the land, the store, even the station, that's my guess."

"Sneaky fucking coon," Dan said.

"But wait a minute, Jimmy," Bill said. "They can't say you was responsible for lynching his kin. You weren't even around then. You didn't have nothing to do with it. And the lynch mob was all wearing hoods."

"Well, that's right," Jimmy said, "and the paper said there weren't no eyewitnesses. But a jury might just decide he deserves to get the property because the attack that Thomas was supposed to do in our store was never proved. There weren't even any trial. And my great-grandfather and great-aunt didn't do nothing to try to stop the lynching."

"Well, I still say they can't prove nothing," Bill said.

"Yeah, well there's more to it than that," Jimmy said. "Listen. I never told you, but my daddy told me that Thomas Phillips used to own this house."

"*He* owned it?" Dan asked.

"Yeah, and it said so in the newspaper article."

"So how did your family get it back?" Bill said.

"The coon's great-granddaddy ran up a tab at the store, and after the lynching the court auctioned the farm to pay off the debt, and my great-great-granddaddy bought it at the auction."

"Yeah?"

"Yeah, and I figure the coon found out about it, and he's gonna try to get the farm back by saying we cheated his great-granddaddy."

"Well, how in hell would he prove that?" Bill asked.

"I don't know. Maybe his family has some records. Maybe they got old letters or papers. Maybe court records say something. I don't know. And who knows what that old woman told him today?"

The rain was falling harder now. Jimmy heard it hitting the metal roof two stories up.

"Nobody's taking this land from me. No white man, no Chinaman, and no nigger."

"No one, Jimmy," Dan said.

"My family's lived on this land for almost three hundred years, and I tell you, no one, least of all a fucking Ne-gro, is gonna take it from me."

"Right, Jimmy," Bill said.

"Never," Jimmy swore.

"So what are we going to do?" Dan asked.

Jimmy told them what he had in mind. As they left, he stood on the porch watching them walk through the downpour as though it did not exist, their boots splashing through the muddy rivulets that rushed down the driveway. They climbed into their vehicles, raindrops drumming on the roofs, and drove slowly into darkness.

～

"The drought must be over," Ron said, looking out the bedroom window. Marty and Rosalie were still in bed, but Wilma was getting dressed.

"Are you running?" Wilma said.

"I think I'll skip it today."

"Too much beer yesterday?"

"No," he said. "It's not my regular day to run, anyway. Say, wasn't that fun yesterday? The kids loved seeing those live crabs. I hope the little monsters didn't give them nightmares. And I enjoyed talking to the neighbors and Mike and Mary's relatives. And the food. Those crabs were great. And that chowder! Mmm. That was rich."

"Do you want to try out a church today?"

"Oh, we have plenty of time for that."

"Why don't you unpack your office, then?" Wilma offered.

"I guess I should. It'll give me time to think, too. I've about run out of leads on great-grandfather."

"Do you think it's time to let it go?"

"Maybe. I just wish I knew what led up to it, why they did it. I know damn well he didn't try to rape that woman in a public place with her brother right there. That's absurd. That's just the excuse whites always gave—the 'nigger' tried to rape her. But what did happen? What was the real reason? That's what I want to know. And what was going on with the land?"

"I doubt that you'll ever find out what happened, Ronnie. It's buried in the past."

"Probably," Ron said.

At quarter of six the next morning, it was still raining. "It must be the monsoon season," Ron said to Wilma. "But I've gotta do it."

"You're going running?"

"Yeah."

"In the rain? It's really coming down."

"I know. But my body's aching for it—my legs, arms, back. I always get wet anyway when I run—wet with sweat—and I'm sure it's a warm rain."

"Have fun. Hope you don't dissolve like that wicked witch."

He put on thin gray sweatpants to keep his legs warm in the rain and a long-sleeve T-shirt. He found his Raiders cap in the boxes, to keep rain and sweat out of his eyes. The last piece of his ensemble was a thin blue nylon jacket with the hood pulled over the cap.

"Oh, in case you don't remember, I have an interview at nine-thirty at Mayville High School. I'll be dropping the kids off at Mary's at eight."

"Okay. I should be back before seven."

He stretched inside the garage, putting his foot on the car bumper. He started his watch and took the path behind the house. The woods were dark in the pre-dawn rain. There was barely enough light to see the path. He came to the stream, which was coursing through the gully, spilling far beyond its normal bounds. *I'm gonna get soaked*, he thought. It took four splashing leaps to cross.

As he ran up the grade toward the bike path, one foot struck liquefied soil and lost traction. He slipped and landed on his face. "Shit." He rose clumsily, mud on his hands and knees, pulling himself up the rest of the bank by grasping saplings. Rain poured down, and wet leaves brushed against him. He was wet, yes, but taking great pleasure in challenging the elements and working his muscles. He entered the bike path and saw the faint glow of headlights on the other side of the bridge over Blake Station Road.

Turning the other way, he ran down the path, mindless of splashes from black pools on the pavement. He passed the houses in his neighborhood, ran through the woods and the abandoned fields. Through the steady torrent, he stopped to glimpse the vague outline of Spring Hill Farm House resting securely on the hill behind the white fence. Into the big woods he ran, with towering kudzu shaped like giant robed monks marking his passage. He slowed at the path to his great-grandfather's house. *Why not?* he thought. *I wonder how wide the stream is down there.* He left the trail and took the path.

After moving gingerly down the hill, he accelerated as the path leveled out and passed the beavers' wetland, twice its normal size. The rushing sound of rain hitting leaves became a low roar, and wet branches lashed his body. Lightning flashed, illuminating dusky shadows, and a crack and boom of thunder filled his ears and shook him. *Great*, he thought. *I'm running between hundreds of lightning rods in an electric storm.*

As he rounded a bend near the house, a figure came out of the bushes and lunged at him. A fist crashed into his face. Ron fell to the ground. Suddenly there were three forms above him. He rolled to the side and leapt to his feet to make a run for it. Again he was hit in the face, and he staggered backward. Two forms began pummeling him— one targeting his head, the other his mid-section. Fighting back, he smashed the taller one in the face with a left uppercut and right cross, but the shorter man burrowed into his abdomen, driving him back with great strength. The taller one recovered and landed a massive blow to Ron's face. As his head dropped, Ron saw the blurry figure of the third form come into view—smaller, and swinging a tire iron. *Jimmy,* he thought. Lurching away from the moving rod, he tried to avoid its arc, but felt a sudden intense pain in the back of his head.

$\sim$

Unaware of how much time had passed, he heard a distant voice. "Dump him in."

"I don't think he's dead."

"Don't matter. He will be soon."

He felt arms around his waist raising him and dropping him on something hard. He felt himself sliding downward, head first. His hip hit an unyielding surface; then he was free-falling, accelerating. Without thinking, he drew his hands in front of his head, and straightened his body. A shock of cold hit him as he struck water. Then he sank, decelerating quickly. His hands and head thudded into the mucky bottom. His body felt trapped by walls pushing against him on all sides. Instinctively, he curled into a ball, somersaulted, and thrust his feet against the bottom, driving himself upward. Breaking the surface into inky blackness, he gasped for air and began bicycling madly in the water. The back of his head stung, his lip and cheek throbbed, and his entire body was electrified by the need to escape the cold water.

$\sim$

"I heard him," Dan said.

"I said it don't matter," Jimmy said. "He's a goner. He'll get cold and drown."

Jimmy tossed the tire iron down the hole. He heard a metallic twanging sound as it bounced against the rocks, and then a splash. "There. They'll never find it. Now slide that lid on over there."

Dan and Bill stood on either side with legs spread and grasped the thick round concrete cover. At a count of three, they slid it over the hole, grunting loudly.

"Ow!" Dan cried.

"What happened?" Jimmy asked.

"Shit! It got my finger." He began sucking the broken skin and crushed nail. He tried repeatedly to shake the pain out of it.

"Okay," Jimmy said. "Loosen the branches."

They untied several nylon ropes holding back bushes, and the concrete cover disappeared into the brush. The rain continued to fall.

SIXTEEN

Wilma had heard the beep of the security system as Ron went into the garage. She sat up in bed, yawning. Sacrificing sleep for the chance to plan her day in peace before the children woke up, she climbed out of bed. She washed her face, dressed, checked e-mail, and printed out a copy of her resume. Then downstairs to start a load of laundry. After pouring a cup of coffee, she looked out the front window for the paper, but it was late because of the rain. She began a list of things to do for the day.

First she needed to go over her resume, to focus her mind for the interview. She would say that she preferred teaching higher-level students, but also had experience with average students and slow learners. Introducing children to great literature, helping them learn to think critically, and teaching composition were her greatest pleasures.

Her mind drifted to wondering how Marty and Rosalie would adjust to new schools and new friends this year and to not seeing their grandparents and cousins, aunts and uncles. She knew the children would miss them. And Ron had been so absorbed in his investigation that she had heard the children ask "Where's Daddy?" more than once.

Maybe they all needed to get away together as a family. Maybe it wasn't too late to find a room near the beach for a weekend and brave the August crowds before school started. It would be good to be together, to get some sun and splash in the surf. She had heard the water was warm on the East Coast. Go on some amusement park rides—Ron could take them on those. Maybe they could even see the wild ponies on Assateague Island near Ocean City—she'd always wanted to see them.

She thought back to fun they had in California—tromping through Disneyland, hiking in redwood forests, watching shorebirds run along the beach, seeing seals relax on wharves in San Francisco, surfers riding waves. She admitted to a pang of homesickness but shook it off, deciding it would be fun to explore new surroundings. She would ask Ron about the weekend before he left this morning, so she could get to work on calling motels this afternoon. She also needed to take the kids shopping for school clothes and supplies.

After putting the clothes in the dryer, she took her cup of coffee upstairs, woke up the children, and finished her makeup. *Seven-thirty*, she thought, glancing at her watch. *Wonder where Ron is.* His keys and wallet were still on the bureau, so she knew he hadn't driven anywhere. At the top of the stairs she called his name. There was no answer, and she went back into the bedroom.

"Marty and Rosalie! Get a move on. We have to leave!" Mary had the day off from the museum and would watch the kids during the interview. Wilma didn't want to be late.

She gathered up some papers from her desk in the bedroom and went to Rosalie's room. The youngster quickly pulled a T-shirt over her head and searched for her running shoes. "Girl, you better hurry up. Bring those shoes downstairs. You can tie them while you're eating. And bring your umbrella. It's raining."

Marty appeared at the door. "I'm ready."

"Well, you bring an umbrella too. It looks like it's going to rain all day."

"Aw, me and Jeff were gonna play basketball."

"You'll find something to do, I'm sure."

She ran downstairs and looked out the window. The paper was in the driveway, so she threw on her raincoat from the closet and grabbed a large umbrella. As she retrieved the newspaper, she looked up and down the street for Ron.

In the house she opened the paper on the counter and called again for the children. They trudged downstairs. Rosalie, who was carrying her shoes, socks and an umbrella, dropped a shoe, and it tumbled down the stairs.

Wilma popped wheat bread into the toaster, and pulled orange juice, margarine, jelly, and raisin bagels from the refrigerator. She glanced at the headlines on the front page, and then poured juice and served toast. "Now hurry up and eat, you sleepyheads," she said, chewing on a bagel. Back to the rear window. *Still pouring.* She looked at her watch again. *Quarter of eight. Where is he?* She pictured him in his white dress shirt—starched and pressed—blood-red silk tie, charcoal wool suit jacket over one arm and briefcase in the other hand. Black shoes like mirrors, kissing her and the children in the kitchen on his way to the garage. *He leaves the house at eight,* she thought, *like clockwork. He's going to be late for work.*

By the time they'd finished breakfast, Ron still had not arrived, so she decided to drop the kids off and come back. She opened the automatic garage door and loaded the children into the light blue Dodge Caravan. It was a short drive down the street to the Hoffmans, where the children ran to the porch without opening their umbrellas and rang the bell. Wilma opened hers and followed them to the door.

"Thanks for keeping them, Mary."

"No problem."

"Do you know what? That husband of mine isn't back from running yet."

"Really? He ran in this rain?"

"Oh, he does that lots of times. But he isn't back yet. He should have been back an hour ago. I don't understand it. He'll be late for work, and he's never late for work. He's very conscientious about that. Is Mike here? Maybe he knows where he might be."

"He just left," she said.

"Well, if Ron's not back soon, I guess I'll have to go out looking for him. Then I'll be late for sure. My appointment's at nine-thirty, and it's a thirty-minute drive, and traffic will be slow in this rain. But maybe he's back now."

"Do you know where he runs?"

"He usually takes the bike trail to Big Oak Road, turns left past the store, then left on Owens Farm Road, and left again on Spring Hill Road and back. But a couple of times he's taken a shortcut from the bike trail through the woods past the Clays' old house and up to the store."

"Oh," Mary said, looking away. "Mike told me he was doing that. I hope he didn't bump into Jimmy Clay down there. I heard Jimmy doesn't like people on his property."

"I told him to stay away from there. He already ran into their big dog once and almost got bitten. But I'm sure he probably just slipped and pulled a muscle or something. If he's not home when I get back, I'll take a drive around and pick up the wet puppy."

Wilma drove back to the house, ran in, and called for Ron twice, but there was no answer. *Hell*, she thought. She activated the security system and left. She decided to take the reverse route, in case he was somewhere along the road.

~

"Jimmy, what were those friends of yours doing here at six-thirty in the morning in the pouring rain?" Annie asked. She was standing at the front door of their house in her raincoat, a few minutes before seven.

"Just paying a visit."

"Yeah? How did you get all wet?"

"I had to go to my truck."

"Well, I'm going. Sure as I open up late, someone'll drive by wishing we was open."

"Everyone'll be late today."

"Not me, Jimmy, and you shouldn't be either."

"Noah will open up."

"Well, what if he doesn't? Maybe he won't be able to get that old pickup going in this rain."

"Yeah, and maybe he will."

"You'll never amount to nothing, Jimmy Clay. I swear."

Annie left. Fury lay on the porch, watching her go.

Jimmy went to the basement door and unlocked the padlock. He picked up the kerosene lantern hanging near the top of the stairs and lit it, heading downstairs without bolting the door behind him. *No need,* he thought. *No one here.*

He set the lantern on the altar, looking at the pictures of his ancestors, and began talking in a hushed, reverent tone. "Everything's okay now. The nigger's dead, just like his great-granddaddy. He'll never take over this place. Not him, not no one else. We gonna keep this place like it always was. Nobody's taking it, least of all some rich, uppity darkie. He's in the ground now, and he ain't coming out, believe me. Jus' like his great-granddaddy down in Hawkinstown—he's in the ground. I'm jus' sorry we couldn'ta strung him up from the big oak like before, but things have changed. They won't let no one lynch no more, so you gotta be sly and get around the law. But don't worry, we did. Word'll get around quick enough that the coons better watch where they go and what they do or they might just disappear. Can you believe he ran right past this house on our property—and more than once, too? And he had the nerve to come on to Annie in the store? Why, he might've raped her. Well, jus' like before, we put an end to it. He ain't no more. That's the last time he'll pull any of that shit." He turned toward the picture of Hitler and raised a stiff right arm. Heels together, he shouted, "Heil Hitler!" Then he fell into a chair in front of the altar and slept deeply in the arms of the past.

～

Wilma drove slowly down Spring Hill Road, leaning across the passenger side shouting "Ron!" through the open window as rain blew in and wet the seat. She turned right on Owens Farm Road through the formerly rural neighborhood, continuously searching the shoulders and calling his name as loudly as she could. The wipers bounced wildly, lifting the veil of water from the windshield and giving momentary glimpses of the gloomy day. Cars approached with headlights on, and to her rear an angry procession gathered. Directly behind her, a car rode her bumper and urged her on with blasts of the horn and hand gestures. *Hellfire!* she thought. *I'll get in a wreck and be late for sure … I won't be able to talk … The rain will ruin my hair.*

She turned right onto Big Oak Road, letting the cars speed past, spraying great fans of water from puddles in the road. She then continued to search and shout. Entering a wooded area, she rounded a bend and passed a gravel driveway on the right with brick columns and black iron gates. On the left was the entrance to Big Oak Station subdivision, and another gravel driveway on the right with lots of warning signs. *The Clays' place*, she thought.

Around another bend and up a hill, the oak tree emerged from the gray, towering over the store and garage like an immense green roof. One bay of the garage was open, and the light was on in the store, so she pulled into the parking lot and went into the store on the chance that someone there had seen Ron. A young woman was sitting on a stool behind the counter reading a magazine and listening to the radio news.

"Can I help you?"

Wilma quickly took in the shoulder-length blond hair, sleeveless T-shirt, small tattoo on her shoulder, suntanned arms, slender shape, and tight jeans.

"Hi. Are you Miss Clay?"

"Sure am. But I don't think we've met."

"No, I don't think so. I'm Wilma Watkins. My husband Ron has been in here a few times."

"Oh?"

"Yes. He had his oil changed here last week. He's tall, and he goes running past here all the time. Do you know who I mean?"

"Yes, I think so."

"Well, he went running this morning—"

"In this rain?"

"Yes, and he hasn't come back yet. Have you seen him this morning?"

"No, I sure haven't. How long has he been gone?"

Wilma glanced at her watch. "It's been over two hours, and he never runs more than one. He's late leaving for work, and Ron's never late." She looked straight into Annie's eyes. "Oh, and a couple of times, he's run through the woods on that path that goes past your house."

"Really? Well, he shouldn't have done that. I mean, we have a real mean dog, you know."

"I've heard about your dog, and I've told Ron several times not to run on your property. I apologize for that, but he's full of curiosity and always wants to know what's around the next bend." It crossed Wilma's mind that her husband was running through the woods past the house of an attractive, young white woman—a skinny blond, at that. A slight frown gripped her eyes. "You didn't see him go by your house this morning, did you?"

"No, ma'am. I've never seen your husband go by my house."

Wilma kept searching her eyes. "You don't suppose your brother has seen him, do you?"

"Jimmy? Well, no, I don't think so. He never said nothing to me about that, and I'm sure he would've if he did."

"Is he here?"

"No, he's still down at the house. But I can call him if you like."

"Oh, would you, Miss Clay? I would appreciate that very much." Wilma recalled Mary's description of Jimmy—a really mean redneck— and felt a twinge of fear.

Annie pulled out her bright pink cell phone, clicked a few buttons, and waited. It rang and rang. "He's down there," she said, annoyed.

"Probably asleep." She hit redial, let it ring, and hit it again. He picked up. "Jimmy. You know that Ron Watkins that goes running past here all the time? You've seen him in the store. Had his oil changed here last week … Yeah, well his wife's here and she says he went out running this morning about two hours ago and he ain't come back. You seen him? … Well if you do, can you call me? … You coming up here today? … Yeah, well, Noah's working on one car and another one just pulled in and—" She turned to Wilma. "He hung up. Said he ain't seen him. Told me not to call him again. But if you give me your telephone number, I'll call you if I see him."

"Thank you, Miss Clay." They traded cell phone numbers and Wilma left.

She decided to stop at the house again and change clothes before searching for Ron along the bike trail—and to call the high school to reschedule her appointment since she would never make it on time.

She pulled into the driveway, ran in, and called Ron's name again. There was no answer. *Damn it all*, she thought. She ran upstairs and quickly changed into a jogging suit and hooded raincoat. She called the high school but was put on hold. She called Mary and asked if she could make the call for her. "Just tell them I have an emergency and can't come, and I'll call back and reschedule later today."

Grabbing her umbrella and cell phone, she reset the alarm and started down the short trail through the woods. The rain was falling steadily and hard. Coming to the stream, she thought, *Oh! I do not want to do this. Why do I have to do this? Damn him. Why did he have to go running today?*

She opted against leaping, not wanting to fall in. Instead, she sought solid footing, hopefully wetting only her feet and ankles. The ford was successful, and she continued, carefully climbing the slope to the bike trail. *Maybe he's on it*, she thought, *but if he is, he must be badly hurt, or he would have dragged himself home.* Her worrying grew intense. *If he's not by the trail*, she thought, *he must be in the woods near the Clays' house—maybe attacked by that dog … or maybe by Jimmy Clay.*

She walked quickly with her umbrella open, pointing it into the wind to keep it from turning inside out.

She passed through the subdivision and field, calling out, "Ron! Ron!" The sound was muffled by the downpour. She saw the brick mansion on the hill, through the scrim of rain. She entered the section of path with forest on both sides, shouting his name until she was hoarse, and came to the bridge. There was no sign of him. She considered returning to the store but then thought about Jimmy Clay. Ron was nowhere to be found, Jimmy had denied seeing him, and Mary had said Jimmy was a mean redneck. Wilma quickly decided that she did not want to encounter Jimmy Clay in the woods or anywhere else, did not want to confront him directly, so she pulled out the piece of paper with Annie's number on it and called her.

"Hi, Annie, this is Wilma Watkins again. Any sign of Ron?"

"No, I ain't seen him."

"Okay, thanks. Bye."

What now? Images of Ron lying on the ground bleeding, unconscious, and even dying riddled her mind like bullets. She called Mary. "I'm on the bike trail near the store and I can't find him anywhere. I called Annie Clay, and she says she hasn't seen him, and Jimmy told her that he hasn't seen him, but I'm not sure I believe him or even her, but I just can't go walking down into the woods to their house, trespassing on their land, with that big dog guarding it, and maybe with Jimmy around too."

"You stay out of there, Wilma. You love Ron, but you're a mommy too. You don't know what kind of trouble you'll get into down there. I mean it, Wilma. Don't you go near that house."

"Yes, I know—but I just don't know what to do."

"Call the police, Wilma."

"But they won't start looking for people for twenty-four hours, will they? And I need help now!"

"Call them anyway, Wilma."

She hung up, and dialed 911.

"Hold, please."

Hold! How can they put me on hold?

She started walking back toward the house. Fighting the wind, she held the bottom of the umbrella handle under her arm and the top with one hand while clasping the cell phone to her ear with the other. After half a minute, the operator came back on.

"I'm sorry to make you wait, ma'am. We're overloaded at the moment. How can I help you?"

Wilma said she wanted to report a missing person. The operator transferred her to the county police. A man answered.

"Detective O'Neill. Can I help you?" The voice was deep and calm and sounded white.

"Yes, detective. My name is Wilma Watkins. I live on Blake Station Circle."

"Yes?"

"My husband went jogging almost three hours ago—"

"In the rain?"

"Yes, and he hasn't come back. He never runs for more than an hour, and I traced his route, and I can't find him. Can you help me find him?"

"Yes, ma'am, but first we'll need some information. I'll need to send an officer to your residence to do a missing persons report. What's your name, address, and phone number?"

"But I'm not home right now."

"Where are you?"

"I'm on the bike trail between Big Oak and Spring Hill Road."

"You're out in the rain?"

"Yes. I've been looking for my husband."

"Are you near your house? I can have the officer meet you there or somewhere else."

"Can I just give you the information over the phone?"

"No, ma'am. We don't take incident reports over the phone. We're required to respond in person."

"Then do you start looking right away? Someone said you wait twenty-four hours before you start looking for people."

"It depends on the circumstances. We evaluate each report individually. If it's a runaway who's left fifteen times before and always comes back, we may not put someone on it right away. If it's an adult who disappears from time to time for one reason or another, we may take that into account. If it's a critical case—like a child or an old person or someone who's mentally ill or disabled—or where there's a crime involved—we investigate right away and put out a press release to alert the public and ask for information. Like I said, we evaluate each case individually."

An adult who disappears from time to time? A press release?

"What else do you do to try to find people?"

"We put out a bulletin to the other police departments in the state to let them know about the disappearance, and we usually file a missing person report with the FBI National Crime Information Center and with the state police missing persons unit and—"

"He didn't commit a crime."

"No, ma'am. That's just what they call it. The FBI handles missing persons, too. But we don't always file the NCIC report. It's not automatic. It depends on the evaluation. The crime may have been committed *against* your husband, ma'am. If there's evidence of a crime, it needs to go in the incident report, anything suspicious or any signs of violence."

"I don't have any evidence of a crime, but I have a pretty good idea where he is. I think Jimmy Clay on Big Oak Road did something to him."

"The one who has the store with his sister?"

"Yes."

"Why do you think Jimmy Clay did something to him?"

"My husband always went jogging by the Clays' house. He trespassed on their property at Big Oak. And Clay has a big dog." The reasons suddenly sounded lame to Wilma.

"Do you think your husband might have stopped in to see Mr. Clay's sister?"

Where did that *come from? Did the detective know Annie's reputation?* "No. I talked to Miss Clay. She hasn't seen him."

"I didn't mean to suggest anything improper, ma'am, but people do unpredictable things sometimes, and we have to consider people's privacy. It's not a crime to be missing, you know."

"My husband is very predictable, Detective."

"Do you want me to send an officer to take the report?"

Wilma was uncertain. *What was she getting into? She didn't want to embarrass Ron and certainly didn't want to risk his job if he'd done something stupid. And if she tried bringing up a hundred-year-old lynching, the police would think she was out of her mind.* In frustration, she kicked some water out of a puddle on the path. "I—I'll call you back." She hung up.

She called Mary when she was almost home. "They don't want to do anything for twenty-four hours, unless it's a child or someone who's mentally incompetent or there was a crime."

"I think that's their policy—they want to see if people will turn up on their own."

"What am I going to do?"

"I don't know, Wilma. But don't worry about the kids. I'll keep them as long as you need me to."

SEVENTEEN

S hocked by cold and energized by fear, he pumped his legs. Flailing his arms, gasping for air, he stared blindly into total darkness.

Shit! he thought. *How long can I keep this up? If I don't think of something, I'll drown down here. And it won't be long.*

Continuing to tread water, he reached out with one hand underwater and touched something hard, rough, rounded, irregular, slippery, in and out.

Stones, he thought, *like field stones.*

His head slipped under and he came up gasping and coughing. Then he reached again for the stones and let his hand follow their contours.

A curved wall—with a small circumference. It's a well. I'm in a damned well. And it must have a cover on it because there isn't any light.

The initial cold shock passed, and his body began to grow numb. He remained breathless. He tried to climb the wall by reaching up and grabbing at rocks with his strong fingers while pushing up with the toes of his running shoes. But the indentations between the stones were slimy and too small for his fingers to take hold. He slipped off and submerged again. Again and again he made the attempt on other parts of the wall—pushing with his toes under water and jumping up and grabbing at a piece of rock with his fingers, only to achieve the same result. He felt like a rat—frantically swimming from side to side, leaping upward and falling back.

Fatigue and claustrophobia surged through him, and his hands thrust against the wall in front of him. He tried desperately to push it away while his back pressed against immovable stone. Then he thrust upward with the heels of his shoes, only to slip down once more under the water. *Entombed in a fucking well*, he thought.

Again he paddled and raised his nose into the air. He pushed both hands outward and extended his arms until they were stiff, wedging himself with his hands on the stone in front and his back and buttocks against the wall behind. His rubber heels found slightly larger depressions in the stones, his legs transferred his weight to the tiny ledges under his feet, and for a moment, he was able to keep his face just above the surface. Straightening his legs, he pushed gently upward, lifted his body, and raised his entire head a few inches out of the water.

Remaining mostly submerged, he rested in the darkness, relieved that the crisis was over, at least for a moment. His jaw throbbed, and the back of his head stung where struck by the steel; his hip burned where it had banged against stone on the way down, and his neck ached from hitting the mud on the bottom. *I must be bleeding*, he thought, *but how much?*

Minutes passed. He felt his arms beginning to tire and knew that he couldn't keep pushing for long. His mind began to lose its focus. He grew colder from lack of movement and began to shiver and quake as frigid waves passed through him. Again he slipped and sank below the surface. Again he paddled. Again his arms pinned his body to the stone behind him until his feet found support and he raised himself slightly.

Then he thought: *hypothermia. The water temperature must be in the fifties, and I don't have the energy to keep paddling to stay warm. How long can I last with the water sucking heat from my body? My clothes might help a little, but not if they stay wet. Eventually, my organs will stop functioning; I'll just slip down and succumb to sleep. I've got to get out of this water.*

"Oh God!" he called out loud. *No!* he thought. *Be quiet. They'll hear you. They'll know you're alive. They'll take off the cover and shoot you—like a fish in a barrel.*

~

Wilma walked into the house. She was frantic. Then hope flashed through her. "Ron!" she called. "Ron!" The answer was silence. She shut the door.

What can I do? Who can help me? I can't risk having the police look into it. And with no evidence of a crime, they probably wouldn't do anything right away anyway. We hardly know anyone here—just neighbors.

She called Mary back. She had to talk to Mike. He was Ron's friend and knew about Jimmy, the lynching, Jimmy's relatives, and the history of the house. And he was white and knew people in the area. He might have some ideas on how to locate Ron.

"Mary, do you think Mike could … come home? I just don't know what to do, and he might have some ideas. I hate to ask, but—"

"I already called him to tell him what happened, and he decided to come and help look for Ron. He's on his way. He should be here in half an hour."

"Oh thank goodness. But I hate to lay all this on Mike."

"Some of the other neighbors might be able to help too, if anyone's home."

"Yes. I can call them."

"You could even have a meeting and see what other people think."

"That's a good idea. Can you ask Mike to come to the house when he gets home?"

"Yes, of course. And if there's anything—anything—else I can do, just call me."

"Thanks, Mary. I'm just so glad you have the kids."

Wilma opened the drawer in the kitchen and pulled out her list of neighbors' phone numbers. Even if Ron had done something wrong, she would rather the neighbors know about it than the police and the FBI. *Neighbors won't tell the IRS,* she thought. *And maybe some of the men in the neighborhood could face Jimmy Clay.* She looked up a number and punched it in.

"Hello?"

"Tabatha? This is Wilma up the street."

"What is it, girl? You sound shook up."

"I can't find Ron. He went out running at six o'clock this morning and never came back. I'm afraid something's happened to him."

"Oh my. What can I do?"

"I hate to ask you this, but I need to hold a meeting right now and see if anyone has ideas on what I can do to find Ron. He might be lying somewhere in the woods half dead. I've gotta find him soon. Can you come right now?"

"I sure can."

"Has Alfred left for work yet?"

"No, he's home. He has an appointment to look at stores with Mary's dad."

"Oh, can you ask him to come too?"

"Hold on, girl. We'll be right down. He can look at stores another time."

Wilma called the Randolphs next. Donna answered. Wilma was surprised she was not at work. Wilma told her about Ron and asked if they could come.

"I'm sorry. Philip is sick today."

"Oh, is he okay?"

"It's just one of those summer colds, I think. But he's feeling real draggy and is still in bed, so I think I need to stay with him."

"What about John? Is he home?"

"He left a few minutes ago."

"I'm really desperate, Donna. How long before he gets to work?"

"He works at Andrews. It usually takes him about forty-five minutes to get there."

"Is there any way to get hold of him?"

"I can try his cell phone. Maybe he can come back for a while."

"Oh, thank you."

"You're welcome."

Wilma called the Haydens next, but there was no answer.

She called the Pierces and explained the situation to Sam. "Can you come up for a while, Sam? I'm at my wits' end."

"I was just going to walk out the door anyway, so I can come right now."

"Can Cherise come too?"

"She's already gone to drop the kids at daycare on her way to work."

"Okay, thanks." After she disconnected, it occurred to her that it might be good to have a lawyer involved—maybe God was sending one to help her know what to do. Then she swallowed hard and tried not to weep at the positive reaction of her neighbors so far. *Thank you, God*, she whispered.

Next, she called the Graffs. The phone rang and rang.

"Hello."

"Arno?"

"Who's this?" he said in a voice thick with sleep.

"It's Wilma down the street."

"Who?"

"Wilma. Ron's wife. In the house with the green siding."

"Oh, yeah. Sorry, Wilma. I had night shift last night, and I just got to sleep. I'm wiped out."

"I'm sorry. I shouldn't have bothered you. Is Judy there?"

"No. She took Robert to day camp, and she's at work now."

"Oh."

"Can I help you?"

Wilma explained.

"Oh my. Well, give me a chance to wash my face and get dressed, and I'll be down."

"You don't know how grateful I am, Arno."

"No problem."

She had just put on a fresh pot of coffee when the doorbell rang. It was Tabatha and Alfred, and down the street she could see Sam Pierce walking up in his long gray raincoat with a black umbrella spread over him.

"Hey, Wilma," Alfred said with concern. "What's going on?"

She took their umbrellas and raincoats. "Hi Alfred. I'm just waiting for all the neighbors to arrive. I'm hoping you all can help me figure out what to do."

The doorbell rang. "That must be Sam," she said.

As Sam came in, Wilma noticed Arno trudging across the street wearing a hooded raincoat over gray sweats, carrying no umbrella.

She took them to the great room and offered them coffee. Seeing the assembled neighbors, she was moved. *Thank you, God*, she silently prayed.

She reviewed the details of what had happened. "I'm really scared, and I have no idea what to do."

"Are you sure he didn't run up to Mayville Road and over to Big Oak, or take some other route?" Arno asked.

"He may have. I guess we should check it out. But he's never gone that way before that I know of, and I think he would want to stay away from traffic as much as he could on a day like this, so he wouldn't get splashed."

"Yeah. He wouldn't wanna get wet," Alfred said.

"I'll check it out, Arno," Wilma said, "but the other thing is, and I haven't told any of you this—" The doorbell rang. "Hold on." She went to the door. It was John Randolph. He greeted her and took off his raincoat, revealing his blue Air Force uniform with gold leaves on the epaulets. His shoes were black and shiny.

"Thanks so much for coming, John."

She brought him up to date on the way to the great room, then went on with her story.

"I haven't told anyone this, but Ron has learned that his great-grandfather grew up right here on this farm we are living on now and was lynched on that big oak tree on Big Oak Road."

"No!" Tabatha said. All eyes were wide.

"Ron thinks the mob that lynched him was led by Jimmy Clay's great-great-grandfather."

"Son of a bitch!" Alfred exclaimed.

She told those who didn't know that Jimmy and Annie own the oil-and-lube and grocery store, and then relayed the specifics about the lynching from the *Baltimore Courier* article.

"Whew," Sam said. "So now you think the Clays may have Ron?"

"I'm just praying he's still alive," Wilma said. As she spoke the words, a look of terror distorted her face, and a tear ran down her cheek.

"Pasty-white mothafuckas!" Alfred shouted. "So now they're trying to lynch Ron!" He leaped to his feet and started pacing.

"Oh, my," Tabatha said. She went to Wilma's side and put her arm around her.

Arno bent over, elbows on his knees, looking straight at Wilma. John stood erect in his uniform in stony silence.

"Oh, and another thing. The Clays have this big German shepherd, and it chased Ron one day, but he faced it down and escaped into the store over there."

"Where do the Clays live?" John asked.

"In a house in the woods across the road from the grocery store. It must be down a long driveway. You can't see it from the road."

"But you say there's a path to it from the bike trail?" Arno asked.

"That's what Ron said. I didn't see it when I walked the bike trail just now."

"What about the police, Wilma?" Sam asked. "Have you called them?"

"I called them about an hour ago. They seemed hesitant to investigate right away. They said people almost always turn up within twenty-four hours, and the only connection I could give them about the Clays was that Ron jogs past their house and has trespassed on their property. Oh, and that Ron had his oil changed there. Not much to make them think they need to check it out. I saw how thin the connection looked to them, and I just gave up. If I had brought up a hundred-year-old lynching, they would have thought I was a nutcase."

"Yeah, they probably would have said you're just blaming Jimmy Clay for something that happened long before he was born," Arno said.

"So where's this Clay dude right now?" Alfred asked.

"I don't know, but I stopped in at the store and asked Annie Clay if she had seen Ron, and she said she hadn't. Then I asked her if her brother had seen him, and she called down to the house, and he told her he hadn't seen Ron either, so I think he may still be at the house."

"Hmm," Alfred said.

"So does anybody have any ideas about what I should do?"

"Well, the way I sees it," Alfred said, "that fucking Jimmy Clay's got him at the house or knows where he is, so we got to get Clay and persuade him to tell us where Ron is."

"Now wait a minute," Sam said. "What's the evidence that Clay has Ron?"

"I got all I need. He's white. Ron's black. Clay's fam'ly lynched Ron's great-granddaddy, who used to live in the same house the Clays live in now. Ron cut through Clay's land, trespassing, more than once. Clay's dog goes after Ron."

"What's Clay's sister like?" Sam asked Wilma.

"Skinny blond with straight hair, a tattoo, and tight jeans. Mary says she has a reputation for coming on to men. You know, Mary's lived here all her life, and she says that Jimmy is real jealous of anyone who talks to Annie."

"Has Ron ever talked to her?" Sam asked.

"Yes. Several times at the store when he was running, and when the dog chased him, and when he got an oil change up there."

"See, I told you!" Alfred said. "There's another reason that cracka went after Ron."

"He's jealous of Ron for talking to his sister," Arno said.

"Can't stand to have a black man talking to her," Alfred said.

"I can just see that white bitch flipping her hair at Ron," Tabatha said.

"Wilma, do you think there's any possibility that there was something going on bet—"

"Don't even say it, Pierce!" Alfred said. "That's jus' what the rednecks always say. We come on to their women, we look at their women, we rape their women! I won't hear that from you or anybody else, 'specially not right here in Wilma's house, niggah."

"Cool it, Alfred," John said, leaning forward in his chair. "Sam's only trying to figure this thing out."

"It crossed my mind, Sam," Wilma said, "but I really don't think so. All he's been able to think about since we moved here is his job and this lynching thing. He hasn't had time to fool around, and I don't think he would if he had the time. And I talked to that Annie at the store this morning. I just don't think there's anything there."

"Except that cracka's jealous," Alfred said.

The doorbell rang. "That must be Mike," Wilma said.

"Mike!" Alfred said. "You asked Mike to come? That's all we need is to have some white boy along when we're trying to persuade that white pig to talk! You can't trust honkies, Wilma. None of them!"

Wilma stopped on the way to the door. "Mike is a good friend of Ron's, Alfred. He helped Ron get the information about his great-grandfather's lynching. Ron couldn't have done it without him. Ron trusts him, and Mike came home from work in downtown DC to help find Ron, and nobody even asked him to."

"You making a big mistake, Wilma."

"Please sit down, Alfred," Wilma said.

"Sit down, Mr. Mance," John said.

"Well, don't any of you agree with me?" Alfred said.

The men shook their heads. Tabatha said, "I think you're right, honey, but it's not what Wilma wants, and Ron's her husband."

Mike came in wearing khaki pants, a navy sport coat, a tie loosely strung around his unbuttoned collar, and nappy brown shoes. "How're you doing, Wilma?" he said.

"Not very well, Mike, but I think we're making some headway. I think we've all concluded that Jimmy Clay may know where Ron is. It's all circumstantial evidence, of course, but Ron had been trespassing on his property and talking to his sister, and Jimmy's supposed to be the jealous type."

"How's it going?" Mike greeted the group somberly, looking everyone in the eye. He turned back to Wilma. "You know, Wilma, the only thing I might add is that from what I hear, Jimmy Clay really hates black people, except for that man that works for him."

"His slave," Alfred said.

"That may be right," Mike said, nodding his head. "Well, I'm just thinking that Jimmy's hate for black people is another reason he might've done something to Ron."

"Alfred thinks that Jimmy has him or knows where he is," Wilma said. "Does everyone agree with that?"

"Sounds likely to me," Arno said.

"I agree," John said. "Didn't you say that trail past their house is the only part of Ron's running route that you didn't check out?"

"Yes," Wilma said. "I was afraid I'd run into that big dog, or Jimmy Clay."

"What do you think, Pierce?" Alfred said.

"This kind of evidence can evaporate quickly. We may well find him up on Mayville Road, you know. But I agree that we need to check this guy out."

"What do you think, Mike?"

"I bet he knows where Ron is. There are too many coincidences— too many connections."

"Tabatha?"

"It's him."

"And we think Jimmy's at the house in the woods right now," Wilma said, "or at least he was an hour or so ago when Annie called him from the store. So what should I do?"

"We need to have a talk with Jimmy," Mike said.

"More than that," Alfred said. "We need to *get* him to talk."

"That won't be easy," Mike said.

"It won't be legal," Sam said.

"Will someone please tell me what choice we have?" Tabatha asked. "We have to save Ron."

"We'll make a citizen's arrest," Alfred said.

"Oh, Christ," Sam said. "Here goes my career."

"We can't let these goddamned Klanners get away with another lynching," Alfred said. "It's gotta stop."

"Now," Mike said.

EIGHTEEN

The heels of his running shoes had only the slightest bearing on the ledge under the water. Ron knew that the least movement would cause him to slip and sink under again. Worse, his arms began to tire as they pushed against the wall in front and wedged his back against the wall behind. *What's the use?* he thought, and he relaxed his arms and bent his elbows until he was leaning forward with his head against the wall in front of him. It was pleasant to rest this way, although his nose was barely above water. He was surprised to find that angling his body made his foothold more secure.

He began to experiment and discovered that it was not necessary for his hands to touch the stone in front of him; he was secure with only his feet on the ledge under water and his head against the stone in front of him. He dangled his arms in the water, flexed them, and shook them. *Oh, that feels good*, he thought. But he knew that his head and neck soon would tire, and the water still sucked heat from his body.

Through further experimentation, he found that by putting the heels of his hands—fingers down—on ledges in front of him and his elbows into his abdomen, he could take some of the pressure off his head. If he pushed upward from this position, he could lift his upper body. If he lifted one leg upward, the other would hold his weight. If he could find a new ledge with the heel of the raised foot and push up on it at the same time that he pushed up with his arms and hands, he might be able to raise his whole body to a higher level. Tentatively, he bent his knee, raised his right leg, moved his foot around till he found another depression between the stones and applied pressure against the stone. Then he released his head from the wall and pushed upward with his arms. It worked. He raised his entire body about six inches.

Once more he made his body rigid so that his weight was on his head and upper foot. Then he raised his other foot to a higher depression and his hands to higher rocks, with his fingers pointing down, and lifted himself again.

~

Mike sat entranced with the search and rescue planning.

Alfred was on his feet again, pacing and punctuating his sentences with his fists. "The way I see it, we gotta take the house by surprise so that white shithead don't have time to get a gun and start shooting or call the police, or beat it out of the house and into the woods. So I see two choices, unless John here can bring in some of his Air Force choppers. We either take the path through the woods off the bike trail and sneak up on the house, surround it, and rush it, or we just drive down the driveway fast, pile out, charge up the steps, bust down the doors, and break some windows."

"Has anyone been back in there?" John asked. "We need a recon. How 'bout you, Mike? Did Ron ever take you in there?"

He felt their eyes on him. "No. He's the runner, not me. But I've seen a map—pretty small scale—but I'd say the house is only about a hundred yards from the road, down that driveway, and maybe two hundred yards from the bike trail. And there's a stream that runs through there. We might have to cross it if we come in from the bike trail."

"A stream," Alfred said.

"We could still do a recon," John said. "Come in through the woods."

"We ain't got time," Alfred said. "We gotta get Ron now, not later."

"I wonder what the house is like," John said.

"I haven't seen it," Mike said, "but judging from its age, I'd bet it's pretty small, a two-story farmhouse with a big front porch."

"What about the dog?" Arno asked. "What do we do about it?"

"Well, that's one thing," John said. "If we come in through the woods, that dog will hear us for sure and come after us. That will alert Clay right away."

"Yeah," Mike said. "That's what happened one time when Ron went running through there. The dog heard him and chased him up to the road."

"I think if we come in fast down the driveway," Alfred said, "we can surprise the dog too, and Clay won't have time to react."

"Sounds like that might be the best approach," John said.

"But the dog will still attack us," Arno said.

"Stop worrying about that dog," Alfred said. "I'll take care of the dog."

"I'm more worried about Clay," Sam said. "What if he has a gun? I bet he does. That's why we need the police."

"They won't help unless they think there's been a crime," Tabatha said.

"Don't worry about guns, Sam," Alfred said. "We ain't going in there unarmed."

"What do you mean?"

"I mean we're going in with our own guns—all of us," Alfred said. "Who all got guns?"

"Oh boy. Here we go," Sam said.

"Wait, hold on," John said. "You want to go in with *guns*?"

"This cracka's got a gun. Believe it!" Alfred said. "We gotta take guns. Now what you got?"

"Well … I have a pistol," John said, "but that won't do much good if he's got a shotgun or an assault rifle."

"Don't worry," Alfred said. "I got all the guns we need. Everyone know how to shoot?"

"I was trained in the Air Force," John said, frowning.

"Sharpshooter, expert, what?" Alfred asked.

"Neither," John said.

"Well, that don't matter, close up anyways," Alfred said, "as long as you can pull the trigger. What about you, Arno?"

"I—I can shoot a pistol—and a rifle, but I—I never shot a man before."

"Well, we ain't shooting anyone unless we have to."

"Great."

"What about you, Mike? What do you know how to shoot?"

"Just penny-arcade stuff," Mike said, "but I have gone duck hunting a few times and shot skeet. I can handle a shotgun, I guess." *Pretty feeble,* he thought.

"Sam?" Alfred asked.

"Listen," Sam said. "Do you all have any idea what you're getting into? Just *carrying* a weapon will get you three years, plus ten if they prove assault. And if it's an automatic weapon, you'll get five to twenty. You all sure you want to go there with guns?"

"What if Clay's got a gun?" Alfred said. "What are we gonna do then? Let him kill us?"

"No, I don't think so," John said. "You're right, Alfred. It would be safer for us if we had guns."

"I don't know," Arno said. "I'm not interested in going to jail."

"Listen," Sam said. "I'm not sure how much help I can be on this thing. You might be better off without me."

"Well, I figured we'd have at least one fucking coward in the group," Alfred said.

"Alfred!" Wilma said. "You can't call Sam a coward!"

"How 'bout yellowbelly chicken, Wilma? All he wants to do is stay out of it so it doesn't hurt his law career! He wants to let the police do it. But they won't do it. And your Ron is out there somewhere, and may be hurt and bleeding, may need us, and this chickenshit yellowbelly is afraid to do something, afraid to stand up to this white world and this white trash honky who's trying to lynch another black man. All this good neighbor wants to do is stand by and let it happen! Fuck that shit! Fuck it, I say!"

He moved to where Sam sat and stood over him. John and Arno jumped up and grabbed him, but Alfred tightened his shoulder and back muscles, and it was obvious to the men that there was no way they could stop him if he decided to attack.

"Honey," Tabatha said, "don't hurt the man! We need him! We need him to ask the right questions—legal questions. We need him to help us find Ron."

"That's right, Alfred," Arno said. "We need him to interrogate Clay, to find out where Ron is."

"Well, is he coming with us, or what?" Alfred asked, still in a rage.

Sam looked shaken, but unafraid. "I'm not going if we take guns."

"Well! What about you, Mike?" Alfred said. "You chickenshit, too?"

"No, I'm not chickenshit, Alfred," Mike said. "But the more I think about it, the more I'm with Sam. We can get ourselves in a lot of trouble if we're not careful. I'll go if we don't take guns."

"I knew we couldn't trust no white boy on this," Alfred said. "He's already backing out."

"No, I'm not," Mike said, gritting his teeth. "I just won't take a gun, and I don't think that's chicken, either. I think it takes more guts to go in without guns."

"Shee-it," Alfred said. "I ain't ready for the pearly gates yet."

"We're taking a big chance going in without guns," John said.

"You know, if Jimmy gets shot," Sam said, "we'll all be found guilty for it."

"And if there are any shots," Mike said, "the police are sure to investigate."

"So what do we do if we go in without guns?" Arno asked.

"Hmmph," snorted Alfred.

"What do we do?" Mike asked him.

"Same as if we had guns. We still gotta surprise him. Still gotta pull up to the house, jump out fast, run up, move in, take control, and just hope and pray he ain't got no gun."

"So, who's willing to go in without guns?" Arno asked.

Mike looked around and softly said, "I am."

Sam slowly nodded his assent.

"I guess I am, too," John said.

"Well, I sure gotta go," Alfred said. "Someone's gotta lead you pussies in there."

"Someone named Alfred's gotta take care of that dog, too," Arno said.

"I think we need to put our hands together and say a prayer about this, everyone," Wilma said. "Let's all stand and bow our heads now."

They rose. Wilma took Alfred's hand in one hand and Mike's in the other, and they formed a circle. She closed her eyes, and the others followed as she began to pray.

"O good and gracious Lord, I'm calling on you at this time because your humble servant is in great need; I'm afraid that my husband is in danger and may be hurt or dying. Lord, I'm calling on you to save his life—the father of my children and friend of my neighbors. He's a good man—"

"Save him," Tabatha said.

"Let him live today, Lord, and help us find this man and bind his wounds and save him—"

"Help us, Lord," Alfred said.

"Help us, and give us strength as we risk our lives. Be with us, and keep us from doing harm to others. In the name of the one who gave his life that we might have eternal life with you, your only son, Jesus Christ, our only Lord and Savior, a-men."

"A-men," the group repeated. They released hands, and Wilma hugged Alfred and then Mike while Tabatha held John and Sam. Mike shared a fist bump and hug with Arno.

Wilma turned back to Alfred. "Do you want me to go with you?"

He shook his head. "No, mama. This here's man work. You

best stay back here by the phone in case we need you. Besides, you need to take care of those children. We don't need you getting hurt looking for Ron."

~

The only sound in the eerie darkness was the lapping of water against the stone walls. Once more he bent his knee, lifted his right leg, and felt with his heel for another hollow between stones. Finding one, he applied pressure to it with his leg while pushing upward on the opposite side of the well with his hands. Again he lifted his body. Now his shoulders and part of his torso were out of water. Then he let his weight transfer to his head while he found higher ledges for his hands and at the same time a higher resting place for the heel of his other foot.

If I can keep doing this, maybe I can raise my whole body out of the water and dry out enough that I won't get hypothermia. Slowly, deliberately, he continued climbing until his entire body was out of the water, the dirty water dripping off his clothes. Then he rested—his head pressing against the stone, feet against the opposite side of the well, arms dangling in air. *Thank you, God,* he thought.

The longer he rested, however, the colder he grew, especially his legs, until again he was shivering and shaking. He returned his hands to the cold stone in front of him to keep from falling.

What is making me so cold now, even when I'm out of the water? I'm freezing! It's gotta be in the fifties down here … Evaporation, that's it. The water is evaporating and reducing the temperature. Shit!

NINETEEN

Mike marched to Alfred's house in a steady downpour. *Going to war,* he thought, *to find Ron.*

Alfred stood on the porch with two baseball bats. John asked for one, and Alfred gave it to him. He offered a tire iron to the others, but they declined. "I got fists," Mike said, "and Clay's smaller than I am."

"Okay," Alfred said. He turned to John. "You drive, bro, and let me ride shotgun, so when you stop, I can jump out and run up them stairs. The rest of you follow me up and smash the windows off the porch to distract him, and John, you go around the house and run in the back door to keep him inside." They piled into Alfred's black Toyota Sequoia SUV. John and Alfred sat up front, Mike and Arno in the second row, and Sam in the rear.

"Alfred and John," Sam said. "I advise you not to take those bats into the house. In Maryland that will probably be considered assault with a dangerous weapon, and that'll likely get you thirteen years, even if you don't harm anyone. You can use them on the dog, but don't take them into the house."

"Shit! You want us to go in there against that redneck with nothing but bare knuckles?"

"You bet your life, Alfred."

"I got an idea, hero. You go first."

～

Annie was taking inventory, checking expiration dates, and occasionally wiping dust off cans of food. It seemed as though she and Jimmy had been living on stale bread and expired food lately. French toast for breakfast, bread pudding for desert. How much old bread could they eat? Only three customers had been in that morning. At times—especially at night—her desperation grew. How could she keep the store going selling hot coffee in the morning, snacks during the day, beer at night, and small purchases where customers didn't care about the price? A few came every day to buy lottery tickets and little else. Today she was bored and feeling alone. It was a slow, dreary day.

Jimmy, she thought. *What was he doing down at the house? And what were Dan and Bill doing there this morning?* There were so many damned mysteries about them. She was sure they were up to no good, but what exactly she didn't know.

And what is in the basement behind that locked door? From the time she was a little girl, she knew that women and kids were not allowed down there. One of her earliest memories was standing at the top of the stairs looking down as her daddy walked up with an angry look on his face. He'd said "Annie, I told you never even to look down here." Then he locked the door, got his belt, and whipped her until she was covered with welts. All the while her mother looked on in passive silence.

She remembered Jimmy's sixteenth birthday—no cake, no candles, no gifts. But after dinner, Daddy had said, "Come, boy. Today we go downstairs." She remembered how frightened Jimmy looked, even though he was as tall and strong as their father. "No need to fear, boy. I ain't gonna hurt you." The door shut and she heard the bolt close on the basement side. She listened at the door, but could hear nothing. They must have been whispering or speaking softly. Hours later she heard their footsteps on the stairs. Jimmy emerged, solemn, proud, and defiant. Annie knew not to ask what had happened.

Dan and Bill had come on the scene after their mother and daddy died, almost five years ago now. Annie remembered the two of them sitting with Jimmy on the porch at night talking in low rumbles that occasionally rose into angry words. She could tell they were not angry with each other. She knew they hated black people and Jews, but they rarely spoke of it in normal voices. Annie disliked the two men. They looked on her with mild disgust, never with desire. They made her feel small and powerless. She responded with hostility or by ignoring them. *Fuck those impotent gorillas!* she thought. She would live in her world, they could stay in theirs, and everything would be fine. But this morning she felt that they had intruded on hers.

∼

Jimmy awoke in his chair in the basement but remained in a trance. He would not go up for lunch. This was a day to fast, a holy day. A day when he had acted to protect his heritage and destroy one more black animal threatening Aryan dominance. A day to commune with the spirits in the room: his great-great-granddaddy Colonel Jeremiah Clay, his daddy, granddaddy, and great-granddaddy, and the others—they all came alive. The white people who stood by the hanging nigger, looking up approvingly. It was a day for communing with the Fuhrer himself. Jimmy studied their faces and felt kinship. He was proud to have proved that he was one of them, to have done his part. He heard the voices of the people at the hanging. He heard the crowd roar when Hitler spoke. He heard the boots of goose-stepping stormtroopers, and the cries of slave mothers pleading with auctioneers not to separate them from their children. *Mules,* he thought, *just mules. That's all they are.* He closed his eyes and drifted again into sleep.

∼

In darkness, Ron braced himself with his hands, elbows, head, and heels, muscles taut, waiting for the shaking to stop, praying not to plunge into the water again. But the shaking would not stop, and he decided that the only way to rid himself of the tremors was to warm his body with exercise. *I've got to keep going,* he thought.

More carefully than before, he began the repetition, bending his knee, raising a foot and finding a secure position, finding higher support for the heels of his hands, pulling his head back, pushing up with his hands and foot, raising his other foot, and repositioning his head against the stones. Now that he was above water, the stones were mortared together, and it became more difficult to gain solid footing. Finding secure positions for his hands was also problematic, since he had to do it by touch in the darkness. On the other hand, repetition made him more sensitive to the depressions, and away from the water the stones were not as slick.

Increasingly, his scalp hurt where it was squeezed between skull and rock, and he was forced to keep changing the position of his head to relieve the pressure. He also had to rest more often with his elbows against his abdomen.

Dream scenes played across his mind. He saw his attackers coming out of nowhere. He was sure it was Annie's brother who hit him with the tire iron. He saw Jimmy in the back aisle of the store when he was paying Annie. *Jimmy despised me at first sight*, Ron thought. *But turning violent, what brought that on? Did he think I was coming on to Annie? Guys go in there all the time, and the way she dresses and looks at men, they must hit on her all the time. So why me? Because I'm black? Is he so much of a racist that he'd try to kill someone just because he ran across his property a few times and looked at his sister? Shit! It must be because I'm black. He is a racist, that's it. The racist of all racists, And the other ones, too. They're all racists. They came after me because I'm black.*

His mind turned to Wilma. *Oh, Wilma. What are you doing now? Oh God, she must be frantic. She's probably out searching for me. Calling my name. Maybe she called the police. Maybe they're out looking. But how would anyone find me in a well with a cover on it? Or maybe she left for her interview before I got back and doesn't even know I'm missing. Maybe no one knows. Maybe they'll start to wonder about me at work. But no one will be home when they call. How will anyone know? Oh, but Wilma wouldn't leave before I came home. I don't care how important her interview is. She wouldn't leave me. She knows me too well. Knows my habits. How long I run. When I leave for work. No, she knows something's wrong. She's searching. Wilma, honey, are you up there?*

And where are the kids? Marty. Rosalie. Are they safe? Could Jimmy and his goons be going after Wilma and the kids next? Be careful, kids, he thought. He closed his eyes and prayed, until he remembered that the kids were spending the day with Mary.

Methodically, he crept upward. Now he was higher in the well. The shakiness was gone, and he was beginning to grow warm inside his sweats.

Then panic filled him. *How will I ever get out? Sooner or later I'm going to slip and fall. Is this how my insignificant life will end? I'm wasting my time. I might as well relax my muscles, fall into the water, slip under, and die now.*

Shit, he thought. *Do I have enough insurance for Wilma and the kids—so she can keep the house and at least one car, and live, have a little fun, so the kids can go to college when the time comes? I don't know.* He did some calculations. *No,* he thought. *Not nearly enough. They'll have to move. And there's no way Wilma can put them through college or even have a decent life on a teacher's salary. She'll have to remarry.*

But it's still an ugly world out there, and I won't be around to protect them. I won't be able to teach them what to watch out for. And all because I wasn't careful enough myself.

Wilma, I love you. Remember that. But I want you to know that you should find another man. For your sake, and the kids'. Wilma, can you hear me? I love you, Wilma. Oh Wilma, I miss you. Where are you?

He felt tears in his eyes and felt his body start to relax. *No, goddamn it! Control yourself. Give yourself a chance. Give them a chance. Think of something else. Occupy your mind. Think about … what?*

He began considering the well, his mind wandering into the past. *Who built it? It's stone,* he thought, *not brick, and not smooth pipe, so it's probably old, maybe built in the eighteenth century even. Probably dug by a slave, and the stones laid by a slave. But how in the world did they dig wells? How did they keep the dirt from falling in? How did they get the dirt out, and put the stone and mortar in? Did they dig until they hit water and then dig some more? What if they ran into solid rock? Did they stop and dig somewhere else? They couldn't blast, could they? I don't think they had dynamite back then. They must have used a pick and shovel. But how would the digger have enough room to swing a pick? The hole must have been bigger before he laid the stone. But if he hit water, the water would slow the impact of the pick, so he would have to stop when he hit deep water, or use a shovel. But underwater, the dirt would slide off. And how did he mortar the stones under water? Oh, wait—they aren't mortared under water. How did he get in and out? By ladder? Could they build a ladder thirty or forty or fifty feet high? How deep am I anyway? Maybe he went up and down on a rope, with a helper at the top letting him down and pulling him up. He would have to have a helper unloading buckets of mud and rock and sending down stones and mortar. But what if the rope slipped? It would fall on the digger's head! That would be the end of him. Maybe they wound the rope around an axle with a handle on it and had some braking mechanism. Couldn't have the rope slip and the load—or the digger—go falling thirty or forty feet down a hole.*

He hung for a moment with his head and feet against stone, arms dangling like oak leaves. The fingers on his right hand tapped on his palm—one-two-three-four-one-two-three-four-one-two-three-four—then curled into a fist.

Pigs. Those fucking racist pigs. Attacking me. Knocking me out. Throwing me down a well. Leaving me for dead. Mothers. Assholes. Another hate crime against another black man. Another lynching. In the twenty-first century. First my great-granddaddy, now me. Whites attacking blacks again, the way they've always attacked us. Wait till I get out. They'll wish they had never even thought of this. I'll kill them all. And they'll suffer first.

He raised his right foot, found a depression and pushed—too hard. His foot slipped on the smooth stone. Instantly, he went rigid. His left foot held, and he caught himself.

Oh Christ! he thought. *God, help me. Save me from this place. Save me from dying in this hole. Make me be more careful. Lord, you've brought me this far. Deliver me. Forgive my evil thoughts. Forgive me.*

Again, he calmed himself and tried to think of other things. *How did I even survive the fall? Water. I hit water. And I instinctively I knew how to break the surface with my hands so I wouldn't hit my head.*

Back he went to digging the well: *Dirt falling in. How did they keep the dirt from falling in? OSHA would be interested in that—trenches and cave-ins and burials and such. Maybe they passed down some kind of a big barrel or hogshead, as they call them here, and the digger worked inside it, and as he dug, the barrel would slide deeper, and maybe the helper would keep adding other barrels on top. Something like that. But did they leave the barrels in the ground and lay the stone inside them, or did they pull them out? And let the dirt fall in, dummy? No, the barrels had to stay in the ground to hold back the dirt while he was laying the stone. Hell, I don't know.*

How did the digger and mason see down here? They must have had a lantern. Wish I did.

His hands passed over the stones again and again, feeling the depressions, searching for solid bearing, and he thought of the hands of African slaves that felt them in the building of the well. *Felt the stones as they picked them up in the field, sorted them for size, loaded them onto a wagon, then into a bucket, and let the bucket down the hole. Then the mason—another slave—picked up each stone, decided which direction to lay it, put mortar on the wall with his trowel, and squeezed the stone into the mortar. But what did he stand on as he moved upward, laying the stones? Boards spanning from opposite sides of the well, resting on the stones?*

How much farther do I have to go? How deep am I? How close am I to the top? If I get to the top, how will I get out? There's a cover. And covers are concrete, to keep out kids. How will I move that while leaning on my head? Impossible. Didn't I read somewhere that old wells are usually filled with dirt to keep people from falling in? Why isn't this one? It must be one that no one even knows exists. No one even knows it's here. So how could anyone find me, unless that goddamned Clay or those other two assholes told them? And they would never tell anyone.

Reality started to bludgeon him: *I'm never getting out of here.*

He took a deep breath and exhaled.

What the hell. If I kick off, maybe I'll come back as a redneck. Then I won't have to fight the Jimmys of the world. Just the Alfreds.

TWENTY

John took the Mayville Road to Big Oak Road so that they could search the shoulders and yards, but there was no sign of Ron. *Come on, Ron*, thought Mike. *Where are you?*

Turning left on Big Oak Road, John went under the bike bridge, passed Big Oak Crossing Road, and slowed down under the oak tree. Mike and Alfred peered into the oil-and-lube, searching for Jimmy, but saw only Noah, sitting in a garage bay looking out. Mike noticed the light on in the store but couldn't see anyone inside.

"This is it," Mike said, and John turned down the driveway into the woods. Around a curve was a two-story house with a long, screened-in front porch.

"Front porch, like you said," Alfred said to Mike. Lights glowed through the drizzle from the first-floor windows. "Okay, let's go. And remember, I go first through the front door. Arno and Mike smash in the windows, John comes in the back door, and Sam, you watch my back."

"And the dog?" Arno asked.

"I take the dog. If he gets past me, mothafucka's your problem."

"Great," Arno said. Mike laughed nervously to himself as he visualized the big dog lunging his way.

John braked hard in front of the house. Alfred leapt out and ran for the steps, bat in hand, followed by Mike, Arno, and Sam. John headed for the rear carrying the other bat.

As Alfred hit the bottom step, the screen door flew open and the German shepherd launched itself through the air toward his throat. Alfred choked up on the bat, and took a vicious swing, catching the dog flush on the side of its head. The rear of the animal hit his chest, and the dog fell to the steps and rolled to the ground, motionless. Alfred tossed the bat aside and jogged to the front door, with Mike and Arno following. He turned the knob.

Mike went to the window to the right of the door and peered through it, but before he could break it, he saw Alfred fly across the living room just as Jimmy came through the door from the basement. Mike jumped to the front door to back up Alfred. He heard the phone ringing, and watched as Alfred smashed Jimmy against the wall with his shoulder, linked arms behind him in a full nelson, and pressed tightly against the smaller man's neck.

"Don't kill me!" Jimmy begged.

"Don't worry, mothafucka. You gonna live. For a while, anyway."

The phone rang a few times and went silent.

Mike and Arno went in and shut the door. Arno had not had time to break his window either. John entered a moment later through the hallway from the kitchen. The men encircled Jimmy in the living room. Sam arrived last.

"You can't break in here and hold me like this," Jimmy whined.

"Where is he?" Alfred demanded.

"Where's who?"

"You know goddamned well who. Where is he?"

"I don't know what you're talking about."

"You got about two minutes to remember, mothafucka," Alfred said, applying pressure to Jimmy's neck. "Arno, check the upstairs. Mike, check the basement." Arno took the stairs two at a time.

Jimmy looked worried. "Now wait a minute. You can't just go through people's houses like this. They'll send you up for breaking and entering, and assault. You can't do this. And you can't go in my basement!"

"Watch us," Alfred said.

Mike glanced at the front door, saw the dog at one of the windows. *Alfred didn't kill him*, he thought. "There's the dog," he said.

"Son of a bitch came back for more," Alfred said.

Then Mike walked slowly down the basement stairs into the dim, flickering lamplight. He heard Alfred taunt Jimmy. "Watcha got down there, boy? Something you don't want us to see? Like maybe you got our bro Ron down there?"

"Ron? Ron who?"

"You know goddamned well who we mean."

"I don't know any Ron."

Alfred was shouting now. "We'll see. Arno? Find anything?"

Mike heard Arno's faint reply from the second floor, "Nothing up here. I checked both bedrooms, the closets, and the bathroom."

The altar and photographs on the wall confronted Mike. He heard Alfred roar. "Okay, Mike? Anything down there?"

"You all better come down here and see this, and bring Mr. Clay along."

"You heard the man, Clay," Alfred said. "We're going downstairs."

"You can't make me go down there."

Mike could see their shock when they reached the basement.

"Jesus," John said. "He's either a Nazi or a member of the Klan, or both!"

"Definitely white supremacist," Mike said. "Maybe a skinhead."

"He got his hair," Alfred said. "Muthafuckin' racist, segregationist pig."

"Neo-Nazi," Sam said.

"Look at this picture," Mike said, staring at a big photo of the lynching. "I wonder if that's Ron's great-granddaddy hanging there. You all know he used to live right here in this house, don't you? God, look at it! That's Clay's grocery store, and he's hanging from the big oak tree right in front of it. And it was probably Clay's great-aunt who accused Ron's great-granddaddy of assaulting her in the store the day before this picture was taken, and Clay's great-granddaddy who led the lynch mob. He lived in the big house up on the hill back there. And now this son of a bitch has Ron! Shit!"

"Where is he, Clay?" Sam said.

"I don't know who you're talking about."

"Mr. Clay," Sam said. "Don't make things worse for yourself. All this circumstantial evidence points to you as the one who has Mr. Watkins."

"What evidence?"

"Where were you this morning, Mr. Clay?"

"I was here all night and all morning. You can ask my sister Annie."

"Well, that's just fine, Mr. Clay. Let's go over the evidence. Fact: Mr. Clay, you were here when Mr. Watkins came up missing. Fact: Mr. Watkins has run across your property many times, including this morning, and you are well known to dislike trespassers, as evidenced by your signs and the dog you let run free. Fact: Mr. Watkins had spoken to your sister a number of times, and you are notorious for your jealousy toward anyone who speaks to her. Fact: Mr. Watkins is black and you are obviously a neo-Nazi racist. So here's the situation, Mr. Clay: You have motive and opportunity. That's the evidence so far."

"That don't mean nothing. That don't prove I did anything to this Watkins guy."

"Oh, I think it's enough to get a judge to hold you until we get the rest. Just wait till they see the photos of this room, Mr. Clay. Watkins' great-grandfather lived in this house right here and was lynched on the big oak tree on your property, and this picture proves that you're proud of it."

"I still say they'll let me go."

"Mr. Clay, you're going to have to make a decision. If Mr. Watkins is still alive and if you tell us where he is now so we can keep him alive, you may only get twenty years with time off for good behavior. If he's dead or if he dies before we find him, you'll get life plus twenty, or the death penalty. This is a hate crime in Maryland, and the moratorium on capital punishment is over. It's your choice. If you're smart, you'll tell us where he is, and no harm will come to you."

"I don't know nothing about it."

"We're running out of time and patience," Sam said. "Please, do yourself a favor and tell us where he is."

"I don't know where he is!" Jimmy said.

"Okay, you redneck cracka. I've had enough of your shit," Alfred growled. He shoved Jimmy violently onto the altar. "Hold him, boys."

John and Mike grabbed Jimmy's arms and held him while Alfred picked up the coiled rope from the altar, cut a piece off the frayed end, and bound Jimmy's hands behind his back. Then Alfred loosened the noose, slipped it over Jimmy's head, and pulled it tight.

"We gonna take you outside and give you one more chance to tell us where Ron Watkins is before we string you up and see how far your neck will stretch."

Mike's adrenaline surged. He pictured the white body of Jimmy dangling limp from a tree limb.

"Makes me think of that Billie Holiday song, 'Strange Fruit Hanging from the Poplar Trees,'" Arno told Mike.

Sam said, "This is not the way."

John stared at the picture of the century-old lynching. "Yeah, you shit-ass. You better tell us where Ron is."

"It would be a new kind of justice," Arno said. "A neck for a neck."

"Yeah, and we could start out by cutting your nuts off," Alfred told Jimmy.

"And everything else," John said.

Mike wasn't pleased with the idea of lynching Jimmy, but he thought they just meant to threaten him, so he kept quiet.

"It's your choice, mothafucka," Alfred said. "Sing or swing. Let's go."

They started walking toward the stairs, but the door at the top slammed shut.

TWENTY-ONE

A pinprick of light projected a luminous dot on the stone. *My God,* Ron thought. *I must be at the top!* He inched another step upward, releasing his head and pushing up with the heels of his hands. His head bumped something hard.

Then he felt a tickle as insect legs ran across his neck. "Shit!" he cursed out loud. *What's that, a spider?* he thought. He grimaced, but somehow controlled the involuntary urge to jump and shake it off. He reached back and brushed his neck with one hand, then returned the hand to its position on the wall. *God, help me,* he prayed. *Don't let me fall.*

And what now? How do I move the cover? And what if they're still up there, guarding the well? He listened intently, heard nothing, and concluded that they were not. *I must take a chance now and try to escape while I still have the strength.* He thought for a moment and decided he might be able to push up the lid with his back.

Taking another step, he found a secure depression, and began driving upward with his leg, pushing up on the cover with his back. He felt it move, but then his foot slipped. Had it not been for the secure position of his other foot, he would have plunged to the bottom. He began feeling the wall with the loose foot until he found a more secure resting place. Again he pushed up with his back. This time it moved upward an inch—not enough to be of any use. *Maybe if I use a rolling motion I can move it sideways a bit before setting it down.* He tried, and it worked. He pushed the cover up and over with his back, set it down, and re-centered his back on the cover. Little by little, he inched it to the side until light flooded the hole and he felt rain on his arm. Then the cover stopped moving. Something was holding it, and it would not move. *Shit!* he thought. Then he wondered if he could move it more the other way—enough to escape. It was his only hope.

Slowly, he began pushing it in the other direction. Up, over, and down. Up, over, and down. Soon he was back to where he started—in darkness again. Then he was moving it the other way. This time he was able to move it almost halfway off before it stopped.

Rain penetrated the well, and he saw it washing down the stone. *The stone will get slick*, he thought. *It's now or never.*

He rotated his body so that his head was out from under the cover by moving his feet sideways to other secure positions. His head against the wall, he reached up with one hand and grabbed the outside of the stone rim, and did likewise with the other hand. He walked his feet up the wall, raised one leg out of the hole, and pushed hard upward with the other leg. Banging his shoulder hard on the cover, he rolled out of the well onto the wet ground. *I'm out. Out! Oh God. Thank you, God. I'm out!*

~

Mike heard the padlock being slipped into place and a voice came through the door. "No one's going anywhere."

"Bill, is that you?" Jimmy asked.

"Me and Dan. Noah called us. Said he saw an SUV full of niggers head down your driveway. Now, if you boys let Jimmy go, you can all come out."

"We're trapped," Mike said in a hushed voice.

"Yeah, but we have Jimmy," Arno said. "They'll have to let us out."

Abruptly, Mike snuck up the stairs, locked the deadbolt on the basement side, and came back down. "They might have guns, and we don't," he said quietly in explanation.

"We still have to get Jimmy to talk," Sam said.

"How the hell are we going to do that if we're trapped in this basement?" John said.

"Okay, you down there," came a voice from upstairs. "You heard what he said." This time it was a different voice. "No one's going anywhere until you hand over Jimmy. Then you can all come out, as long as you ain't armed."

"Right," Mike said in a loud voice. "Then you Nazis can kill us all."

"We still got the key," Alfred said. Then he shouted up the stairs. "You boys got the wrong idea. We got a noose 'round Jimmy's neck right now, and we's getting ready to string him up from this beam down here. So here's the deal: You put your weapons on the floor, unlock your side of the door. Then you step back from the door, put your hands in the air, and we march up the stairs with Jimmy in front of us. If you do that, we won't hang him. Otherwise, your friend is dead meat."

There was a moment of silence, then Bill's voice again. "You kill Jimmy and you're all dead. We might just put a match to this place and leave. Jimmy? You all right, Jimmy?"

"Yeah, I'm okay. They—aaaaah!" Alfred had grabbed him from behind and was twisting his arm nearly out of its socket.

"Quit hurting him!" Bill said, "I'm warning you, anything you do to Jimmy now, you get back twice as bad later. You better let up on him."

"Better do what he says," Sam told Alfred.

"So what are we supposed to do," Alfred said. "Just stay here till our asses all starve?"

"We got cell phones, if they'll work down here," Mike said. "Should we try to call Wilma?"

"What's she supposed to do?" Alfred said.

"Maybe we should call the police," Mike suggested.

"Not till we find Ron," Alfred said.

～

Ron looked around, unsteady and disoriented. *Where am I? In the woods near the Clays' house. But where's the path?*

The rain was lighter now, but water on branches and leaves was soaking him so he zipped up his jacket. He left the hood down, so it would not muffle his hearing.

He started walking downhill toward the stream, hoping he might stumble across the path on the way and follow it home. He wanted to avoid the Clays' house at all costs, having no interest in being caught by Jimmy and his gang again.

Soon he saw a light through the trees. He was much closer to the house than he had thought he was. Fearing that the dog would alert its master and come after him, he slowed his pace and began to walk more cautiously. He was grateful that the rain was still falling and the wet leaves were absorbing his sounds.

Anxious about the dog's whereabouts, he gazed past the shed and ice house to the Clays' house itself. There in the driveway beside the house, he noticed a white pickup, white Cadillac, and black SUV. *That's just like Alfred's*, he thought—*a big Toyota Sequoia. Could Alfred be down there trying to find me? Maybe he thinks Jimmy knows where I am. And maybe Wilma's with him!*

After taking a few more steps, he saw a full-size green Ford pickup. *I know that truck. It was parked on the road when I went running that day. Or is this just another coincidence? But I even think I've seen it on our street. Is that how Jimmy and his gang knew where I ran so they could ambush me? Were they tailing me? Maybe that guy's in there, too. Maybe they're all in there. With Alfred. And—shit—maybe with Wilma, too!*

He looked around, armed himself with another stick, and crept down the trail in a crouch. But the dog didn't appear. *If he's here, he must be asleep or drugged*, Ron thought.

As he moved behind the shed, he stepped on something sharp, and a long handle rose from the deep grass. He pulled it out—a rusty garden rake. He dropped his stick in favor of the rake, and continued toward the house, running low. Closer, now, he could make out the license number on the SUV. He was certain it was Alfred's.

Diving behind a bush by the porch, he rested on one knee. Suddenly he heard a growl and a few sharp barks. The German shepherd charged through the screen door and leaped toward him. Ron rose and swung the rake sharply, the only swing he would have, and caught the dog on the neck with the teeth of the yard tool. It ran staggering around the corner of the house, howling and yelping in pain, its tail between its legs, as Ron resumed his crouch behind the bush.

"What's that?" Ron heard through the door. "Dan, see what's the matter with Fury. I'll guard the basement door."

~

Annie was still stocking shelves when Noah came in the back door. *Now what does he want?* she thought.

"Miss Annie, I think we got trouble."

"What is it, Noah?"

"A while ago, I saw this big SUV full of colored fellas turn down your driveway and didn't come out. I called Jimmy, but he didn't answer. Well, I didn't want to bother you about it, so I called Bill, and he and Dan went to check on Jimmy, and they never came out."

"What? Anything else?"

"Just that I heard Fury howling and crying a little while ago."

"Hell."

"I don't know what's going on, but I thought I better tell you."

"You should've told me before you called them dumb friends of his. Damn!"

"Sorry, Miss Annie."

"It's okay, Noah, but I think I better call someone to check this out. Thanks."

"You're welcome, ma'am."

As he went back out, Annie pondered the situation. *What do I care if someone hurts Jimmy? He doesn't care about me none. If he dies, I get my freedom. I get the farm, or what's left of it, and the house, including that basement. And I can do with it what I want. And then I won't have a brother around telling me what to do and threatening me and scaring men away. Why, I could even bring someone to the house if Jimmy weren't there ... But it's just a dream. He's still flesh and blood. Damn him anyway.*

She picked up the phone, but wondered who to call. *Bobby Miller?* She knew him. He was a cop and a straight shooter. He'd check out the situation. And it would be a good excuse to see him again. He was married, but a few years back he and Annie had spent some time together. She'd even put out for him a couple of times trying to lure him away. This would be a good chance to see if he was still married, maybe get together again. She still hoped to find the right guy, someone who would treat her right, and that just might be Bobby.

"Bobby?"

"Annie?" he said.

"How did you know it's me?"

"Caller ID. But I recognized your voice too. Long time no see, honey. How're ya doing?"

"Doing just fine."

"Well, it's great to hear from you."

"Yeah. It's nice to hear you too."

"We had some great times together, Annie. I think about you lots."

"I think about you too, Bobby."

"Remember that time in the park? I scared out that couple, and then we did it right in the patrol car. Whew, baby, you sure can get it on! I can feel you all over me right now."

"That was fun, Bobby. You sure like to ride, now don't you, cowboy."

"Yeah, baby. We ought to do it again sometime. What do you say?"

"Sounds good to me, sweetie." She wanted to ask about his wife and whether they were still together but decided not to rush things.

"So what's on your mind, little girl?"

"Well, something funny just happened. I tell you what, it's probably nothing, but Noah saw a car with some black guys go down our driveway about an hour ago, and you know something must be wrong about that. You know what a jerk Jimmy is about black people."

"Yeah, I heard he has a problem with black people, and not just from you."

"And then Noah called a couple of friends of Jimmy's to go in and check them out, and they've been in there a long time, and no one's come out yet! And then he heard the dog barking and howling, and, well, we just don't know what's going on. Probably nothing, but I was just wondering if you could cruise down there and check it out for me. Something's gotta be wrong."

"I sure can, Annie. Me and Carl can do it. Carl's my new partner. Good cop. We'll check it out for you."

"Thanks, Bobby. I'm at the store. Let me know what you find out. And give me a call sometime, and we can have a little fun."

"Can't wait, baby."

~

A short, muscular man in a black T-shirt stepped out onto the screened porch with an AK-47 rifle cradled in his arms. The man looked all around, seeing nothing unusual. He opened the screen door, stretching the spring with a twang. As he took a step down toward the ground, Ron reached up by the steps and caught the man's foot with his hand, making him tumble forward. When the man threw out his hands to break his fall, he released the rifle. Ron scrambled out from behind the bush, grabbed the rifle, rolled once, and came to his knees. The man was already on his feet, coming after Ron. When he came close, Ron rose and struck him in the face with the butt of the rifle, knocking him to the ground. As the man shook his head and stood up, ready to come again, Ron addressed him in a matter-of-fact voice.

"You're one of the guys who ambushed me in the woods—the short one. You're dead, man, if you move or make a noise. And I know where I can dump the body. I mean it. Don't move. If you make a noise, it's all over."

The man froze.

"Raise your hands, turn around, and go back up the stairs. We're going in, unless you decide to do something stupid. Then you're dead, motherfucker. Move."

The short man walked up the steps, and opened the screen door, with Ron right behind him.

"Keep going."

The man opened the front door, and they went inside.

"Dan, what did you find out?" The taller man stood by the door holding another AK-47. Then he saw Ron and turned his weapon toward him.

"Drop it on the floor or you're both dead," Ron said, sticking the barrel into the shorter man's back. "Throw it over this way."

The other man went pale, his eyes wide—like he had seen death. "You!" he said. "How did you get out of the well?"

Ron spoke in the most vicious voice he could find. "I turned into a ghost and flew out, asshole. Now drop it, or you're both dead. I mean it!"

"Do it, Bill," the short man said. "He'll kill us if you don't."

Bill hesitated, then surrendered, still staring at Ron. "All right, all right. Don't shoot." He tossed his rifle on the floor toward Ron.

"Okay, now both of you lie face down on the floor over there with your hands behind your heads. Now!" Ron barked. The two complied.

Ron heard Alfred shouting in the basement. "What you two mothas doing up there?"

"Is that you, Alfred?"

"Ron?"

"Yeah, it's me. Back from the dead like the ghost of Count Dracula. Why don't you come join the party? Who's with you?"

"Arno, John, Sam, and Mike, and we got Jimmy Clay with a noose around his neck. Unbolt that door and let us up!"

The neighbors emerged from the basement. John tied up the three men while the others stood guard.

"God, what happened to you?" Mike asked, looking at Ron's face. "You're all black and blue."

"Don't start," Ron said with a grin.

"So where were you, man?" Alfred asked Ron.

"They threw me down a well in the woods."

"Shee-it. A well? How the hell did you get out?"

"Walked out, man. With my head and hands on one side and my feet on the other."

"Can't keep a good man down," Arno said.

"What did happen to your face?" Mike asked with concern. "It looks bad." Ron had developed a puffy shiner under one eye, and his lower lip was split.

"I think if you look at those guys' knuckles, you'll find out. So what are you all doing here?"

"Came looking for you, bro," Alfred said. He told Ron how Wilma had called them together, and how they had captured Jimmy and taken him down into the basement. "But he wouldn't tell us nothing, so I figured we could scare him into talking by taking him out and starting to lynch him. But then these other crackas came and locked us in the basement until you came. How the hell did you take them anyway?"

"Got the short one with gravity. Tripped him on the stairs and grabbed his gun. Got the tall one with bullshit, man. Told him I was gonna kill both of them—you know—just like they say it in the movies. I think I had him spooked. He thought he was dealing with a ghost, 'cause they thought there was no way anyone could get out of that well."

"Would you really have shot them?" Arno asked.

"Maybe—if I could've figured out how to get the safety off."

Jimmy looked disgusted. Bill and Dan glared.

Ron picked up the phone and called Wilma. He glanced at his watch. The display was cracked, but the stopwatch was still running, the numbers were racing toward five hours. He turned it off. "We're all at the Clay house," he said. "Jimmy and two of his buddies attacked me in the woods and threw me down an old well, but I got out and was able to rescue the neighbors from Jimmy's buddies. We captured them all and tied them up. We're getting ready to call the police."

"That didn't make much sense, Ron. Are you all right?"

"Yes. Everyone's all right. I'll be hurting when the adrenaline wears off. The sons of bitches beat me up before they threw me down the well, and I hit my hip on the way down, so it's bruised. But other than that, I guess I'm okay. Damned Nazis. What century is this anyway?"

"I'm just glad you're still alive."

"Me too."

"When will you be home? Should I come pick you up?"

"No. I expect we'll all have to go to the police station to fill out reports, so I'll have to call you later."

"Thank God you're all right."

"Yeah. Thank God."

∼

They finished tying up the three men and took the noose off Jimmy. Sam called the police and explained what happened.

"Can you send some officers to Jimmy and Annie Clay's house in the woods? ... It's on Big Oak Road just past Big Oak Crossing Road and that big oak tree and Clay Grocery ... Turn left down the driveway into the woods ... Good. There are some people here you'll want to take to the station."

He hung up. "They already have a car on the way—I don't know who called them—and another coming for backup."

Sam called everyone together away from the captives, and spoke in a low voice. "Okay, listen. I'll do the talking. Here's our story. We came here looking for Ron because he used to cut through the property here on his runs. Wilma had searched everywhere else, and she couldn't get the police to come. The door to the house was open, and we went in to look for Ron. We found Jimmy, and he let us look through the house to prove that Ron wasn't there. We were searching the basement with Jimmy when these other two arrived, with guns. They trapped us in the basement. Then Ron came, disarmed the two who had the guns, and let us out of the basement. Ron, you can tell them about being attacked, and getting out of the well, and so on. Okay? Any questions? Remember: Stick to the story, don't say any more than you have to, and let me do the talking first."

"Fucking honkies," Alfred said, still angry.

"Just incredible," Mike said.

Ron asked Mike a question that had been bothering him since he saw Jimmy. "Where'd that noose come from anyway?"

"It was on a table downstairs, Ron," Mike said. "You need to check out the basement before the police come. You won't believe what's down there."

Mike and Ron went down into the dim light, and Ron's eyes immediately went to the large photo of the bloody man hanging from the big oak tree.

"God! That must be my great-grandfather. There he is. Right in front of the store. Those assholes."

"Horrible."

Ron's eyes perused the photo. "Shit. Look at all these people in the crowd. Look at their faces looking back at the camera. Some of them look proud, like they were showing you a big buck they just bagged. And look at the defiance in their eyes, daring anyone to do anything."

"Daring blacks to cross the line again," Mike said.

"And shit, Mike. Look at the kids."

"They're all in school—being taught by their elders."

"And look at this girl with long braids and freckles, maybe ten or twelve years old. She's the only one that looks a little scared and uncomfortable—like she doesn't know how she's supposed to act. A little ashamed, even. Maybe she's old enough to have her own thoughts. And look at that blond boy looking up bug-eyed at my great granddaddy."

"They're being taught to hate," Mike said.

"Being taught white supremacy."

"I'm just glad things are different today," Mike said.

"Yeah? How? I was lynched today, man. Today! But I was able to survive it."

"With a miracle."

"Look at this boot with a bone in it and a shackle on it. Where did they get that bone? What kind of bone is it? Not a human bone, I hope. Not—"

"I don't know."

"And all this Nazi stuff. And these photos. My God, he's got one of Dr. King after he was shot. And this must be a slave auction. Good God almighty!"

"Oh man," Mike said.

"What?"

"That rope upstairs, with the noose on it—I bet it's the one they hung your great-grandfather with. We found it on the table here. One end was frayed where they cut it."

"Damn!"

"Hate lives, man."

Ron's eyes landed on the postcards on the altar, then the books— *Mein Kampf* and the small black one without a title. Curious, he picked it up and opened it.

"Ron and Mike," Sam called down the stairs. "The police are here."

Ron closed the book, slipped it into a side pocket of his jacket, and stuffed the post cards into the other pocket.

TWENTY-TWO

Ron and Mike went upstairs into the living room and found Bobby Miller and his partner Carl, who was taking notes in a small, spiral-bound pad. Bobby was medium height, white, thick, and strong. Carl was tall, black, and built like a middle linebacker. Both had short hair and were dressed in county police uniforms.

"I was just telling them about how they threw you down the well," Sam said.

"You the one?" Bobby asked Ron.

"Yeah."

"What's your name?"

"Ron Watkins." *I better give them more information so they know who they're dealing with,* he thought. "I live on Blake Station Circle. I work for the Internal Revenue Service downtown."

"So what happened, Mr. Watkins?"

"I was jogging through the woods this morning, and they were waiting for me by the path."

"Who?"

"Those three right there." He pointed to the three bound men sitting on the floor.

"He's lying," Jimmy said. "Don't believe him."

"Be quiet," Bobby said. "We'll hear from you later. Then what happened?"

"They came out of the bushes and attacked me—the tall guy and the short guy. The tall one hit me in the face a couple of times while the short one hit me in the stomach. Then Jimmy hit me with what I'm pretty sure was a tire iron and knocked me out."

"He's lying!" Jimmy shouted.

"I said be quiet!" Bobby said. "Let me see your head."

Ron turned his back, showing the cut on his scalp, still oozing.

"Nasty," Bobby said. "What happened next?"

"Next thing I knew they were throwing me down that well. I hit the water, then the bottom, did a somersault, and came to the surface. Then they put the concrete lid on the well. That cut out all the light."

"We never threw nobody down a well," Jimmy whined.

"He's a liar," Dan said.

"He can't prove anything he says," Bill sputtered.

"How do we know you're telling the truth, Mr. Watkins?" Bobby asked.

"I don't know. My pants are soaked."

Jimmy laughed. "He was running in the pouring rain."

Ron ignored him. "You can see my face, and look at the tall guy's knuckles. See if they're bruised or cut."

"You mean the guy with the black eye?"

"Yeah. I caught him with an uppercut and a right cross. Got him pretty good. But he got me too."

"Hmm. Carl, check the big guy's hands, will you? What else?"

"You might find some of their footprints around the well, if the rain hasn't washed them away, and see if that mud on their boots matches."

"Okay, what else?"

"See if they left any DNA on the well cover when they were taking it off or putting it back on. Oh, and one other thing: I think I heard some kind of metal twanging sound and a splash as soon as my head came out of the water. I'd check the bottom of the well. I bet they threw that tire iron down there."

"He couldn'ta heard nothing with water in his ears," Jimmy said.

"We'll check it out," Bobby said. "So how did you get out of the well?"

"Tall guy's got a cut on the knuckles of his right hand," Carl interrupted.

Bobby wrote a note in his book. He turned to Bill. "What's your name?"

"Bill Wolfe." Carl and Bobby wrote it down.

"How did you get that cut on your hand?"

"I bumped it when I was splitting some firewood this morning."

Carl expressed disbelief. "You were splitting firewood in August in the rain?"

"I'm getting ready for winter. You gotta let the wood dry out."

"How did you get the black eye?"

"A piece jumped up and hit me."

Carl smiled at Bobby. "Okay."

Then he looked at the hands of the shorter man. "This one's got a cut on the side of his left index finger. The tip of the finger is mashed pretty bad too. Might lose this nail. Got dried blood under it." Eying Dan now, he asked, "What's your name?"

"Daniel Black."

"How'd you get that mashed finger?"

"Slammed it in the car door this morning."

"My, my. You guys must be accident-prone. Well, Mr. Black, tell me, how'd you get your face bashed in like that?"

"He hit me with my rifle butt," Dan said, nodding at Ron. This time, Ron laughed.

"So these rifles do belong to you," Bobby said. The trio was silent. Carl was writing rapidly.

"So, Mr. Watkins," Bobby said. "Now tell me: how'd you get out of the well?"

"I was able to get my heels on some of the stones, lean forward with my head against the other side, and push up with the heels of my hands, and just slowly climb out. When I got to the top, I pushed the lid off with my back."

"God, you know that's kind of hard to believe. All you guys are hard to believe."

"But my story's true. You don't want me to tell you I changed into a ghost and flew out a hole, like I told them, do you?"

"No."

"Well, I really don't want to go back down there, but if you tie a harness around me and lower me down by rope, I can show you how I did it. I'll do it again."

"Hmm," Bobby said, still sounding dubious. "So what happened next?"

"I saw the house through the woods and came here because I saw that SUV outside. It looked like my neighbor's car, and I thought he might be here looking for me, and my wife might be with him. Then I saw the pickup truck outside and remembered seeing it parked on the street when I was leaving the house to run one day. I thought it was strange that the same truck would be here."

"So you came to the house."

"Yes, and on the way, I found a garden rake. When I got to the house, that big German shepherd of Jimmy's came at me, so I hit him with the rake. I think I hurt him, because he ran away howling. Then the short guy comes out carrying one of those rifles."

"Was not," Dan said.

"I grabbed his ankle when he came off the porch and made him fall down the stairs. Then I grabbed his rifle, and then he came at me and I hit him with the rifle butt. Then I made him go in the house. The tall one was guarding the basement door. He had the other rifle. I threatened to shoot both of them unless he dropped his rifle, which he did. Then I let my friends out of the basement, and they tied these three up. I called my wife. Then we called you. That's how it happened."

Bobby made some notes in his book, and then looked up.

"Okay, now it's your turn, Mr. Clay. What happened?"

"When are you gonna untie us? We ain't done nothing. It's them that need putting in jail."

"I'd be careful, sir," Sam said. "They're neo-Nazis. The evidence is downstairs."

"I heard that before. I don't know if it's true or not, Carl, but I think we better leave Mr. Clay and his friends tied up a while longer, till we hear his version and get some backup. There are too many people here and too many weapons, and I still don't know who's telling the truth. So what do *you* say happened, Mr. Clay?"

"These men broke into my house and punched me. Then they held me while they looked all through the house, and made me go downstairs."

"Is that true?" Bobby asked Sam.

"No, officer," Sam said. "We came in here looking for Mr. Watkins, because he often runs through the woods on the edge of the Clay property. Mrs. Watkins alerted us when he didn't return from his run. She looked everywhere along his running route except here, so we concluded he might be here. That's why we come here. No one answered when we knocked, and the door was partly open, so we came in. That's when we ran into Mr. Clay coming up from the basement. No one punched him. We asked him if we could look around, and he said yes. You may want to take a look at the basement. It will tell you a great deal about Mr. Clay."

"Hmm," Bobby said. "Mind if we take a look at your basement, Mr. Clay?"

"You got a search warrant?"

"We're trying to conduct an investigation. Why don't you want us to see it?"

"It's private, that's all."

"He don't want you to see it 'cause there's pictures down there of Clay's family lynching Ron's great-granddaddy from that big oak tree by the store," Alfred said.

"What?" Bobby exclaimed.

"That's right. Ron's great-granddaddy used to live in this house, and Clay's great-granddaddy got a mob together and lynched him. Clay's got photos on the wall showing it. And then Ron cuts through Clay's land, and Clay thinks he'll just lynch Ron too."

"The nigger's lyin'," Jimmy said.

"Cracka, you using the N word in front of us when you's tied up on the floor?"

"Stay cool, Alfred," Ron said.

"What's your name?" Carl asked Alfred.

"Alfred Mance." Carl wrote it in his book.

"You know, Jimmy, we can get a search warrant by this afternoon," Bobby said.

"Do it, then. After I call my lawyer."

"Who's that, Mr. Clay?" Bobby asked.

"Well, I can't remember his name right now, but gimme a phone book, and I'll find him."

"There'll be time for that. Now, Mr. Clay … did you and these two men attack Mr. Watkins in the woods and throw him down a well?"

"No. I never seen him before we come up those stairs and he was pointing that rifle at Bill and Dan."

"He saw me in the store twice talking to his sister," Ron said, "and he saw me when I came in for an oil change."

"And you never hit Mr. Watkins with a tire iron or anything else?"

"No, never."

The other police arrived. Bobby greeted them. "This is some weird shit we got here. Do me a favor and keep an eye on the three guys on the floor, will you? Watch those rifles and keep an eye on everyone else. It looks like we have some kind of a crime scene here, but I haven't sorted it all out yet. And how 'bout calling back and having forensics come out? We may need to take some plaster casts of footprints and look for evidence in the woods. And we'll need a warrant to look in the basement here. Tag those rifles as evidence."

~

Annie pulled up in her Camaro and was surprised to see three police cars, a black SUV, two pickups, and Jimmy's old DeVille. The driveway looked like a used car lot.

She walked into the house to find Jimmy, Dan, and Bill tied up on the floor surrounded by four white cops, a black cop, and six other men—five black and one white. *What the hell is this?* she wondered. She recognized Bobby. "What's going on?"

"Afternoon, Ms. Clay. We're not quite sure. Maybe you can help us figure it out."

"Sure, if I can."

"Well, this man here claims that Jimmy and his friends attacked him in the woods this morning and threw him down a well."

"Oh," she gasped. "Mr. Watkins. Oh shit, what happened to your face? Did Jimmy do that?"

"You know him?"

Jimmy erupted. "No, she don't!"

Shut up, she thought. She glared at Jimmy and gritted her teeth. "Yes, I do," she said. "He's come into the store several times when he was running. Bought some water and this and that. And one time Fury chased him up out of the woods—I guess he was running too close to our house—and he turned on Fury and faced him down in the street and somehow got into the store without getting bit. I couldn't believe that. He told Jimmy he better keep his dog tied up, or someday the dog would bite someone, and then he'd get sued."

All the officers were taking notes now.

"Annie!" Jimmy barked.

"Hush up, Jimmy," she said. "I'm talking now."

"Go on," Bobby said.

"So Jimmy told him it wouldn't happen again, but he had a mean tone in his voice. I wonder what he meant by that."

"I'll kill you, you traitor bitch!" Jimmy said, struggling against the rope.

"That'll be enough of that. Better cuff him, Carl," Bobby said. Carl took the suggestion.

"Hey, what're ya doing? They're the ones that need cuffs, not us!" Jimmy said.

"I don't think so, Mr. Clay," Bobby said. He turned back to Annie. "So your brother has met Mr. Watkins before today?"

"Oh yeah, several times. Ron had him change his oil once too. Jimmy didn't care for him. Course he don't care for nobody, at least nobody black."

Jimmy glowered at her even more fiercely.

"What about this morning? Did anything unusual happen this morning?"

She thought back. "Maybe. I was getting ready to leave for the store and I looked out the window and saw those two."

"Who?"

"Those two sitting there next to Jimmy—Dan and Bill—Mutt and Jeff."

"Go on."

"I noticed them walking toward Bill's truck in the rain."

"What time was that?"

"Shut up!" shouted Jimmy.

"About six-thirty. I noticed Jimmy was wet and wasn't getting ready for work and I asked him how he got wet. He said he had to go to the truck in the rain. And then I asked him what those two were doing here, and Jimmy said they were just paying a visit."

"And then?"

"Well, I told Jimmy he shouldn't be late to the garage even if it was raining 'cause Noah might not show up. But Jimmy, he never did come to the garage. I don't know what he was doing at the house."

She noticed that the basement door was open. "Have you been down in the basement?" Just the thought of seeing what was down there filled her with curiosity and trepidation.

"Not yet," Bobby said. "Gotta get a court order."

She stood transfixed for a moment, then thought, *I'm going down there.* "Will you go down with me, Bobby? I've never been down there, and I want to see what's down there. You don't need a court order. This is my house, too."

"No, girl," Jimmy said. "You get away from that door. You're not allowed down there. Daddy'll kill you if you go down there. He'll beat you till you're dead."

"Hey Carl," Bobby said. "Can you stuff a rag in his mouth? He's getting on my nerves. Let's go, Annie. And Carl, can you come down with us?"

Bobby advised Annie not to touch anything and led the way down the steep stairs in the flickering lamp light. "Wonder how come he didn't put electric lights down here?" Bobby groused.

Annie followed him, walking almost sideways on the narrow stairs, one hand on Bobby's shoulder. "I think he didn't want anyone down here."

Bobby pointed to the swastika looming out of the darkness. "Damn Nazi," he said. "People always said he was a Nazi. There's proof."

"Oh God," said Annie, looking at the large photo of the crowd in front of the store under the tree—seeing the hanging body.

"That's a lynching," Carl said, "right down the lane."

"Oh God, that's my store! And the big oak. They hung that man right in front of my store!"

"And he might have been Mr. Watkins' great-grandfather," Carl said.

"What?"

"The big African-American man upstairs—the one they call Alfred—he says that Mr. Watkins' great-grandfather used to live in this house, and that Mr. Clay's great-grandfather lynched him. Do you know anything about that?"

"No! I never knew nothing about that. Jimmy and my daddy never let me down here. I don't know nothing about it at all."

They looked at the slave auction, the field hands, and the German stormtroopers and tanks. They saw the boot with bone gripped by the shackle. They saw the copy of *Mein Kampf*, but Annie did not recognize the title. She looked at the pictures of her relatives and recognized the portrait of her great-grandfather in his wide-brimmed slouch hat. She picked his face out of the crowd at the lynching, his face looking directly at the camera, exuding pride and defiance. *My family*, thought Annie. *Murderers. And now my brother did this.*

When they emerged, she was sobbing. Bobby was helping her walk, his hands at her elbow and wrist.

Through her tears, she expressed horror at what she had seen. "I'm so ashamed. Right in my own house. I never knew I was living over a cesspool."

Suddenly, she broke away from Bobby. She ran to Jimmy and hit him in the face with her fist. "You animal!" she shouted. The officers restrained her before she could strike him again.

"I've heard enough," Bobby said. "Let's put a lock on the basement. Call for a van and get these three down to the station. Everyone else will have to come down and fill out statements. Mr. Watkins, do you think you can find this well for us?"

"You bet I can," Ron said.

~

Ron and Bobby walked outside with Carl. Ron led them past the shed into the woods. The rain had stopped. Bobby carried a large roll of yellow tape imprinted with POLICE LINE DO NOT CROSS.

"Is that true, what Alfred said?" Bobby asked Ron. "Did your great-granddaddy live here? Is he the one being lynched in the picture in the basement?"

"Yes, it's true," Ron said. "It's in the records in the state archives, and it was in the newspaper back then. There's even a 105-year-old woman in a nursing home here who remembers it happening. I think Jimmy found out somehow that I knew, and that's why he came after me. But I really don't understand why he tried to kill me. He wasn't the one who killed my great-grandfather, and people don't usually try to kill people for trespassing. That's uncivilized."

"I've been having trouble with the motive too," Bobby said. "But I know the world is full of nuts. Did you ever come on to Annie?"

"I talked to her several times, but that's all."

"Do you think Jimmy might have thought you were hitting on her?" Carl asked. "He's got a reputation for being really overprotective of his sister."

"To tell you the truth, I don't know *what* that maniac thinks."

They stayed off the path, in case it contained footprints of the attackers. After much searching, Ron found the well, camouflaged as it was with saplings. The concrete lid was halfway off as he had left it. Bobby asked him to stay several steps back, and pulled the tape in a large circle through the brush to mark off the crime scene.

"Watch out," Bobby said. "There are some footprints right there." He and Carl covered them with plastic sheeting.

"Now, tell me again how you got out of that well, Mr. Watkins."

"I put my heels of my feet on stone ledges, leaned forward against the other side, and pushed up with the heels of my hands. If you don't believe me, you'll either have to put me on a lie detector or put me back in the well on a rope and let me show you how."

~

Back at the house, Ron watched as Bobby had the three suspects remove their boots and bagged them as evidence. Additional police arrived and took everyone to the local precinct in Mayville. At the station, detectives questioned each person individually and took statements. Jimmy, Bill, and Dan each maintained sullen, stubborn silence during questioning. After their interviews, they were put into the lockup. Ron and his neighbors were free to leave.

TWENTY-THREE

Ron's office phone rang. His assistant told him Sam Pierce was on the line. He sat up straight. "Thanks, Jennifer. Put him through ... Hey, Sam. What's going on?" His fingers slowly rotated a pen.

"Ron. Got some news for you. I'm doing some work down at the county courthouse, and I just heard from a friend in the district court that the police filed charges of attempted first-degree murder against Jimmy, Bill, and Dan. The court commissioner issued a charging document against them. He determined that there is probable cause based on the statements from you, Annie, and Noah, and the physical evidence. Turns out that some of the footprints from around the well matched their boots, and the soil samples did too. And on the bottom of the well cover they found blood and skin tissue that matched Dan's DNA and blood type. They found the tire iron at the bottom of the well, but couldn't get any prints from it. And they took that big photo of the lynching from the basement to help establish motive."

"Sounds good."

"And they found a plastic film can in the basement with Jimmy's fingerprints on it, and Bill's, and yours. On the film itself, they found additional prints from you and Jimmy. The film contained the *Baltimore Courier* article on the lynching of your great-granddaddy."

"Really? Bill must have tailed us and been in the library watching us when we were working. He must have watched me take that one off the spool and set it on the shelf because he knew which one to pick up when we left. These guys are something else."

"The police think they have an ironclad case against them."

"That's terrific. They won't be released on bail, will they?"

"No. Not when the charge is attempted murder."

"And a hate crime?"

"I don't know if they'll prosecute it that way or not."

"What happens next?"

"The state's attorney will take the charges to a grand jury and ask for an indictment, and then it will go to trial. My friend says the police think the verdict is all but certain."

"I would hope so, but you never know. They still have to prove that I was in the well. Jimmy'll say I wasn't. Hey, thanks for the call, Sam. I really appreciate it."

"You bet. See you tomorrow night."

~

"Counselor!" Ron said, lifting his beer bottle in a toast to Sam. "To the man who talked our way out of jail!"

"To the counselor," the group shouted.

It was the Saturday night after the incident. The neighbors had gathered to celebrate at Sam and Cherise's—Mary and Mike, Alfred and Tabatha, John and Donna, Arno and Judy, and Wilma and Ron. Black divas sang softly on the stereo in the background. The furniture was white wicker, and the walls decorated with fine-arts prints. Flowers decked tables in the kitchen and family room, and a bust of Martin Luther King watched from a slender wooden pedestal in the corner.

"Hey, hey, and hear, hear," Alfred said, raising his glass of scotch.

"You didn't do so badly yourself, Mr. Watkins." Sam held his wine glass high. "To Mr. Watkins, who got one Nazi with gravity and the other two with bullshit." They all laughed.

"Yes. To Mr. Watkins, the rock climber," John said, raising his beer bottle.

"To the human fly on the wall of the well!" Arno said, holding up his soda can like the torch of the Statue of Liberty.

"Once I altered the earth's gravity and made the well horizontal, there was nothing to it."

"To the neighborhood magician," Arno said.

"And may your swelling go down, so you don't scare little children any more," Sam said. "And may your bandage disappear, and your hair grow back."

"Thanks a lot," Ron said.

"And to our fearless leader, Alfred," Mike said, "who knocked out that dog with a single blow and thought he killed it, and then charged up San Juan Hill without a gun!"

"Didn't knock it out for long," Alfred said. "What a beast."

"To Alfred!" they all toasted.

"What makes me mad is that we all risked our necks to save Ron's ass," Alfred said, "and he ends up saving ours!"

"Yes, but you guys caught the really bad one—Jimmy Clay."

"To us!" shouted Mike.

"To us!" the group roared back.

"I bet you're glad it's over," Mike said to Ron.

"I just wish I had some evidence of Thomas's innocence."

"You know, Ron, you should file a civil suit against Clay," Sam said, holding his wine glass casually in his right hand near his waist.

"Yeah, man," Alfred said. "Sue the motha!"

"You think so?" Ron said.

"Why not?" Sam said, waving the glass to the side. "You could take the house, store, garage—everything they have."

"Yeah, we black folk never get nothing unless we take it," Alfred said.

"You can have it all," Sam said, "and I'm sure that old house holds a lot of sentimental value for you too, since your great-grandfather lived and died there."

"Fuckas lynched him," Alfred said, "just like they tried to lynch you. Face it, man. You already own it. You and your family bought it with your blood. It's reparations time, man. And time to drive that white trash out. They're ruining the neighborhood."

"Reparations," Ron said. "I've been thinking about that. I've been thinking that if you add up what they owe us for all of the horrible things they've done to us—beating us, shooting us, starving us, making us work for nothing or for slave wages, taking our wives and children away from us, stealing our farms and property—"

"Yeah," Alfred interjected.

"—and you add in punitive damages, award for mental anguish and pain and suffering and breach of good faith, as well as lost wages and the opportunity cost of the money we would have made with the better jobs we should have had, and if you calculate in the appreciation of all the property we would have owned if we had received the money they owed us, and then adjust it for inflation and calculate the present value of all that, you end up with white society owing us trillions and trillions of dollars. Yes, trillions. I agree, we deserve to get every penny of it."

"Right on, man," Alfred said, "and that's why you gotta sue. For reparations. Take what they owe us."

"Sue them for that much, and they'll just declare bankruptcy," Arno observed.

"There's no way they could pay it," Ron said.

"No way they would pay," Sam qualified.

"Correct. It would bankrupt the country. We're already deep into deficit spending. They would have to raise taxes a lot or just print more money, but then that would bring back inflation, and that would tax us all—everything would cost more. Poor people and old people and people without property would suffer the most."

"Well, they wouldn't have to give it all to us," Alfred said. "Just some of it."

"Yeah, like forty acres and a mule,'" Ron said ruefully, recalling the Oscar Brown, Jr. song.

"Fuck!" Alfred said. "How many black folks even got that?"

"What do you think, Mike?" Arno asked. Everyone turned their attention to the white man. "Do you think there should be reparations?"

"I don't know. I personally don't feel like I owe anything. I've always tried to treat everyone the same, and I'm only a fourth-generation American. We came here long after slavery ended. What, you want me to speak for my whole race?"

"You always make us do that," Sam said.

"Okay, I'll try … It seems to me that there should be reparations of some kind, for justice, and so no one forgets what we did to black people, to give African-Americans more of a level playing field."

"Justice!" Alfred whooped. "Fuck yes, justice. You know, Mike, you ain't too bad for a fucking honky, 'cept justice would be where we beats you, and sells your children, and works you like animals, and lynches you when you look at our women, and keeps you poor by keeping you out of schools and good jobs. Now that'd be justice. You all do what we tell you to do for a few hundred years—that'd be justice."

Sam ignored Alfred. "Mike, do you even know what 'level playing field' means? Do you know about white privilege? About whites being able to invest in new homes after World War II—homes that are now worth twenty or thirty times what they were then—when our parents couldn't buy in because they were black? Whites inherited all this wealth from generations and generations, long after slavery was outlawed, and your family benefitted too, Mike."

"Blacks couldn't even buy a house around here in the sixties—till Congress made discrimination illegal," John contributed.

"And whites had 'affirmative action' too," Sam added. "Their children could attend any college they wanted to. And they could get even more 'affirmative action' if their parents or grandparents went there. Legacy admissions, getting in because daddy went there."

"And what about job discrimination?" John asked. "White affirmative action in hiring and promoting other whites. At least the military has made strides, but it didn't begin until Harry Truman integrated the services."

"We ought to get off Mike's case," Ron said. "He's not the problem."

"Right on, brotha," Alfred said.

"I *can* see how my family and I have benefitted from the system, though," Mike said.

"Suing the Clays might really turn off some white folks," John warned. "Black folks, too. They'll say that you already have everything, but it's not enough. We rich brothers are never satisfied, always have to get more, leave poor blacks farther behind."

"Maybe," Alfred said, "but none of this matters anyway. This is about Ron Watkins getting lynched by Jimmy Clay, and I still say you deserves to have that house and that land. Clay's going to jail anyway. He won't be needing it where he's going."

"Justice," Ron said. "That's what we're talking about. Justice for our race, in the face of hundreds of years of slavery and Jim Crow. Justice for my great-grandfather, who was lynched and robbed, and justice for me."

"Right," Alfred said.

"The only thing I'm not sure about is whether it's just to punish Annie for the crimes of her brother."

~

"You must have died a thousand deaths that day," said Judy. The women were gathered around the kitchen table.

Yes, I did, Wilma thought. "It was awful. First, I got mad at Jimmy Clay." She gritted her teeth and shook her head rapidly. "Then at Ron. Then I cried. And then I prayed."

"All right," Tabatha said.

"And then," she shrugged her shoulders, "I don't know what time it was, but the phone rang. It was Ron saying he was all right."

"Thank God almighty," Tabatha said.

"And I asked him what happened, and he told me," she said, smiling and slowly shaking her head. "And then he said he might have to go to the police station and fill out a report."

"Okay, okay," Cherise said.

Wilma's strength left her and her body slumped in her chair. "We hung up, and I just fell apart and had a good cry. I went to sleep and woke up a half an hour later. I got the kids from Mary. They asked 'Where's Daddy?' and I told them he wasn't home yet. Then late in the afternoon, he called. Said the police wanted him to go to the hospital and get checked out."

"Puh-leez!" Tabatha said.

Wilma straightened and shook her head again. "He finally called later and said they were keeping him overnight and didn't call again until six in the morning. He asked if I could bring him some clean clothes. So I got the kids dressed and asked Mary to take them again, and she said she would. I told the kids that Ron had been in an accident and was in the hospital but was all right."

"Mm, mm, mm," sang Cherise.

"Well, when I saw him, I almost cried again." Her arms tensed and her hands became fists. "Damn those criminals! His eye was black and puffy, his cheek swollen, the back of his head bandaged. And he had a bad bruise on his hip and cuts on his knuckles. He said he was just exhausted and hurt all over."

"Oh my," Mary said.

"They had X-rayed everything the night before, and there were no broken bones, but an MRI showed a mild concussion and—"

"No!" Tabatha said.

"—that's why they kept him overnight. We couldn't pick him up until that evening, but he was dressed and ready to go when we got there. The kids were really worried when they saw his face, but he put on a smile. He told me later that they wouldn't release him until they had done another MRI. And they made him walk a straight line to make sure his balance was all right, and read the letters on an eye chart, follow the doctor's fingers with his eyes, count backward from a hundred by sevens, all that."

"What? I can't do that," Judy said, smiling.

"On the way home, he made us stop at a store and buy makeup to hide his black eye when he went to work. The kids thought it was hilarious."

"I bet they did," Tabatha said.

"It did help the way he looked. He was stone-cold ugly!"

"Is he wearing it now?" Mary asked. They all looked across the room at Ron.

"Oh yes," Wilma said.

Ron noticed the women looking at him and gave them a puzzled smile.

"I bet he was glad to get in bed with you," Tabatha said.

"Sure was. Climbed in, rolled over, and sweet dreams in fifteen seconds! A new record."

"You know what I can't figure out," Judy mused, "is how he got out of that well. I've never heard of anyone getting out of a well before."

Wilma looked at Ron holding court around the kitchen island. "Ron, honey."

"Yes?"

"Honey, show everyone how you got out of that well."

He looked at her and grinned. "Okay everyone, pay close attention, in case someone throws you down a well sometime." He walked over to the hallway leading to the entry and turned sideways. He put his feet against one wall with his toes touching the floor, leaned his head against the other wall so his body formed the hypotenuse of a triangle. The palms of his hands went against the wall in front of him with his fingers pointed downward.

"Looks to me like he's drunk," Arno joked.

"Or leaning up against the bathroom wall taking a leak."

"Alfred!" Tabatha said. Everyone laughed.

"There," Ron said. "Now, you just walk up the wall with your feet while you push up with your hands. It's easy." To everyone's amazement, he climbed two feet up the wall before rejoining them.

"Right, it's easy!" Mary scoffed.

"He's a damned well-walker," Alfred said, "doing the well walk."

"I can't believe you did that," Mike said. "That's not possible."

"Oh yeah?" Ron said.

"How deep was that well?" Mike asked.

"Oh, I don't know. Thirty feet, maybe more."

"How did you figure out how to do that?" Arno asked.

Ron shrugged. "I don't know."

"He just used his head," Judy said. Several people groaned.

"God was with him," Tabatha said. "He didn't think of that himself."

~

Later that night, Ron and Wilma lay in bed, propped by pillows, each reading a book. Ron read the small black book he had found in Jimmy's basement.

"What's that?" Wilma asked.

"It's Jeremiah Clay's diary for the year of the lynching—1907," Ron said.

"Where did you get that?"

Confession time, Ron thought. "Off the table down in Jimmy Clay's basement. I slipped it into my sweatshirt."

"I swear, Ron. That's gotta be illegal. What if it has evidence they can use against Jimmy Clay in the trial?"

"If it does, I'll just turn it in and say I borrowed it and didn't know any better."

"Honestly, one of these days you are going to get into some serious trouble," she joked. "But seriously honey, you better read that book fast and turn it in to the police."

"I will. I'm almost halfway through already."

"Does anyone know you have it?"

"Just Mike. He said he wouldn't tell anyone."

"What does it say?"

"Well, it's pretty exciting stuff. Every day he gives the weather report and talks about articles in the newspaper. Apparently, he loved to read the paper every day. The diary is full of little summaries of articles about Jim Crow and lynchings, automobiles, airplanes, train wrecks, and the new inter-urban trolley line. He also liked playing checkers with his granddaughter. And riding horses, and going to church. And playing poker with his cronies in the store."

"But what about Thomas's lynching? What does he say about that?"

"I jumped ahead and read through December, and he does write about it. It's just like the newspaper account. He claims that Thomas assaulted his daughter Agnes, and that his son John saved her, and that a mob came and lynched Thomas. But he doesn't admit to having any part in it, and doesn't implicate any of his family. There's nothing here that proves Thomas was innocent."

TWENTY-FOUR

A few weeks later, the Watkins family went to Mike and Mary's house for dinner. Marty and Rosalie immediately went to the basement to play with Jeff and Jason.

"I like your outfit, Mary," Ron said. "What are those—"

"These guys on my T-shirt? They're Mayan pictographs. I bought it at the museum store." The T-shirt hung loosely over her white shorts. On her feet were brown leather sandals. "And you guys look great, too," Mary said. "Wilma, I love that blouse." Wilma's top had three-quarter-length sleeves and a colorful, African motif. She wore it over black slacks. Ron wore a white knit golf shirt and pleated khaki pants.

"Mike," Mary called up the stairs. "They're here."

"Your house looks beautiful," Wilma said, glancing into the small sitting room to the right.

"We keep working at it."

"I love those still lifes," Wilma said. On the wall hung paintings, one depicting a bowl of fruit, the other a flower arrangement.

"Oh, do you like those? My grandmother Margaret did those."

"They're lovely."

"She did hundreds of paintings. She was kind of a quiet woman and loved to spend time alone with her paints and brushes. She painted until her eyes started to fail her in her eighties. Then she spent most of her time listening to classical music on the radio."

"When did she pass?" Ron asked.

"In 1985. She was ninety. I was nineteen or twenty, I think. I was still at Maryland, and she was living with Mom and Dad. She lived a long life. Outlived my grandfather by ten years."

"Born in 1895," Ron said. *That would make her twelve years old in 1907,* he thought absentmindedly in his recent habit of relating things to that year.

"I guess so."

"Were you close to her?" Wilma asked.

"You know, I was. I think I was closer to her than my mom was, even though Mom took care of her. Granny was a very private person, but she and I used to talk a lot. Would you like some snacks while we wait? I don't think Mike is ever coming down."

She led them past the stairs into the great room, which contained a large seating area with high ceilings, windows, and fireplace, a dining area, and the kitchen. The latter had cabinets and appliances on three outer walls surrounding the central island on which Mary had arranged plates of vegetables, crackers, cheese, crab hors d'oeuvres, chips, two bottles of white wine, and a corkscrew. Liquor and glasses sat on the counter beside the sink. A round wood table in front of windows facing the woods was set for four. Mary had brought out white china, cloth napkins, and glistening stemware for the occasion.

"Dinner won't be ready for a while, so help yourself. Can you open that wine, Ron, while I work on the main course?"

"Sure," Ron said. Wilma began nibbling while he opened the wine. "What wonderful smell is emanating from the oven? Is that a roast?"

"Sure is. Do you like rib roast?"

"I love it," Ron said. "Mary, you sure can cook. I'll never forget your chowder from the crab feast. It was great. All those little clams swimming around in whipped cream and sherry. Marvelous!"

"It really was good," Wilma agreed.

Mike came in from the entry. "Hey, everybody. How's the Watkins family today?"

"Just fine," Wilma said.

"Sorry I'm late."

"Late to your own party," Ron said. "All you had to do was stumble down the stairs."

"I've been operating on that CP time you were talking about."

"I think you've mastered it."

"Wilma, would you like some wine?" Mike said.

"Oh, just diet cola, thanks."

He poured Wilma's drink. "Well, you sure look better," he said to Ron. "You were pretty ugly after your encounter with Jimmy Clay and the boys."

"Thanks a lot. And I see you're getting a little color in that pasty white face of yours now that the monsoon season is over."

"Yep. Would you like a drink?"

"Sure. The usual—scotch on the rocks with just a little water."

"Coming up."

"You really do look better," Mary said, studying Ron's face. "You don't look all puffed up anymore. And you took that bandage off your head."

"I got tired of people asking about it."

"You reminded me of an Amish woman in a little white cap," Mike said as he poured the scotch.

Wilma and Mary laughed.

"That's the first time I've been mistaken for an Amish woman."

Mary was removing refrigerated dough from cardboard tubes and placing it on baking sheets. "I think you looked like one of those boxers you see in the paper—after the fight."

"The people at the office were certainly impressed. They moved out of my way when I walked down the hall, and spoke to me with more respect."

"I used to have a punching bag I respected a lot," Mike said, handing Ron his drink. "After I slugged it, I moved my head so it wouldn't hit me back. You should try that next time."

"You're crazy," Wilma chuckled.

"I'll drink to that," Ron said.

Wilma said, "I better check on the kids." She headed down to the basement.

"Thanks, Wilma," Mary said.

Ron and Mike talked boxing while Mary put the rolls on baking sheets, took out the steaming roast, and carved it with a sharp silver knife. Finishing her work, she set the steaming cut of meat on the island. Then she put the rolls in the oven.

Wilma returned with a report. "They're doing fine. Rosalie and Jason are playing with cars, and Jeff and Marty are racing them on the PC. No sign they're starving yet."

"Freshen up your drink a little?" Mike asked Ron.

"No, but I'll have another one."

"Okay, big guy. I'm not gonna argue with you, now that you're a prizefighter."

Mike fixed another drink while Mary set up a buffet line on the island—the roast, a large bowl of peeled white potatoes, whole carrots, sweet onions, and a bowl of horseradish sauce. She asked Mike to set out water and pour wine. Then out came the rolls. She put them in a basket, and set a stick of butter and a knife beside them.

"Oh, that smell! Roast beef and warm rolls!" Ron said with a hungry air.

Wilma asked if it was time to call the kids. Mary said yes, and the children soon appeared in the kitchen. Mary served up plates, which the children took to the basement, Wilma carrying their drinks down behind them. Once Wilma returned, she and Ron bowed their heads for a moment of silent grace. Mike and Mary joined them.

"Well, here we are," Mike said, once grace had been said. "Let's have a toast." He raised his glass, looking at Ron, Wilma, and Mary. "To our lifelong friendship. May we never be divided."

"I'll drink to that," Ron said. "To us."

All four raised their glasses and took a sip.

"Well, Ron, have you heard anything about what happened to Jimmy Clay and his gang?" Mike asked.

"Nothing new. They were charged with first-degree attempted murder, which carries the same penalties as first-degree murder. They're still being held without bail. I guess they could get the death penalty. Wilma doesn't believe in that. I used to agree with her, but after getting thrown down that well, frankly, I wouldn't care if these guys got the max."

"I just want them put away for a long time," Wilma said.

"We're with you, Wilma," Mike said. "We're against the death penalty. We don't think vengeance is justice, and we don't believe in 'an eye for an eye and a tooth for a tooth.'"

"And the appeals take ten or twenty years, which is hard on the victims' families and expensive for the state," Mary added.

"So you all think I should've turned the other cheek and let Jimmy throw me down the well a second time."

Wilma ignored him. "Most people I know are against it. There have been so many cases where the system has been prejudiced against blacks, where blacks don't get good representation and get the death sentence for the same crimes that white criminals just get prison time. And look at all the cases where they've convicted people and found out later they were innocent. Thank goodness for DNA testing."

Ron looked away from Wilma and shook his head. "I don't think there's any question that Jimmy and his buddies are guilty."

"I just hope the prosecutors don't do something stupid that will let them off," Mike said.

Ron shrugged. "They have plenty of evidence. Sam thinks it's an open-and-shut case with my testimony and Annie's and the testimony of the old guy that works for Jimmy at the garage. Consider all the physical evidence—the DNA on the well cover, the footprints around the well, the tire iron in the well, and all that neo-Nazi stuff in the basement."

"But they never did confess, did they?" Mike said.

"Nope. They're a tough bunch."

"They're just punks," Mary said.

They consumed the dinner with pleasure. Everyone had second helpings.

~

Mike dished out ice cream for the children, and they went right back to the basement. Next, he spooned champagne-flavored sorbet into small bowls and put three tubular cookies in each. The adults took their desserts to the living part of the great room. The furniture was in a U-shape with a twelve-foot sofa facing the stone fireplace. Two-story windows on each side of the fireplace looked onto the woods. An eight-foot sofa lined up with one stack of windows. Two stuffed easy chairs with a lamp table between them were on the other side. The upholstery fabric of the furniture resembled Mayan quilts. Ron and Wilma sat at opposite ends of the long sofa, Mike in a chair near Ron, and Mary on the other sofa near Wilma.

"Oh, I forgot to tell you all," Mary chirped. "My dad looked at store sites with Alfred, and he's working with him on a business plan. He's sure they can put something together and get him a store around here."

"That's wonderful," Wilma said.

"How did he feel about riding around with a black man?" Ron said.

"He said it felt a little strange, but he knew Alfred was a friend of ours. He knows that things are changing around here, and he needs to respond to the market. 'Business is business,' he said."

"Let's hear it for the almighty dollar," Mike said, "the great leveler."

"And here's to Mary's dad," Ron said. "Mike, can you get me another scotch so I can drink a toast to Mary's dad?"

"Sure thing, big guy. Anyone else?"

"I'll have some more wine," Mary said.

"Another diet cola, please," Wilma said.

"I'll help you," Ron offered. He and Mike walked to the kitchen island.

"So what did you find in that diary?" Mike asked Ron.

Mary heard him from across the room. "What diary?" she asked.

Ron saw her staring at him, awaiting his response.

"Jeremiah Clay's. I picked it up in Jimmy Clay's basement."

"So what did it say?" Mike asked.

"Not what I hoped. There's a lot of stuff in it about the prices of tobacco and wheat, and Teddy Roosevelt, and how farmers couldn't get good field hands. And every day there were notes on what he read in the newspaper. Lots about lynchings."

"Yeah, but what about the lynching here?" Mike said.

"He mentions it in the December entries. His account agrees with the newspaper. He doesn't admit to having any part in it and doesn't implicate any of his family. Now I'm reading it from the beginning looking for clues. I'm still sure he had something to do with it."

"He must have," Mike said.

"I suppose I won't ever find out exactly what happened. Like whether Thomas really owed the store more money than he thought, whether he really did assault Agnes. But it's damned hard to believe."

"It's time to forget about it. Let it go, just be glad you're alive," Wilma said.

"I know. I just hate to quit without proving that Thomas was innocent. But I will if I hit a dead end. I've already started thinking about other things."

"What, like me and the kids?" Wilma kidded.

"Honey, this *is* all about us and the kids—and black pride."

"You're sure it's not about Ron's ego?"

"Ooooh," Mike hooted.

Mike and Ron brought the drinks back and sat down.

"I see you have lots of new things on the walls," Ron observed.

"Yes," Mike replied. "We spent several hours this morning hanging pictures."

"Wilma and I did that a few weeks ago," Ron said.

"We finally hung the family pictures too."

"Oh, I'd like to see those. I want to see if you have any people of color in your family."

"Hard to say. I'll let you decide for yourself. You can study their complexions. The pictures are over there." Mike showed him the photos, hanging along a wall several feet behind the big sofa.

"I have my light meter right here in my pocket."

"Start here. That's my mom and dad, Bob and Dottie. And here we all are with Randy and Lonnie, you met them all at the crab feast. And here are my grandfather and grandmother on my dad's side with all their kids.

"Definitely a lack of melanin," Ron said.

"Here's Mary's mom and dad, Beth and Frank, with me and Mary, and Mary's sister, Heather, and her husband, Greg. Bored yet?"

"Getting there. No black folk I can see with the naked eye."

"And here's Mary's granny and her husband, on Mary's mom's side, and her grandparents on her dad's side. They all look white to me."

"So that's Margaret, the one who died in 1985?" Ron asked. "The one who painted and was real close to Mary?"

"I think so. I never met her. Mary, is this your granny Margaret, the painter?"

"Yes, that's her."

"I just wanted to put a face on your story, Mary. Thanks."

She and Wilma resumed their conversation.

"And these are some prehistoric relatives of Mary's who died a hundred million years ago," Mike continued. "I don't know who they are."

Ron looked at the next picture. Something caught his eye. "That girl," he said, pointing to a young girl. "Who's she?"

"Mary, Ron wants to know who this girl is in this picture."

Mary looked across the room. "Oh, that's Margaret again, when she was a girl, along with her mom and dad and brother and sister. Why?"

"I've seen that girl before," Ron said slowly.

"What?" Mike said. "Where?"

"I ... I saw her in that picture ... in the basement ... at the Clays." Ron spoke softly. "She's the one with the braids and the freckles."

Mike bent toward the picture, studying the little girl. "It, uh ... it, uh ... I guess it does kind of look like her."

"And that little blond boy next to her," Ron said. "Who's he?"

"That's her brother, Luke. My grandmother's brother," Mary answered from across the room. "Why are you so interested in them?"

"What in the world are you two talking about?" Wilma asked.

"Ron thinks he recognizes the kids in this picture—Mary's grandmother and her brother," Mike said.

"Well, that's weird," Mary replied, puzzled. "Where do you think you saw their pictures before?"

"They were ... well, I don't know how to say this. They were in the picture of the lynching, Mary." He watched her turn red.

"What?" Wilma said, rising and walking to the picture.

"She was ... at the lynching. I can't forget her. Her face was turned back toward the camera. She looked scared and maybe even a little ashamed. It's her. I'm sure of it. And that blond boy may have been the one next to her in the picture."

"Ronald Watkins. How can you be so certain it was her?"

Mary looked at Ron nervously but made no denials, gave no information.

"I'm sorry, Wilma, but ... I'm just sure I'm right. And this man in back of her, the old man next to him in the center. My God, I think they were in that other picture in Jimmy's basement ... on the wall at the end of the table. They look like—you know what, I have that postcard of the lynching at home. I took it off the table in the basement. It's the same picture. I'll go get it."

Mary's shoulders drooped. Her eyes filled with tears. "You don't need to do that, Ron." She put her hands together, elbows stiff, and began pacing in front of the fireplace. "You're right. Granny was there, she and her brother."

"Was her brother the blond-haired boy?" Ron asked.

"Yes. Luke. That was his name. They were both there."

"What?" Mike cried. "At the lynching? Did Granny tell you that?"

"Yes. They were both there. Granny told me about it."

"I can't believe you never told me about that," Mike said. "What else did she tell you?"

"I'll tell you. I'll tell you all about it. Please, everyone, sit down. I'll tell you." They sat and stared expectantly at her.

"Granny was there at the lynching," Mary said, wringing her hands. "So was her brother, Luke. Their parents made her and Luke come. They went over the morning after the actual murder. Granny said that word had spread all over the county that a man was hanging from the big oak. People came from everywhere. They even cancelled school so the children could come see it."

"Lord, Lord," Wilma said.

"But who were the two men in your family picture?" Ron asked.

"The younger man was Granny's father, and the older man with the horseshoe moustache and cavalry hat was her grandfather."

"And what were they doing in the picture in Jimmy Clay's basement?" Mike asked. Mary looked out the window by the fireplace.

"What were their names?" Ron asked.

She turned toward Ron. "Her father's name was Manley Strickland."

"Strickland?" Mike said. "Where have I heard that name before?"

"That was Agnes's last name," Ron replied. "You know, the bookkeeper at the store."

"Were they related?" Mike said.

"Yes, yes, yes," Mary cried, tears rolling down her face. "Granny's mother was Agnes Strickland."

"Agnes was the one who accused Thomas of assaulting her," Ron said. "And her daughter was Margaret? Your granny?"

"Yes, that's right," Mary said.

"And Agnes was Jeremiah Clay's daughter?" Ron asked.

"Yes, Agnes was Jeremiah Clay's daughter."

"So you're related to Jeremiah Clay," Mike said.

"Yes!" Mary cried, her face anguished. "Jeremiah Clay was my great-great-grandfather."

"And that means you're related to Jimmy and Annie Clay," Ron said.

"Yes, yes. They're fourth or fifth cousins—I don't know."

"Why didn't you tell us?"

"Well, do you think I'm proud of all this? I'm so ashamed of it all I can hardly stand it!" She sobbed and shook.

Wilma put her arm around her, and guided her back to the sofa.

"Do you know them—Annie and Jimmy?" Ron asked.

"Leave her alone," Wilma said. "Stop badgering her."

Mike pulled out a handkerchief and gave it to Mary.

Between sobs, Mary spoke. "It's okay, Wilma. You all have a right to know about this. I … I went to high school with Jimmy and Annie, but I never spoke to them. My mother told me they were not the kind of people our family associated with. I've only been in the store a few times in my whole life."

Ron looked her suspiciously, his head cocked to the side. "Did you know you were related to them?"

"Distantly, yes."

"What about Jimmy? Did he know you were related?"

"I don't think so. At least he never let on that he did."

"Did you see them much after high school?" Mike asked.

"No. I went off to Maryland and lived on campus."

"But you heard some things about them."

"Correct. I heard about their parents getting killed in that wreck—their father was driving drunk. And I heard that Annie went kind of wild with boys after that, and that Jimmy got mean and did a lot of drinking like his father did. Then every once in a while there would be a rumor—from people who went to the store, I guess—about Jimmy abusing Annie. But I didn't know he was dangerous. I didn't know he was a neo-Nazi."

Ron wasn't satisfied. He shook his head, his eyes on the floor. "Why didn't you tell us about this?"

"She said she was too ashamed," Wilma said.

"I would have told everyone if I had known he was dangerous, Ron," Mary said, looking up at him. "I swear I would have!"

"She warned us about him, Ron," Wilma said. "She told me that Jimmy was mean and that you should stay away from him, and I told you she told me that, but you didn't listen."

"I know. I didn't listen."

"That's because he thinks he's immortal," Wilma explained facetiously.

"He thinks no trespassing signs mean, 'Welcome! Come on in'," Mike joked.

"You can't blame Mary for anything, Ron," Wilma said.

Ron held Mary in a steady gaze. "I don't blame her a bit."

"You better not, Ron Watkins," Wilma said.

"I know, I know. I'm sorry, Mary, if you thought I was blaming you."

"That's okay, Ron," she gasped with a sob. But Ron thought he saw a stony glint in her eye. *I wonder,* he thought.

He stood up and circled the end of the sofa.

"But I'm still trying to figure out how the lynching happened … Did your granny tell you any more about the lynching, you know, what led up to it and all?"

"Ron, stop," Wilma pleaded angrily.

"It's okay," Mary said. "Yes, we talked about it a few times. I had just graduated from high school when she told me about it. It's so horrible … You see, it all goes back to 1899, when Jeremiah's wife

Elizabeth convinced him to sell one of his tenant farms to her brother, Harley Archer. Granny said that Jeremiah knew Harley was a drinker, didn't like him, didn't want him as a neighbor, and figured he would fail. But he figured that if Harley did fail, he could then buy back the property for less than he had sold it to him for."

"Real nice," Mike scoffed.

"We can't pick our parents, and we sure can't pick our ancestors, honey," Mary said.

"This was part of Spring Hill Farm?" Ron asked.

"Yes. It included the house at the bottom where the Clays live now, but I think the parcel was a lot bigger than what Jimmy and Annie have now."

"Yes, it was," Ron said. "I searched the deed on the property. It said the original farm was thirty-seven acres, but before Jimmy and Annie got it, Jeremiah and his descendants sold off thirty-two of them."

Mary's face showed surprise at Ron's having such detailed information about her family.

"So what happened?" Mike asked.

"Well, Granny said that everyone said Harley was lazy and drank a lot. But if he missed some payments, it wouldn't matter because Elizabeth's father would give him some money. Her father had plenty."

"So, did he default?" Mike asked.

"Yes. He quit paying. But Jeremiah's plan didn't work out the way he thought. Harley hated Jeremiah, and instead of selling the farm back to him, Harley found a buyer's agent and sold the farm through him. He even sold it for more money than he paid Jeremiah to buy it."

"I bet that made Jeremiah mad," Mike said.

"Yes, but what really made him furious was that the agent bought it for a black man. For Thomas Phillips."

"Oh!" Wilma said.

"Thomas borrowed the money for the purchase from his father, Henry."

"My great-great-grandfather."

Ron moved to the counter and shoveled some cold crab hors d'oeuvres into his mouth. "So that's how we got the land ... but wait, how did Granny know all this? She was just a little girl then."

"She said she overheard her mother talking to Jeremiah. Later on, when she was older, Melinda, the family housekeeper, told her that Jeremiah had started plotting right away how to get the farm back. He simply could not stand to have a black farmer live right next to him on his old land."

"How neighborly. So what did Jeremiah do? Start harassing Thomas and his family, to get him to sell out?"

"No. Granny said he couldn't do that because both Thomas and his father were known in the area as 'good Negroes,' who were honest and worked hard and treated white people with deference and respect—although that wasn't what Granny's mother called them."

"What was that?"

"She referred to them as 'new niggers'—'the wild, uppity kind that couldn't be controlled and didn't know their place.'"

Ron shook his head.

"Mary, where did Henry Phillips get the money to lend to Thomas for buying the farm?" Mike asked.

"Melinda told Granny that Henry had steady work on the railroad and saved his money, even gave Thomas an interest-free loan."

"So what did Jeremiah do?" Ron asked.

"Well, Jeremiah had heard that a company was planning to build an electric trolley line through the area, from Washington to Baltimore. He went to the county seat and to Annapolis and talked to some friends. Tried to convince them that if the right-of-way was coming nearby, it should pass through his land but not through Thomas's farm."

"Figures."

"But he failed, partly. The right-of-way went through both of their farms, and stations were planned near both properties—where the trolley crossed Big Oak Road and Spring Hill Road. Both farmers received a payment from the trolley company. That made Jeremiah even madder, the prospect that Thomas might make money by selling lots near the station, might even sell lots to blacks. And Jeremiah wanted that money—he thought it was his right, his money—so naturally, he wanted Thomas's farm back even more."

"So what was his next plan?"

"At first, he hoped to buy Thomas out when the farm failed. After all, Thomas was young and had no experience running a farm. The problem was that Thomas did well. He grew corn, raised hogs, smoked hams—which all brought a good price. Sold chickens, eggs, and vegetables too. Thomas had a lot of kids—I think Granny said nine— and they all worked about as soon as they could walk. But Thomas didn't raise tobacco. It wasn't profitable anymore, because it took too much labor."

"Interesting," Mike said.

"How did you learn all of this?" Ron asked.

"Just listening to Granny talk about it, over and over."

"Granny knew the older children in Thomas's family. She said she and her brother and sister used to sneak down and play with them in the woods, at least while they were growing up. Granny knew she wasn't supposed to play with 'pickaninnies' because they were black and dumber than sticks—that's what her mother said—and they were black because they were dirty, and they didn't go to school with white children because they couldn't learn anything. Granny's mother said they were just like mules."

"Just like mules. Dumber than sticks, huh?" Ron said.

"But Granny said that she and her brother Luke were down at the woods one day and they saw some of the Phillips kids peeking at them from the bushes, so she and Luke hid from them to show how stupid they were. But in a few minutes they saw the Phillips kids looking at them again. None of them smiled; they just looked. So Granny and Luke ran away and hid again. Before long, those kids were looking at them again, this time with little grins on their faces.

So they ran and hid again. But this time, the Phillips kids didn't come, and she and Luke laughed about how dumb the black kids were. Then Granny and Luke decided to go looking for *them*, so they could sneak up and scare them. They snuck around through the bushes pretending they were Indians, lifting their feet high and putting them down in the leaves as quietly as mice. But they couldn't find them. Then suddenly, out of the bushes, the Phillipses leaped up and hollered and waved their arms. Scared her and Luke half to death. And they did that again and again. Granny said they would play hide-and-seek for hours. Later on, they did it right, by turning their backs and counting out loud to a hundred so fast that no one could understand what they were saying. Sometimes Granny and the older Phillips boy would run and hide from the little kids and jump out at them. The older boy's name was George. She said he was big and strong, dark, and a year older than her."

"Kids will be kids," Wilma observed.

"Some time later, Granny found out that the older kids could read and write and do arithmetic. They went to their own school when they weren't needed in the fields. Once she asked George what six times seven was, to stump him. He shook his head and said, 'I sure don't know that one, missy, 'cept I do think I 'member someone told me once it was forty-two.'"

"Ha!" Ron chuckled.

"Granny was shocked."

"Sly devil," Mike said.

"I didn't think blacks had schools then," Ron said.

"They didn't have many," Mike said, "because white people were afraid they'd want social equality if they were educated."

Ron looked back at Mary. "So what else did Granny say?"

"One time she snuck a checkerboard down to the woods and taught George how to play. Granny said she beat him several times. Then he started beating her."

"Yes!"

"Then he started letting her win, but she knew it and got mad, told him not to do it."

"Most women I play with want you to let them win," Ron said.

"Ha!" Mike said.

"What women do you play with besides me?" Wilma asked.

"I'll never tell."

"Hmm. So did Granny's mother ever find out she was playing with the Phillips kids?" Wilma asked.

"She probably had her suspicions. Then one day, when Granny was older, she was riding one of Jeremiah's horses through the field near the woods. The horse stepped in a hole, fell down, threw her, and then ran home. She hit her head and shoulder hard, was knocked unconscious. The next thing she knew, she saw a big black man kneeling over her. He was patting her forehead with a wet cloth. Behind him stood young George. She squealed and tried to get away but couldn't make her body respond. It was George and his father, Thomas, who were caring for her. Thomas asked her if she was badly hurt.

"Granny could feel a sharp pain in her shoulder and another on her forehead, and she pointed to them. Thomas suspected that she had a broken collarbone in addition to the nasty bump on her head. He used George's shirt to make a sling for her arm, and they went down the path through the woods to the Phillipses' house. Granny said George's mother was hoeing the garden, but ran to their side when she saw them. Mr. Phillips asked his wife to take Granny home in the wagon—he didn't want his neighbors to see Granny with black men—and urged her to say that his wife, Becky, had found her and helped her, not he and George. So Mrs. Phillips took Granny home and told Agnes about the accident. Granny didn't know why she had to lie, but she did. Her mother looked at Mrs. Phillips and Granny like they were lying. She always said that niggers lied all the time anyway. But the important thing was that Margaret was home safe.

"Agnes told Granny later that Becky Phillips had been offered a job as the Stricklands' nanny, but had turned the position down—a rejection that led Manley and Agnes to conclude the Phillipses were uppity. But George told Granny that his mother just needed to work on the farm and take care of her own children and that his father didn't want her around white men."

"Good for Thomas," Ron said. "He wouldn't let Becky work in that house."

"Did Granny stay away from the Phillips kids after that?" Mike said.

"Mostly. But once, about a year later, she was out riding General Jeb—one of Jeremiah's best horses—and saw George down by the woods. She offered to let him ride but didn't tell him whose horse it was. He climbed up behind her, put his arms around her, took the reins, and off they went across the meadow. I remember what Granny said: 'Oh, George could make Jeb fly,' she said. 'Fly!' After that Granny and George had many conversations together."

"Uh-oh," Wilma said.

"Did the Phillipses have any horses of their own?" Mike asked.

"No, just a mule and wagon," Mary said. "No horse, no buggy. They were too poor."

"Did the family ever catch Granny with George?" Wilma asked.

"Yes, but not until much later. One day, Jeremiah was riding in one of the far fields and saw Granny standing by Jeb, talking to George at the tree line. He shouted at her to come. George ran off into the woods, and Granny rode to her grandfather. Jeremiah laid down the law to her, said she was never to speak to that boy again, told her that black men were animals, that they would hurt her and do mean things to her, and maybe even kill her and take her clothes and dump her body in the crick. Granny cried. She knew George would never hurt her. He was her friend."

"How old were they then?" Wilma asked.

"Granny was twelve, and George thirteen, I think, when Jeremiah caught them."

"Almost old enough," Mike said. "What happened then?"

"She rode behind Jeremiah all the way to her home, which was on the next farm over. When they got there, Jeremiah talked to Agnes, and she took Granny to the bedroom and lit into her, telling her the same thing Jeremiah did, except she added something. She said that nigger men wanted to force their things into white girls and make them have black babies. And then the white girls would have to kill themselves because no white man would want them after that. I guess that shocked Granny because she didn't see George after that."

"Lord, Lord," Wilma said.

"Can we go back a minute, Mary?" Mike interjected. "I'm curious about how Thomas got so good at farming. Didn't you say his father worked on the railroad?"

"Yes, I think he was a Pullman porter. But Granny said Thomas's wife was from a farm family, and Thomas had worked on farms when he was growing up. I think he must have learned a lot from black farmers he talked to—tenant farmers and sharecroppers and the like."

"Interesting," Ron said. "So what happened next?"

"Well, I guess it really made Jeremiah mad to see Thomas prosper. So he decided to try to get his farm back by getting Thomas hooked on credit at the store. He told his son John to be friendly to him and offer him credit. Jeremiah knew that if he could get Thomas to buy on credit, he might be able to gradually get him into a position where he couldn't quit buying from the store and would get deeper and deeper in debt. Eventually Thomas would have to sell out to Jeremiah, if it worked."

"Peonage," Mike spat.

"Sort of," Mary continued, "except the goal was to get him to sell, not keep him working. But things didn't end up the way Jeremiah wanted."

"What happened?" Mike said.

"Thomas would hardly buy anything at the store. The Phillipses kept a dairy cow for milk and butter, grew their own vegetables and fruits and canned them to eat them over the winter, and ate a lot of corn and cornbread and bacon they smoked themselves and eggs from their own chickens. Sometimes they bought a little sugar, flour, salt, and soda to rub on the hams, and occasional articles of clothing. But they were frugal and always paid with cash. In winter, they sold firewood to neighbors, and they were always bringing around pies and jellies to the door and selling ham and bacon at the store.

"It wasn't until 1907 that they ran into a string of bad luck. Their cow died in the winter and they had to buy another one. Then there was a late, wet spring. Heavy rain washed out their garden and a lot of their corn. Thomas had to buy more seed and fertilizer from the store to replant. When they were making hay late in the summer, it rained more, and a lot of the hay got moldy in the field. He ended up having to buy hay instead of selling it to other farmers. He even had to buy some cornmeal and food at the store."

"On credit?" Mike said.

"Yes. He finally gave in."

"The slippery slope," Ron said.

"And at the end of the year, just before Christmas, Thomas came into the store. Granny's Uncle John asked him when would be a good time to talk about his account, since they had to close the books for the year. Thomas said, 'Any time's all right with me, Mr. John'—at least that's what Granny said he said."

"How did she know what Thomas said?" Ron asked.

"She was in the store helping her mother stock shelves. Agnes was the bookkeeper for the store, but did lots of other things, too."

"More scotch?" Mike said to Ron.

"I'm fine," Ron said, his eyes fixed on Mary.

"So what happened then?" Ron said.

Mary slumped a little. She took a deep breath. "Granny said that her mother brought her Uncle John the ledger book. Her uncle went over each item in Thomas's account quickly and gave him the total. Then Thomas turned and looked at Granny, who was standing across the room, and stared straight at her with a big grin on his face, rocking his head back and forth. He started talking rapidly, like he was agitated, but all the while grinning. He said in a polite tone that there must be a mistake, that he couldn't have spent that much, that he knew he hadn't. But he did not take his eyes off Granny. It was like he knew she was a good child and a friend of his family, that she would believe him even if no one else did."

"I wonder how that made Granny feel?" Wilma said.

"In fact, she told me she was really uncomfortable with him staring at her like that, this man who'd been so nice to her when she broke her collarbone and whose son was her friend. Here he was grinning and staring like a madman."

"God," Ron said.

"Then her Uncle John slammed the book and said, 'That's what the book says and that's what you owe.' Thomas glared at Agnes, the one who kept the books, and swung his head back toward Granny and spoke the unspeakable. She would never forget it. Through gritted teeth, he said 'Ah got my own book, and Ah wrote down ever'thing in it, and Ah knows what Ah owes, and that's way more than Ah owes.' Granny said his face was horrible—all distorted—a mixture of mirth and hate."

"Mm, mm," Wilma murmured at the story's tension.

"Granny didn't know what made her uncle madder—Thomas looking at her like that, or questioning Agnes's figures, or saying that he had his own books. Of course that wouldn't have mattered because black people couldn't testify in court against a white person. But whatever it was, her uncle flew into a hateful rage, screaming at Thomas that he was a lying, thieving, ungrateful, disrespectful, biggety nigger. That no black brute was going to look at his niece like that with lust pouring out of him and call his sister a liar like that, and that Thomas better get out of the store right then before he took out his pistol and shot him dead on the spot."

"Oh, Lord Jesus," Wilma said.

"Always the lust," Ron muttered. "But what really happened is that Thomas caught him dead in a lie and called him on it."

"I guess we know what happened next," Mike said.

"What did Granny say happened?" Ron asked.

"Well, she said that Thomas did indeed run out of the store and down the lane to his house. And then her uncle told her she didn't have to be afraid—that nigger would never get a hold of her—he'd see to that. And then he told her mother that they better go talk to Father about it, that Uncle John knew what he wanted to do, but Father had the say. So they locked up the store, hitched the horse to the wagon, and rode up the hill to see Jeremiah.

"When they got there, he was on the porch. Agnes told Granny to go inside. Granny could tell that she was really angry. And Granny did go inside, but she hid by a window to the porch so she could eavesdrop and peek out."

"What did they say?" Mike asked.

"Uncle John told Jeremiah how they had gone over the books with Thomas, just like they had talked about, but then Thomas had denied it, explained that he kept his own books, while staring at Margaret and briefly at Agnes.

"Granny heard her grandfather say, 'Keeps his own books, does he?' and watched as he bent over and let a lip full of tobacco juice slaver into his spit can. Then he said something like 'That's what happens when you let them go to school—they start keeping their own books. And then they say your books are wrong. But it doesn't matter because no one would take the word of a nigger over a white man or woman anyway.'

"Uncle John told him he was afraid what Thomas might do to Agnes, since he as much as called her a liar, and Uncle John also said he was afraid what Thomas might do to Margaret, the way he kept staring at her with that crazy smile on his face.

"Agnes told Jeremiah that Thomas was so mad she was terrified he would do something violent, especially since they tried to overcharge his account—"

"There," Ron said. "Agnes admitted they tried to cheat him."

"Yes, she did," Mary said. "And then she said she wanted something done about Thomas. She was a woman, and she expected her men to do right by her and to protect her and her children from these beasts. Because if they didn't do something, that angry, vengeful nigger might just find them in their beds at night and ravage and murder them both. She expected the men to do something to keep that from happening."

"Nice," Ron said. "Who was giving the orders here?"

"Granny said that's when she saw her grandfather's jaw set. He said he knew it was going to come to this with Thomas, and it was time to do something about these brutes, that they were taking more and more license, doing whatever they wanted, acting white. He said it was time to make an example of one of them, and he didn't care how many people thought Thomas was a good nigger, that sometimes it's best to get rid of a good one to let all of them—good and bad alike—know that it could happen to them, too. And that we shouldn't forget that he's sitting right on our land that he swindled out of us by buying from that crooked agent. Jeremiah said that it was time to show those niggers working on the railroad and trolley line, and them with all the jobs in Washington, and every field hand and sharecropper in the countryside—it was time to show them who is master and who is slave. And that everyone should remember how the niggers ran wild in those riots in Atlanta and how the whites had to put them down and show them who was in charge. Granny said there was a big riot in Atlanta in 1906 with lots of blacks killed and buildings burned down."

"Mm, mm, mm," Wilma said.

"Then Grandfather told Uncle John—he said, 'John, it's time for a lynching,' and Uncle John said, 'Yes, sir, it is.' His father said for him to ride out and tell the neighbors what happened—that the nigger kept leering with his filthy eyes at Margaret, and when Agnes said something about it, he went after her, and thank goodness John was there to pull him off of her and run him off. He said tell them that it's time to teach these animals a lesson. He told Agnes to have her husband Manley get his rifle and grab a few neighbors, to ride down to Thomas's house and watch over it to make sure he didn't try to get away. Then he told Uncle John to spread the word to come after dark, bring their guns and wear grain sacks over their heads, if they want. The plan was to take Thomas at about ten o'clock at night. They wanted as many as possible to show these niggers what happens when they attack our women, and so there would be no trouble if the sheriff showed up."

"So they didn't tell anyone about Thomas questioning his account at the store?" Ron asked.

"No."

"They wanted to touch the hot button," Ron said. "It was rape or attempted rape that set everyone off."

"Did Granny say how she felt about all this?" Wilma said.

"Oh yes. She was terrified that they would kill him. She couldn't believe that they were going to lie to everyone about what happened and use her as part of the excuse for whatever they were going to do to Thomas. That made her mad, she said.

"But her grandma Elizabeth came into the room, and accused her of eavesdropping. Agnes heard their voices and was through the front door in an instant. Grandma Elizabeth told Agnes that she'd found Margaret listening through the window, and her mother scolded Granny. She and her mother drove home, and Agnes talked to her about how she was going to have to be punished for spying on adults like that.

"When they got home, Agnes spoke to Granny's father, but Granny didn't know what they said. She knew her little brother Luke wondered what was happening; he was too young to understand. Through the window, Granny saw her father leave the house with his rifle, go to the barn, and ride out on his horse.

"Granny was really frightened and mixed up. She guessed that Thomas had done something really bad, but she also knew that her mother was not telling the truth about everything. She wanted to be obedient to her parents, but she also wanted to warn George's family, to tell Thomas to run away. So she opened her bedroom door a crack and told her mother that she wanted to feed the horses in the barn, but her mother forbade it."

"So Granny stayed in her room?" Ron asked.

"Yes. She thought about slipping out the window and just running to Thomas's farm, but she was already in trouble and was really afraid of what her parents might do if she disobeyed them now. And she still thought they might be right."

"Couldn't she tell her brother to go?" Ron said.

"He was too young," Mary said. "And she didn't want to get him in trouble. No, if anything was to be done, she would have to do it herself."

"So how long did she have to stay in her room?" Ron said.

"At dinner time she could smell the food cooking and she opened the door, but her mother told her that her next meal was breakfast."

"That was mean," Wilma said.

"I think Agnes wanted to make sure that Granny stayed in her room until it was all over," Mary said.

"Did she?" Ron asked.

"Yes. She cried herself to sleep. The next thing she remembered was sitting bolt upright at the sound of rifles going off in the distance. Then she remembered tossing and turning because she couldn't sleep, and then her father riding in and talking to her mother. He was loud and braggy, and Granny thought that he had been drinking.

"Then Granny heard him say what she had feared. 'It's done. That uppity nigger's hanging from the big oak for everyone to see, with more holes in him than a beehive.' That Agnes should have seen him grovel and beg down in the basement while his nigger woman and all them little pickaninnies were just screaming and wailing. That Jeremiah's son Matthew and his son Christopher held her back and John took out his whip and put the lash to him and told him to tell the truth, that he did look at Margaret with lust and did attack Mrs. Strickland. And Thomas said, 'No.' John whipped him until the skin on his back was sliced to ribbons, and he finally admitted it: 'Yes! I did it. Jus' don't hit me no mo'.' Little did he realize his false confession was only the beginning of his suffering. They dragged him outside and threw him down. Thomas wasn't halfway up before John shot him in the leg. John bragged to Agnes about asking the crowd, 'What do we do with a rapist brute that tries to run?' Someone in the crowd had shouted 'Shoot him!' And a couple of shots were fired, hitting Thomas in the arm and side. Then a sudden fusillade riddled him. And then it was over, and Uncle John told how he had tied a noose around Thomas's neck. And while he did that, some folks started cutting off pieces of him for souvenirs—fingers and toes and such—and then someone reached inside his pants and cut off his 'you-know-what'—that was Granny's term, not her father's. And John finished his triumphant story: they dragged Thomas's body behind a horse up the hill to the road, threw the rope over that big limb that hangs out over the road, and pulled the body up in the air so that everybody could see it."

Ron, Mike, and Wilma were silent. Then Ron spoke. "How many were in the mob?"

"Granny said over a hundred—maybe two hundred in the mob that lynched him."

"Farmers, doctors, preachers, lawyers, teachers, cops," Ron bitterly said.

"She didn't say, but I guess a lot of these lynch mobs included prominent people."

"So what happened with your granny?" Wilma asked.

"She couldn't stand any more of the awful story. She ran out of her bedroom toward her father, and started beating on him with her fists. Then her mother grabbed her from behind. 'You stop that. Your father didn't kill him—the mob did, and they did it to protect you and me from that animal!' Granny told her mother that it was a lie. Agnes slapped Granny so hard across the face that she knocked her down. 'Don't ever say that again!' she said. 'You remember how that nigger looked at you. Remember that! And you remember that those niggers hate us, and that they will hurt us if we don't keep them in their place.

And you remember that you're a Clay and a Strickland, and you are white!'

"Granny said that in the morning they made her put on her Sunday clothes—her plaid dress with long sleeves and lace down the front—and Agnes did her braids so they were neat and tight. Her father hitched the horses to the surrey, helped Agnes and the children up, climbed up himself, and took the reins wearing his black suit and fedora. Agnes sat beside him in a full-length dress suit, cape, and fancy dress hat. Granny sat with her brother in the back. Agnes told her that if anyone asked her what happened in the store, she should say that Thomas looked at her funny and made her afraid, and that she didn't want to talk about it.

"It was a warm and sunny December morning. Granny said they hadn't gone far when they found the road blocked with wagons and buggies and horses. Manley pulled to the side of the road, tied the horses to a tree, and helped the family down. They started walking up the road. As they came around the bend, there was the body—dangling from the thickest limb of the big oak tree. The black skin was covered with coagulated blood. All of the fingers and toes were gone, and the back was covered with maroon stripes. His head was bowed solemnly, as if in prayer, and his ears were missing. It didn't seem real to Granny. She wasn't even sure it was Thomas. But the more she dared look, the more certain she became."

"Did many people come?" Ron asked.

"To view the body? Granny said hundreds. She saw most of her friends from school, their parents, her minister, and storekeepers—but mostly people she didn't know—all around the tree, in front of the store, and at the intersection of the roads. Her Uncle John had opened the store and was doing a brisk business selling candy and soda pop from the fountain. Granny said people were smiling and pointing and laughing. It was like a circus, but Granny could hardly keep from crying. Lots of people were taking pictures, mostly with small box cameras. She heard her name spoken behind her, then someone called, 'Margaret.' As she looked back, someone kneeling snapped her picture. She wandered through the crowd, and a boy shouted at her, 'Hey, Margaret. Did that nigger try to get you?' Granny stared at his grinning face and dutifully told him, 'He looked at me funny and it made me afraid, but I don't want to talk about it.'"

"Did Granny and her family stay long?" Wilma asked.

"Yes. It seemed like her mother and father had to talk to everyone there. Spin control, I guess. But after asking her mother, for the second time, if they could go soon, she asked if she could go back to the horses, and her mother agreed. So Granny walked through the crowd and down the road through the wagons and buggies. She passed the driveway to Thomas's house and glanced into the woods.

"There stood George. His face was swollen from crying, but he stood strong and erect. Granny looked at him and erupted into tears. Sobbing and shaking, she leaned back against a wagon, holding on with both hands. Again her eyes fell upon George, tall and somber. Her head waved back and forth. Then his eyes filled, and he began walking toward her. She turned and ran back up the hill into the crowd. She loved that boy, Granny said, but to cross the line with him was to kill him."

"Oh Lord," Wilma said.

Mike rose. "Anyone need a refill?" Mary asked for a cold bottle of water.

"I'll take ginger ale this time," Ron said. "Straight."

"Coming right up."

Mike walked to the kitchen and Ron turned his attention back to Mary.

"Is there more?" Ron asked.

"I'm afraid so. Granny said that after the lynching, her grandfather filed a lawsuit against the estate of Thomas Phillips, and the court awarded a judgment for the amount of Jeremiah's claim and ordered Thomas's property to be sold at auction."

"What then?"

"By the day of the auction, Thomas's family had moved out of the house. Jeremiah and Granny's father and uncles and some others came, and they all brought weapons with them—guns, clubs, and whips."

"Were any of Thomas's family there?"

"No. Granny was sure they were afraid to come. Hardly anyone came except Clays."

Mike handed Ron his soft drink. Ron thanked him without taking his attention from Mary.

"Did any black people come?"

"No."

"Was the auction advertised?" Mike asked.

"I don't know. She said there was a small sign about it on Big Oak Road at the top of Thomas's driveway."

"Was your granny there?" Wilma asked.

"Yes. They made her go. She stood in the back. She said that everything was in piles in front of the house, separated for inventorying— tools and farm equipment, wagon and harnesses, kitchen utensils, furniture, and so on."

"So how did the bidding go?" Ron asked.

"It was over in a few minutes. Jeremiah bid twenty dollars and the auctioneer awarded him the farm."

"Twenty dollars?" Ron was incredulous.

"That's what he asked for."

"Enough to pay off what they said Thomas owed at the store," Ron said.

"So what happened?" Mike asked.

Mary looked at the floor. "Granny said Jeremiah barked, 'Twenty dollars.' Then he laughed and glanced at his sons with kind of a hard sneer, and walked toward his buggy, while the auctioneer was still saying 'Twenty dollars going once. Twenty dollars going twice. Sold to Jeremiah Clay for twenty dollars.'"

"There were no other bids?" Ron asked.

"No."

"None? Everyone else was afraid to bid?"

"No one else came to bid."

Ron folded his arms and began pacing. "It was robbery! He stole it back. The son of a bitch stole the farm from Thomas's family!"

"That's what Granny thought too."

They were silent for a moment. Then Ron asked, "Is there more to the story?"

"Not really," Mary said, "except that Granny more or less stopped talking to anyone after that. She said there was no one she could talk to. All she wanted to do was paint and play the piano. George was gone, and all she felt was helplessness and loneliness."

"But she did get married," Mike said, "or you wouldn't be here."

"Yes, eventually she did, but I think it was kind of a stoic relationship, on her part at least. I don't think she ever opened up to my grandfather and let him into her inner world. And he did not share her attitudes toward black people."

"Oh?" Ron said.

"He thought blacks were inferior to whites, and mixing should not be allowed. I think my mother may have absorbed some of his prejudices, too—she was her daddy's little girl."

"How do you remember all of this?" Wilma asked.

"I lived through these stories with Granny many times. It was our secret world. And I guess I've been holding it in and waiting to tell it for years and years. I'm sorry I never even shared it with you, Mike. But I was the only one Granny trusted to tell. My mom and dad don't know any of this. It was a part of Granny's life that she could talk about with me and never erase. It just lay in her belly like some monstrous cancer that kept growing and would never go away no matter how many beautiful paintings she did and no matter how many sonatas or fantasias she played. She spent the rest of her life regretting that day, wondering if things could have been different if she had run down that hill." Mary's head dropped to her chest. Then she looked up. "That's the end of it."

"What a story," Wilma said. "Sure seems to answer all the questions. It answered yours, didn't it, Ron?"

"Seems like it." He closed his eyes and rubbed them with his fingers before resuming his pacing. "But you all will have to forgive me if I'm still hot about the notion that Jeremiah murdered Thomas and then stole his farm from his family."

"You have good reason to be," Mary said.

"Calm down, honey," Wilma said.

"So Mary, what you're saying is that your grandmother was in love with one of my great-uncles."

"Yes, I think she was."

"Wow," Mike said. "Small world."

"And that makes us sort of like cousins, doesn't it?" Ron said.

"Brother, what are you talking about?" Wilma said.

"I'm just ranting a little—letting my mind wander through this maze."

"Stop," Wilma said.

Ron felt his body tense. He crossed his arms, crushed them against his chest, and grabbed his upper arms with his hands. "Oh—and yes!" he said. "Some things are certain: Mary's descended from the Clays. Mary's related to Annie and Jimmy. And Mary wasn't going to tell us about the lynching."

"What are you getting at, Ron?" Mike asked.

"I don't know. It just seems like a lot of white people conveniently forget the past."

"What?" Mike asked in disbelief.

"You know, there are too many pieces to the puzzle, and there are so many different shapes, and I'm not sure how they go together. But another I have now is that my family has a legal right to the Clays' property. Something else Mary wasn't going to tell us about."

"She told you everything, Ron, every detail," Mike said, "and I resent you implying that she didn't want you to know about that property."

"Mary," Ron said. "Did you try to hide this from me?"

"No, Ron, I didn't. I tried to tell you everything I know—everything I could remember of what Granny said."

"Every detail?"

"Ron," Wilma said angrily. "Maybe we should go home if you're going to act like this."

He felt like he was in the well again, floundering in icy water. "Wilma, look at the facts. First, she knows that I'm looking into this lynching, and she tells me nothing about it. Then she knows I'm trespassing on Jimmy Clay's land, and she knows how dangerous he is, but she says nothing."

"That's not true, Ron. I told Mike and Wilma to tell you to stay away from Jimmy, that he was mean. But I didn't know how dangerous he was—that he might try to kill you. You have no right to imply that I knew he was dangerous and didn't warn you."

"She's right, Ron," Mike said. "Absolutely."

"And then when I came up missing, she still wouldn't tell Wilma or Mike what she knew about Jimmy Clay."

"I already told you I didn't know how dangerous Jimmy was. I didn't even know them. We didn't associate with them, and all I heard about them was second- or third-hand."

"That's the truth, Ron," Mike said. "Back off."

"It just seems possible that she may be protecting Annie and Jimmy," Ron said, "and trying to help them keep what's left of the old estate. Isn't that right, Mary?"

"No, that's not right."

"Well, why didn't you tell me that your family stole that land from mine?"

Mary jumped up, put her left hand on her hip, and pointed at Ron with the right. "That was a hundred years ago! *A hundred years ago*! It's ancient history. Anyway, you don't have any legal right to that land."

"What?"

"You heard me. You have no proof of ownership. No proof that it was stolen. You don't have anything! So what difference does it make if I told you or didn't tell you?"

"Spoken like a true white woman! Or a white lawyer."

"Ron!" Wilma cried.

"It makes a lot of difference, Mary." He turned his back to her, and spoke over his shoulder. "I may not have proof, but you know I have a moral right to it. I have the moral right to take that land back from the Clays. I can sue their asses for everything they have and take it back and sell it and put the money in my pocket for my family, and I have every right to do it. That's what difference it makes." He turned toward Mary, steaming now. "And don't tell me I don't have the right to do it, that I would be wrong, after your family stole that land from mine, lynched my great-grandfather, left his family to starve, and tried to do the same to me in that fucking well. Don't tell me I would be wrong!"

"Ron!" Wilma shouted, getting to her feet. "Keep your voice down. The children will hear."

"Sit down, Wilma," Ron said.

"Ron," Mike said. "I think you better leave."

"No, no, no," Mary said, starting to cry. "We've got to get through this. Ron, listen to me. You've got to believe me. I didn't know Jimmy was mean enough to kill, but I did warn you about him through Mike and Wilma. And maybe you do have the right to that land. Maybe you should take it. It's just a swampy old woods and falling down house, but I can see what it means to you. And Jimmy Clay does deserve to lose everything he has."

"You're damned right he does," Ron said.

"But what about Annie?" Mary said. "Does she deserve to be thrown out of her house and the source of what little income she has? She didn't know Jimmy was that evil, and she lived with him. She never set foot in that basement. She was afraid to. She didn't know about your great-grandfather's lynching, and she certainly didn't know that Jimmy and his gang were going to try to kill you."

"Yes, yes. But what I want to know is why you didn't tell me what you knew when you first learned I was investigating the lynching."

"Ron," Mary said. "Do you have any idea how embarrassing it is to have something like this—you know—liars, thieves, and murderers—

in your family? My great-great-grandfather, my great-grandmother, and my great-uncle—all of them were liars, thieves, and murderers! That's *my* past. That's where *I* come from. Those are my roots. How could I tell you about that? I wanted you to like Mike and me. Oh, I wish it hadn't happened! I wish they hadn't killed him. I wish it wasn't my family. I wish it was someone else's, but it's not. Do you think I'm proud of it?"

"No."

"I'm not," she said, shaking her head, tears rolling down her face, "but I am proud of Granny. She survived."

"Uh-huh."

"But can't you see how it hurt her? The guilt, the shame."

"Yes. I can see. They killed part of her, too."

"Can you see how my parents are trying to change?"

"They're making an effort, at least. I can see that," Ron said.

"Can you see why Mike and I moved into this neighborhood? We're trying to live together, trying to learn and work out new relationships, to put the past behind us. And other white people are, too. Can you see that?"

"Yes, but it just pisses me off that not only do we have to live with all this shit from the past, we're expected to help white people overcome their ignorance and guilt, too."

"I don't know what else to do. We're trying to be friends and get over this thing. But you've got to help us, Ron."

He was silent, then looked softly into her eyes.

"I'm ashamed," she said. "I'm deeply ashamed of all of this. I'm so sorry it happened. I know that's not adequate, but I apologize for what they did back then, and what Jimmy did to you. Please accept my apology. What else can I say? Please accept me, Ron." She stepped forward, put her hands on his arms, and looked up at him. "Please, Ron."

The breath came out of him. He took her into his arms, and she rested her face on his chest.

Mike rose tentatively and looked at Wilma. They both walked forward and joined the hug.

Wilma said, "I think we need to pray."

"Yes," Ron said, "but this time it's my turn." They closed their eyes. "Dear God, help us all to do to other people what we would want them to do to us, and forgive our sins. Forgive me, Lord, for blaming Mary for things she didn't do and not seeing what she did do. Help us all not to forget the sins of the past, but help us to change because of them. We all have to change, Lord. Help us be friends and live together … in harmony and equality and justice. And help us to be fair and equitable and forgiving in our dealings with others. And help me find hard evidence of Thomas's innocence—to protect my children. In Jesus' name, we pray. Amen."

TWENTY-FIVE

A few days later, Wilma answered the phone. It was Annie Clay asking for Ron. She called him to the phone and he picked up.

"Hi, Annie. How're you doing?" Wilma resisted the temptation to listen in. Ron and Annie heard the click.

"Mr. Watkins?"

"You can call me Ron, Annie."

"Thanks, Ron. But what I'm calling about, and I don't know if you have any interest at all, but I was wondering if you wanted anything from the basement." They both were silent for a moment. "I know your great-granddaddy and his family lived here, and I don't know if there's anything left from then, and I don't know if you want any of that other stuff, either, but I'm figuring on cleaning it all out and throwing everything away, so I can start trying to forget about what happened here."

"I see."

"And, you know, the state is making me fill in that well. They don't want anybody else falling in there. They're afraid something might pollute the water in the ground, so I have to call a well driller and have him come out and do it. He's gotta fill it with some kind of clay and concrete and file a report with the state that says it's been done."

"Who pays for that?"

"They're making me pay, of course, even though I don't have the money. I'll see if I can sell Jimmy's car and truck, if he'll let me. I don't think he'll be needing them. The Cadillac was Daddy's. We got it when they died in that wreck, so I have a right to it, too."

"Did they have a will?"

"No. The state just split everything, gave Jimmy half and me half.

"Well … good luck."

"But you know, Ron, I was just thinking. I'd like to just throw all that crap from the basement down that well before they fill it up. I thought that might be a fitting burial for that stuff, to put it at the bottom of that well they dumped you in. Then we could bury everything at once."

"Hmm."

"I was thinking you might just like to help me do it, since we're both related to those people back then. It might mean something to both of us to do it."

Yes, he thought. *We are connected. And maybe it would be a fitting gesture to bury those things in that well.*

His mind raced. *What will Wilma think about it? Should we bring the children?* As much as he feared telling Marty and Rosie about the lynching, he still wanted them to see where it happened. And the well he'd been thrown down. He wanted the chance to explain it all in a way that they would know that Thomas was innocent and would not be afraid something bad would happen to them, and would not fear and hate white people.

Mike and Mary might want to come, too, since their family was also involved. But he would not tell any of the children that the Hoffman family was related to the men who did the lynchings—Jeremiah and Jimmy. He would leave it up to Mike and Mary to decide whether to tell Jeff and Jason.

"You know, Annie. I think you're right. That would be a good thing to do. And I would like to do it with you. Do you mind if I bring Wilma and my children?"

"No," she said hesitantly. "I … I think they got a right. It's about their kin too."

"Yeah, it is. I'll talk to Wilma about it. But I'm pretty sure she'll support the idea."

"Good."

"And oh, another thing. I think I'd like to bring a couple of friends along who helped me learn about my great-grandfather's lynching—Mike and Mary Hoffman. Mike was one of the guys who tried to rescue me, and Mary's his wife. I think she's a distant cousin of yours. Her grandmother was Jeremiah Clay's granddaughter. Her maiden name was Fletcher."

"Oh my God! I went to school with a Mary Fletcher. Mom said we were related, but the Fletchers were always too snooty to talk to us."

"Mary's not that way. Is it okay if they come?"

"Well, sure, if you want them to."

~

They planned the ceremony for the following Saturday. Mike and Mary told Ron they wanted to come, but did not want to bring Jeff and Jason. After talking to Marty and Rosalie, however, the children insisted on going. They all wanted to see the well that Ron had escaped from. Wilma told Ron she was concerned about telling the children about the lynching, but he finally persuaded her.

Saturday morning came, and they picked up Mike and Mary and the children in Wilma's Caravan and drove to the Clay house. Ron and Mike sat in front with Mary and Wilma behind them. The children were crowded onto the back seat, talking excitedly.

Ron and Mary were quiet, each feeling residual soreness from their verbal battle. *Well,* Ron thought. *Time to break the silence.* When he stopped at a light, he said, "Mary, I want to thank you again for telling me what your granny told you about Thomas. It really meant a lot to me."

"I'm sorry I didn't come forward sooner, Ron."

"And I'm sorry I got angry. We're still okay, aren't we?"

"Yes."

He turned back to the road. "You filled in a lot of blanks for me. I just wish I had some hard evidence of Thomas's innocence—you know, something besides oral history—something I could get my hands on."

"I could write it all down for you, and then you would have that, but that would be second-hand evidence—like hearsay—since I would be telling what Granny told me." He saw her look out the window, then down at her lap.

"That would still be great, if you have time. I can't find anything definitive in Jeremiah's diary—just his claim that Thomas assaulted Agnes."

At the house, Ron introduced Annie and Mary, and the two distant cousins spoke briefly.

Once inside, Ron asked Annie for a last favor. "Let Mike and me go down first alone. I want to take some pictures."

They descended the steep stairs. The men photographed the altar with the slave paraphernalia, and the walls with the posters, lynching photos, and family photos. They removed the photos they thought would be disturbing to the children. Then they invited everyone downstairs and explained to the children what had happened there. Annie and Mary stood by, embarrassed.

"This used to be your great-great-grandfather's house," Ron told Marty and Rosalie. Mike urged Jeff and Jason to listen. "He owned this farm. But one day some bad people came in and shot him and hung his body from a limb of that big oak tree."

"They shot him and hung him from that tree on Big Oak Road?" Marty asked.

"Yes, but it was a long, long time ago—a hundred years ago. Things are very different now."

"Why did they do that?" Rosalie asked.

"I don't know, Rosy. People were mean back then. They wanted to steal his house and farm from him and his family."

"Will anyone come in our house and kill us?" Rosalie asked.

"No, no, no, no. We have a security system. And police. And good neighbors, like the Hoffmans. And people are a lot nicer now. They don't do things like that."

"And your dad is too big and strong," Mike added. "He wouldn't let them."

"Yeah, but they tried to kill him, too" Jeff said. "They threw him down the well."

"Yes, but he climbed right out and caught them all, and now they're going to jail for a long, long time."

"How long?" Jason asked.

"Probably for the rest of their lives," Mike explained.

"Okay," Ron said. "Let's go bury this stuff."

Everyone picked up something and carried it upstairs. They went outside and started up the path into the woods. The day was bright, but cool for a Maryland summer. Sunlight filtered through the leaves of the large trees, and an occasional fly buzzed them.

"Here we are," Ron said. "Uh-oh. They put a new cover on it. I hope I can move it." Everyone gathered around. He reached down and bent his knees to grasp the lid, then lifted it to the side a few inches. "There. That should be enough."

"Is this the well they threw you in, Daddy?" Marty asked.

"Yes."

"Cool," Jeff said.

"Can we look in?" Marty asked.

"Sure."

Everyone crowded close, but they could not see far into the dark hole with their eyes adjusted to daylight.

Ron turned away. He was just as glad that he could not see into the place where he had suffered.

"And this is where you climbed out?" Rosalie asked.

"Yes."

"Wow. That's way cool, Mr. Watkins," Jeff said.

"The human fly," Mike smiled. "Well, should we throw the stuff in?"

Ron was silent. He looked at the effects again. "Wait, wait, wait, wait, wait, wait. I'm sorry. Now I think we're making a mistake. We can't do this."

"What?" Wilma asked.

"We brought all these things up here, and now you don't want to throw them in?" Mike asked.

"We can't do it. We just can't bury all this stuff at the bottom of a well."

"Why not?" Annie asked.

"Annie, it's one thing to forgive. But we just can't forget about all this."

"I was wondering about that myself," Mary said. "So much has already been lost."

"I don't know what to do with it all, but we've got to save things like this. It's evidence—to prove what happened back then. Throwing it away would be like destroying all the slave cabins."

"Yeah," Mike said. "Sooner or later people will say it never happened."

"Right," Ron said.

"Like neo-Nazis saying the Holocaust never happened."

"Yes. We need to see if some museum wants this stuff," Ron said.

"The Smithsonian might want some of it," Mary said. "I can call some people about it."

"Great," Ron said. "And the Blacks in Wax Museum in Baltimore might want that boot with the bone in it with the shackle on it, and the whips, and some of the photos—that slave auction and the field workers, maybe. Is there anything you want to keep, Annie?"

"I just want it gone. I don't ever want to see any of it again. It makes me sick to look at it."

"Even the photos of your relatives?" Ron asked.

"Especially them. If you want anything, take it. Anything else I want to throw down the well."

"I'd rather the family photos not be displayed in a museum," Mary sighed. "But I know it's better if they are, so that no one forgets."

"Mary's right," Annie said.

"I'll take it all, then," Ron said. "We'll figure out what to do with it later."

"You mean we have to carry it all back down the hill?" Marty asked.

"You're big and strong," Ron said. "You can do it."

"Let's pray," Wilma said. They stood around the hole and bowed their heads.

"Dear God, we are here today putting to rest evils of the past that inspired crimes of today. We know we are blessed, and we thank you for your eternal grace. We thank you for saving your servant Ron from death inside this well. We thank you for showing him how to climb out of it and for helping him save our friends. Dear God, bless this good woman here who owns this property. We thank you for helping her love all people and for helping her speak the truth. We honor her today for her righteousness, Lord. Help her through the travails of life and bless her richly as she deserves. In the name of Jesus Christ, our lord and savior, who gave his life that we might live. Amen."

Carrying the relics once more, they all started back down the hill. Annie asked Ron if she could speak to him in private. "I need to ask you a question."

"Shoot."

"You ain't gonna sue us, are you? You know, for what Jimmy did?"

Ron thought back to being in the well and Mary's story of the lynching and the auction.

"Ron?" Annie said, trying to call him out of his thoughts.

He spoke softly, slowly. "We certainly deserve to get your land, Annie—the store, garage, house, everything. And not just because Jimmy tried to kill me."

"Why else?"

"Because Jeremiah Clay stole your land from my great-grandfather's family in 1908, right after he lynched my great-grandfather."

"What? How do you know that?"

"It's in the county land records, Annie. After the lynching, Jeremiah bought the farm at auction for twenty dollars. There were no other bidders—the Clays kept them away."

"Oh!"

"Twenty dollars. He stole it from us, Annie, after he killed my great-grandfather. We deserve to get it back. That's justice, isn't it?"

"Yes—it is—but ... but what about me? What'll I do if you take it?"

He descended into thought again. *What about her? Which is it, love and forgiveness? Or justice?* Annie had grown in his respect and affection, but the farm belonged to him.

He remembered wondering how the old store could stay in business and pictured Annie selling lottery tickets. Then he recalled her volunteering the truth to the police. She didn't have to do that—she could have remained silent. And she'd never even been in the basement. She wasn't responsible for what her relatives did back then, just like Mary. *But what about reparations? When do we get what they owe us? When?*

He looked at Annie, and a rush came over him. *No!* he thought. *I can't do it. Get justice for a crime committed a hundred years ago? That doesn't excuse hurting Annie today. In this case, justice demands forgiveness. But what if I do want the property some day? Maybe she should offer it to me first, before she sells it.*

"Ron?"

"I ... I'm not going to take it from you, Annie. You don't deserve to be punished for what Jeremiah and Jimmy did. I'm not going to sue. All I want is right of first refusal if you decide to sell. I don't know if we'll want to buy it or not, but I want the opportunity."

"Oh, thank you, Ron. You know, I don't have anywhere else to live. I gotta have the store and garage to keep going."

"I won't sue you. You can keep it. What do you think I am, some kind of monster that slithers out of a hole in the ground—like a well, maybe?"

She threw her arms around him. "Thank you, Ron."

"Wait, baby. What will people think?"

"Ooooh, Dad," Marty teased musically. "I see you hugging that woman. I'm telling Mom."

"See?" Ron said.

When they arrived at the cars, he asked Annie about the future of the businesses. "So, is Noah going to run the garage?"

"That's what I was planning—same as always. He'll do the work and I'll take the money. Jimmy never did nothing anyway."

"Sounds good."

TWENTY-SIX

S everal days after the visit to Annie's house, Ron went running. He came to the path leading to the old house, and considered taking it. He would enjoy seeing the beaver lodges again. The crime scene and the well still held a morbid fascination for him. Suddenly a vision filled his mind. He saw Margaret and George—children, white and black—riding through the fields. Then Thomas bending over an injured Margaret, patting her forehead with a wet cloth, he and George helping Margaret through the woods. He pictured Annie in the house, getting ready for work. It was six-thirty, so she might still be there. Maybe he could visit. Quickly, he rejected that idea. He had no interest in getting tangled up with her. Then he thought of Fury, bounding off the porch, and the possibility that Jimmy and his friends had somehow escaped or been released and would attack him again, this time bent on revenge. That clinched it. It was time for him to explore new paths.

When he arrived at the bridge, he looked over at the store and the big oak, imagining the bled-out black body swaying from the huge bare limb. He saw the road full of people eating licorice, drinking sodas, laughing, and talking, their horses, wagons, and buggies waiting beyond. Shaking away the picture, he turned right onto Big Oak Road and took a new route home. He stopped in front of his house and clicked off his stopwatch.

Mary approached in the Hoffmans' minivan. Ron waved her

down, flashing a big smile. She lowered her window and he greeted her. "Good morning!"

She was lethargic and gloomy, but managed a weak smile. "Hi, Ron."

"You don't look like you're awake yet."

She summoned some spirit. "You know, I don't understand people like you—how you can just get up and run like that. They made us run in school and I hated it. I've never run an inch since."

"Different strokes."

"For very different folks."

"In some ways ... Well, have a good one."

"You too." He turned away. "Wait, Ron." She reached into the glove compartment. "I've been meaning to give this to you."

He leaned his hands on the open window. "Give me what?"

"It's a letter Granny wrote me. I think it may contain what you need to prove that Thomas was innocent. She sent it to me just before she died." Mary sensed Ron's renewed frustration. "I know you wonder why I didn't give it to you before. It's just that I didn't want my family to know about it. I didn't want my parents or the kids to be hurt. You'll see what I mean when you read it. I'll give you a copy of it. But first, I need you to promise me that you will not show it to anyone before my parents die and my children are grown."

"What? The whole reason for me getting evidence was to prove to my kids that their great-great-grandfather wasn't a criminal."

"But I don't want *my* children to know that their ancestors were criminals, either. Can't you just put off telling your children about the letter for now? Tell them that you know Thomas was innocent and can prove it to them some day, just not now?"

"I can't promise that, Mary. I can't do that. I—I can promise I won't show it to them unless they start asking questions about whether Thomas did anything to deserve being lynched. But then I'll have to show them whatever evidence I have."

Mary thought a moment. "But you won't have to connect the letter to me, will you?"

"No. I don't have to say anything about that. But I won't lie to them, either."

"They're such good friends with Jeff and Jason, and I'm afraid that—"

"I understand. It might hurt their friendship. I'll remember that."

"All right." She handed it to him. He began reading the shaky writing:

My dearest granddaughter Mary,

I am writing you now because I feel like I may never see you again. My health is failing, and I grow weaker day by day. So it is that now, while I still am able, I want to express my wishes to you regarding the information I have given you on my mother and father, uncles, and grandfather, concerning the lynching of Thomas Phillips; for if this episode ever becomes public, I want it known that not all of your relatives were of the same evil character as your great-great-grandfather, Jeremiah Clay.

If all these ancestors were nefarious and their evil deeds became known, then these facts might forever trouble any children you may have in the future and the other descendants of Jeremiah Clay. For because of Jeremiah's greed for another man's land and money, he and his family did in fact conspire first to cheat Thomas at Clay Grocery by falsifying his account in an effort to eventually seize his property and second to organize the lynching of that man and the taking of his farm from his wife and children in a rigged auction in which he kept bidders away by threat of violence.

I suppose it may sound self-serving of me to write here that I am not part of that infamous legacy. But I want it known that Thomas, that poor man, was a good, honest, and hardworking soul who, contrary to the newspaper reports, did not attack my mother, never looked at me with lascivious intent, and, in fact, helped me when I broke my collarbone.

I also want to declare that I truly loved George Phillips, Thomas's son, first as a friend and then with all my heart, as well as caring deeply for his parents and siblings. I only wish I had had the mental and physical fortitude to escape the confinement of my house the day of the lynching, run down the hill, and warn Mr. Phillips about the impending attack.

Now, I—perhaps the last living person to know the facts of this abomination—am providing this letter to record the truth. And although I would prefer that the letter remain confidential to protect our family name, still yet, should false information on Thomas Phillips from newspapers or other sources ever be told to future generations, I ask that you make this letter public in deference to my wishes and my love and respect for the memory of George Phillips and his family.

Always, your loving grandmother,
Margaret

Ron read rapaciously, and looked up. "My God. This is what I need, Mary. This is what I've been looking for. Thank you for sharing this. You have no idea how much I appreciate it. She was a courageous person, Margaret—just like her granddaughter."

"Thanks, Ron." Mary nodded her head and drove away.

It's finished, he thought. *Unless Marty and Rosie have nightmares about the lynching and the well.*

THE END

AUTHOR'S NOTE

Certain places described in this work are real, and certain events described did take place. However, this is a work of fiction. All characters, names, places, incidents, organizations, and dialogue in this novel are either the products of the author's imagination or are used fictitiously.

The lynching statistics in the novel are historically accurate. There is no official record of a lynching occurring between Washington DC and Annapolis, Maryland, in the year 1907. However, according to the Maryland State Archives, two men were lynched in Maryland in 1907: James Reed in Crisfield on July 28, 1907, and William Burns in Cumberland on October 5, 1907. There were sixteen lynchings in Maryland between 1895 and 1911, and forty-three between 1854 and 1933. This included Jacob Henson in Ellicott City on May 28, 1895; James Bowens in Frederick on November 17, 1895; Edd Watson in Pocomoke City on June 14, 1906; William Lee in Crisfield on July 26, 1906; and two in Annapolis—Wright Smith on October 5, 1898 and Henry Davis on December 21, 1906. In Prince George's County, an unknown victim was lynched in October 1869. In Upper Marlboro, the county seat, John Henry Scott was lynched on March 23, 1875; Michael Green on September 1, 1878; Joe Vermillion on December 11, 1889; and Stephen Williams on October 20, 1894. My description of the lynching in the book draws from incidents that occurred in Maryland and around the country.

Newspaper quotations in Chapter Six are actual quotes from *100 Years of Lynchings*, ©1962, 1988 by Ralph Ginzburg, Black Classic Press, Baltimore, Maryland.

The graffiti incident at the beginning of the novel mirrors the one that occurred in Bowie, Maryland on April 25, 2006, as reported in the *Washington Post* and other newspapers, and on WTOP radio and NBC4 television news.

I changed the name Prince George's County to Patuxent County to make the story less site-specific. This story could have taken place in most southern states, if cotton were substituted for tobacco, or in most any of the tobacco-producing border states. Descriptions of the county and its history are mostly true, but the names of nearly all the roads and places I use are fictitious. The massive white flight that has occurred in the county after the integration of schools and subdivisions is factual, as is the concurrent development of the most affluent majority African-American county in the nation.

My background research in writing this novel included the *July 1993 Illustrated Inventory of Historic Sites*, published by the Maryland-National Capital Park & Planning Commission (MNCPPC), and Susan Pearl's *African-American Heritage Survey, 1996*, also published by MNCPPC. I also made use of the 1861 and 1878 maps of Prince George's County, which I obtained from the Prince George's County Historical Society, and research materials obtained from the Bowie State University Library. My descriptions of the Maryland Archives, Maryland Law Library, which archives the *Baltimore Sun* (I called it the *Baltimore Courier*), and county deed office are generally accurate since I conducted research for the novel at those places.

Other books I found particularly instructive were Leon F. Litwack's *Trouble In Mind* (1998), *Without Sanctuary* by Congressman John Lewis, Leon F. Litwack, Hilton Als, and James Allen (2004), Ralph Ginzburg's *100 Years of Lynchings* (1962), James W. Loewen's *Sundown Towns* (2005), Sherrilyn A. Ifill's *On The Courthouse Lawn* (2007), Robert J. Brugger's *Maryland, A Middle Temperament 1634–1980*

(1988), Barbara Jeanne Fields' *Slavery and Freedom on the Middle Ground, Maryland during the Nineteenth Century* (1985), and Sharon Ann Holt's *Making Freedom Pay: North Carolina Freedpeople Working For Themselves, 1865–1900* (2000).

Finally, although it is certainly possible to walk out of a well, not everyone has the ability to do the well-walk as well as Ron. I do not recommend that non-athletes attempt to do so. It takes skill, strength, and agility to walk up a well. The technique can be practiced at home in a hallway three feet wide using shoes with non-skid soles and rubber gloves. I take no responsibility for bruises and fractures incurred in this pursuit.

I would like to thank my wife, Barbara Morris, as well as William and Stephanie Byers, Joe Herring, Carol Herring, Steve Buckingham, Deon and Winfred Merene, Janis and Don Rose, Audrey and Rick Engdahl, James and Agnes Chittams, Virginia Grove, Jennifer Ruby, William Gilmore, and Svend Lauritsen for their many contributions to this book. I also thank the editorial staff at iUniverse.com for their excellent suggestions during their editorial review process. Most of all, I thank Barbara for her constant encouragement, thoughtful consideration of issues, wise counsel, and endless readings and proof-readings over the nine years I have been working on it.

Hyattsville, Maryland
September 2009

Breinigsville, PA USA
19 February 2010

232791BV00002B/3/P